It should have been a perfect night out. Instead, Mark and Donald collide with tragedy when they leave their favorite night spot. That dark October night, three gay-bashers emerge from the gloom, armed with slurs, fists, and an aluminum baseball bat.

The hate crime leaves Donald lost and alone, clinging to the memory of the only man he ever loved. He is haunted, both literally and figuratively, by Mark and what might have been. Trapped in a limbo offering no closure, Donald can't immediately accept the salvation his new neighbor, Walter, offers. Walter's kindness and patience are qualities his sixteen-year-old nephew, Justin, understands well. Walter provides the only sense of family the boy's ever known. But Justin holds a dark secret that threatens to tear Donald and Walter apart before their love even has a chance to blossom.

I0590577

BASHED

Rick R. Reed

A NineStar Press Publication

www.ninestarpress.com

Bashed

Printed in the USA

Print ISBN: 978-1-64890-064-8

NineStar Edition, August, 2020
Originally Published in March 2009

Also available in eBook, ISBN: 978-1-64890-063-1

WARNING:
This book contains sexually explicit content, which may only be suitable for mature readers, graphic violence, depictions of gay bashing, homophobia, and death of a loved one.

For all the victims of hate crimes. May you find peace, and may you see the day when such atrocities are a piece of history only.

Prologue

The night had turned cold while they were in the Brig, one of Chicago's oldest and most infamous leather establishments. A strong wind out of the north had blown away the cloud cover that allowed the city of Chicago to retain a little Indian summer heat this late October night. With the wind, the temperature had plunged nearly twenty degrees, from a relatively balmy sixty-two, down to the low forties. But the wind had also revealed a sprinkling of stars, visible even with the ambient light from downtown. And the moon had emerged, almost full, lending a silvery cast to North Clark Street.

Donald wrapped his arms around Mark as they headed south on Clark, toward the side street where they had left their car. Even with his chaps, biker jacket, and boots, Donald felt the chill bite into him, vicious. He couldn't imagine how Mark was faring, wearing only a T-shirt and jeans. He'd get his boy into leather one of these days! It was just past three a.m., and the far north side neighborhood called Andersonville, once the province of Swedes and working class folk, and now the home of yuppies and gays, was quiet. A lone taxi headed north up Clark, looking for fares. Someone even unsteadier on his feet came out of the adult bookstore ahead of them, blinking rapidly, and looking around, perhaps for more excitement than he had found in the bookstore. Donald thought that, once upon a time, he could have been the sad, singular man emerging from an adult bookstore while the rest of the world slept, but things had changed since he had met Mark six months ago.

"I feel almost—almost—like we're the only two people on earth," Donald said to Mark, drawing him in close for a sloppy, beery kiss. When he pulled his mouth away, he flashed the crooked grin he knew entranced his boyfriend and completed the thought with, "And that's fine by me."

Mark grinned back, then rubbed his upper arms. "It's not fine by me. Not when it's this frickin' cold! Let's get home!"

They wrapped their arms around each other to ward off the cold, much as they had done the night they met, back in March, in the same leather bar. And once again, they were just a bit boozy and flushed with need for each other. Tonight, the weather outside may not have been as frigidly cold as it had been last winter when they had first laid eyes upon one another, but the heat and electricity passing between them was still burning as brightly as that very first night.

Donald stopped again in the middle of the sidewalk, pulling Mark close and planting a kiss on his cheek. There was no one around, and in this neighborhood, such displays really were nothing to worry about, Donald thought. Hell, most anyone they encountered would either be sympathetic or jealous. He nipped at Mark's earlobe and whispered, "I love you, you know that?" He paused to breathe in Mark's scent and to nuzzle his nose in Mark's blond curls.

And Mark stopped, right there in the middle of Clark Street, on an early Sunday morning, and placed his hands on Donald's shoulders, so he would stop walking and so he could look right back into Mark's penetrating stare.

"And I love you, Donald." He gave a small grin and looked down at the ground for just a second, almost as if he was embarrassed, and then said, "And I always will. This is a forever thing."

Donald felt a rush of warmth go through him at the exact same moment a harsh wind, full of chill and with the smell of dark water, glided east from over Lake Michigan. He pulled Mark close and kissed him full on the mouth, his tongue lifting Mark's and doing a little duel with it. Neither of them closed their eyes, preferring instead to stare into each other's rapt gazes. Just as they were breaking apart, they stiffened as the roar of a souped-up engine shattered the still of the night. The backfire issuing forth from the car's muffler made both men jump. They gave each other a quick glance, then laughed.

The car, an old maroon Duster that had been tricked out beyond good sense, taste, or fiscal responsibility, slowed across from the pair. Three shadowy figures moved inside. One of them rolled down a window, and a young male face, pale and marred by acne in the moon's light, emerged making a kissing sound, exaggerated and prolonged. Donald heard the other guys in the car laughing. He stiffened and felt a trickle of sweat roll into the small of his back, in spite of the chill in the air.

Just as suddenly as they had arrived, they roared off, leaving them in a wake of sour-smelling exhaust. But they did not leave without casting a parting shot out the window. "Fucking faggots!"

Donald shook his head, glancing over at Mark, whose young face was creased with worry. "Don't let shit like that get to you. They're idiots. And chickenshits... It's pretty easy to call names at people from a speeding car."

The pair continued south. Up ahead, they needed to turn east to make their way to the little side street where they had parked Donald's Prius. The street could usually be counted on for a spot, even on a busy Saturday night. Donald thought it was more the fact that the street was hard to get to than the fact that it ran along the northern border of St. Boniface Cemetery that made it such a good parking bet.

"I know. They're just a bunch of assholes," Mark said as they continued east. Donald could feel the defeat and fear in his voice. He hoped the hotrod homophobes hadn't broken the spell of their night. Because Mark was much younger, he hadn't been exposed to some of the same ridicule and taunting Donald had, growing up in the late sixties and seventies.

Donald bit his lower lip, suddenly feeling all the shame and embarrassment he had once associated with being gay rise up again. *It never really disappears, does it?* His face felt flushed, and a curious mixture of emotions warred within him. First, there was the shame, which he chastised himself for, but he still couldn't stop the little inner voice that scolded him for the public displays of affection, even on an early Sunday morning and in a part of town that was very gay. Second, there was a more recent, more reasonable voice that was enraged and asked "How dare they?" This voice was ready to chase after the speeding car, shouting epithets right back at the cowards who hid behind the car's macho posturing and tinted glass. And the final voice, the other half of the fight or flee duo, just wanted to grab Mark's hand and run back to the car, jump inside, and make sure all the doors were locked before roaring off into the night themselves. Thank God they had a secure garage to park in at home.

"Yeah...assholes," Donald whispered, then spoke up. "I need to be getting you home, young man. It's way past your bedtime." Donald quickened his pace so Mark would match his step and tried not to let the name-calling weigh too heavily on the evening. He was pissed about how a mood could be so easily shattered, especially by some more-than-likely suburban rubes that were not entitled to it. Fuck them! He wished he could make the mood come back, but not now, not with the "fucking faggots" still ringing fresh in his ears.

Maybe when they got home, Donald could put things right. No maybe about it! He would light candles, open a bottle of wine, put on some trance music, and urge Mark over to the couch. He would undress him slowly, gliding his strong hands over every inch of Mark's silky skin as he exposed it. He could already taste Mark's lips and the clean heat of his mouth.

They were almost to their car when they both tensed, slowing as they heard the growling muffler of a car behind them. Donald closed his eyes, thinking, *Oh God, please not again. Not them.* They both stopped for just an instant. Donald didn't have to look back to know who was in the loudly idling car behind them. His heart began to thud, and he resisted an impulse to simply grab Mark's hand and run the three or four feet it would take them to get to the car. But such a sissy maneuver was probably just the kind of thing those assholes would take particular delight in seeing. And the hot pursuit of a couple of scared queers would be the perfect capper to a boring night.

Donald spoke quietly, out of the corner of his mouth. "Let's just walk to the car. Don't look back. Don't even give them the satisfaction we're aware of them. We both know who it is. But to look back will just open the door to more shit."

Mark kept pace. "Right." His voice was clipped, and Donald could pick up on the fear and tension in it.

Behind them, they heard the kissing sound again, over the beat of some heavy metal music, the bass throbbing hard enough to shake the car's frame. "Hey, boys!" A falsetto voice, mocking, rang out through the autumn night. Donald wanted to freeze in his tracks and could tell Mark did too by the way he tensed. But Donald had enough presence of mind to keep moving forward slowly, cautiously, the way one would back away from a lion about to pounce. No sudden moves. No eye contact. Donald had to remind himself to breathe.

A wolf whistle cut through the night air. "Hey, if you guys are gonna suck some dick tonight, can we get in on the action?" The car's passengers erupted with laughter.

Donald dug in his tight-fitting Levi's for his keys. His hand was trembling. His stomach was churning. He wished they had left much earlier. He wished they had parked on busier, more brightly lit Clark Street. He wished they had taken a cab. He wished he had left his leather gear at home, just for tonight. He managed to grasp the keys just as they arrived at the car. Mark hurried around to the passenger side. When Donald met Mark's gaze, he saw that the younger man's eyes were bright with fear. He mouthed the word "Hurry" to Donald.

The sound of car doors slamming behind them made Donald's hands shake so badly he dropped the keys into the gravel by the side of the road. "Fuck," he whispered. They were off busy Clark now, and the side street was dark. Empty. He couldn't see where the keys had fallen. He could see where they should logically be, but of course, that's not where they were.

Mark said, in a tense voice, "Hurry up, Donald."

Donald didn't have to look behind him to know the car's occupants were no longer in the Duster and were getting closer. Each slam of a car door caused his heart to beat a little faster, his breath to quicken. One of their voices sounded almost right behind him.

"So what do you say, guys, how about a little head?"

Snickers. High fives. Laughter all around.

Donald swallowed painfully, his throat dry. He tried feeling around in the cinders beside the road with the toe of his boot and came up empty. He did what he had to do, bent down to grope in the gravel for his keys.

"Nice," one of the boys hissed behind him. "Hey, Justin, look at that. He's getting ready for you."

Donald straightened quickly, the keys in his hand now, hoping the two of them could get in the car before the guys drew any closer.

He had his finger on the remote button that would unlock the door to the Prius when he felt the blow to his lower back. He tried to suck in some breath, but it seemed there was no air. The pain, rushing up, white hot, from his kidneys was fierce, intense, and agonizing. He saw stars. There was no air. He dropped the keys again and groaned, slowly reaching back to rub at the spot where something hard had landed powerfully against the tender area of his back. Through pain-blurred eyes, he looked down and saw the keys lying on the gravel once more, glinting back at him mockingly in the moonlight. He didn't know if he could reach down and get them, couldn't imagine how the movement might ratchet the pain in his back up to unbearable levels. And then he groaned again, not because of his own pain, but because he saw one of the other guys, his face hidden by a shadow from the Chicago White Sox baseball cap he wore, grab hold of Mark from behind and pull him close to his chest. The guy whispered something in Mark's ear and made that infernal kissing sound again. Only this time, no one was laughing. He lifted Mark, whose bright, terrified eyes seemed to reach out to Donald across the hood of the car, pulling him aloft for a second and away from the car. Another of his buddies, this one wearing a do-rag and a leather jacket that would have looked very much at home in the Brig, stepped up, pulled back his arm, and punched Mark savagely in the stomach. Mark let out a great whoosh of air and then a groan.

The guy in the Sox cap let him go to watch Mark stumble, clutching his stomach. Donald heard Mark whisper, with what was left of his breath, "Please...no." Donald attempted again to reach for the keys, but the pain, searing, prevented him.

And then another of the trio stepped up behind Mark, and Donald saw the hard, blunt object that had just so painfully connected with his own kidneys, an aluminum baseball bat. This guy wore no cap and had the face of a boy: ruddy, matching the dark red hair that topped his head. He handed the bat to the guy in the leather jacket, smiling. The man in the leather jacket took the bat from him, gripping it firmly around the base. "Batter up!" the guy in the Sox cap called and then guffawed. The guy in leather's face was a mask of grim determination as he raised the bat and prepared to bring it down, with great force, on top of Mark's head.

Donald cried out, heedless of his pain. "No! Get away from him, you son of a bitch." Blindly furious, Donald stumbled forward, around the back of the car, to try to do whatever he could to stop that bat from connecting with Mark's skull. But as in nightmares, his movements were agonizingly slow, as if he were moving through something thick and viscous, even as the beating on the other side of the car seemed to speed up, as if in fast-forward motion.

Donald stood frozen near the back bumper, breathless and wheezing, as the bat came down and landed with a sickening thud on Mark's head, sounding like a watermelon being squashed. Mark dropped to the ground, and Donald rushed to help him.

Like a pack of animals, they were on Donald, and it was only seconds before he too was on the ground, watching as booted and running-shoed feet kicked at him everywhere they could find that was soft: his stomach, his balls, his face.

He rolled into a little ball and had enough presence of mind to chastise himself for not being able to save Mark. He also thought, in that split-second moment, how quiet it all was. And how fast—how very fast—everything was moving.

He turned to look up. The guy with the leather jacket stood above him, swinging the bat; on his face an expression that was a curious mixture of glee and rage. He smiled, and Donald noticed details: the gap in his teeth, the stubble on his face, how his nose skewed to one side, as if it had been broken once. But the last thing—the most horrible thing—Donald remembered seeing was the bat whistling down through the air toward him. He rolled away, hearing someone whisper, "Get him. Get the cocksucker." He reached out for Mark's foot, which was only inches away.

And then everything went black.

Chapter One

Justin was breathless, shaking, and it felt like the fries, Italian beef sandwich, and five beers he had consumed that night were about to make a hasty and searing exit from his gut at any moment. He and Ronny were covered in blood. The smell, its sharp metallic tang, was one of the things that made Justin fear losing the contents of his stomach. The other thing was the violence they had just perpetrated. How had some innocent name-calling morphed into something so brutal? He couldn't allow himself to think about that now, couldn't allow that hot touch to his memory. But somehow, he managed to hold the bile back, tasting its bitter acid in the back of his throat, because he knew Ronny would think he was a wimp. Just like he thought Luis was a wimp for running off into the night after they bashed those fags down in Andersonville. Justin simply thought Luis was smart, scared, and yes, sensible, to want to get away from him and Ronny and the bloody mess the three of them had just made less than an hour ago.

Justin wasn't sure how much longer he could hold things together. He had started trembling after the attack and was still shaking. They had put a serious hurt on those guys, and he wasn't sure how, or if, they were getting on. Earlier, in the car, he had begged Ronny to let him call 911 from his cell to report the attack so that someone might send an ambulance.

Ronny had sneered at him, a Marlboro clamped into the corner of his mouth as he steered with one hand. "What are you, fuckin' nuts? They got GPS or some shit on those phones. They'll find us, dickhead. Is that what you want?" Disgustedly, he dragged in on the cigarette, making its cherry glow in the dark interior, and angrily exhaled through his nose. "They're a couple of fags, dude. They got what they deserved."

Justin had just stared quietly out the window as they sailed up Lake Shore Drive, headed for Sheridan Road and the far north side neighborhood known as Rogers Park, where Ronny had his own little studio on Morse. Ronny must have been doing eighty or ninety, and Justin wondered just how smart that was. What if they got pulled over, covered in blood as they were? How would they explain that away?

But Justin knew better than to nag at Ronny about his speed. It wouldn't be the first time his best friend gave him a backhand across the mouth. Justin simply slid down in his seat and kept his own counsel. Hopefully, there would be no cops out on Lake Shore or Sheridan tonight.

And now, here they were in Ronny's tiny, filthy bathroom, crowded together, in nothing but boxers. They had thrown their bloody clothes into the tub and were scrubbing vigorously with soap and steaming water at their hands and faces to remove any trace of splatter. Ronny had already wiped down his leather jacket and was satisfied it was clean.

Ronny shut the water off and placed his hands on Justin's shoulders, looking him over. "Sweet, man, clean as a baby." He pulled him close and sniffed at his neck. "No smell, no tell." He leaned back and grinned. "We'll bag up the clothes and drop 'em in a dumpster."

Justin continued to shiver, trying to tell himself it was from a chill and not from the fact he was still scared. "Uh, so you think we'll be okay?"

"No witnesses, man. And those queers will keep their mouths shut if they know what's good for them."

"And Luis won't say anything?" Luis was the friend they had hooked up with earlier in the night at the arcade on Belmont. He was half Mexican, half Irish, and up for anything.

"Nah. Unless he wants to implicate himself."

Justin shivered.

"You cold, little bro?"

Justin nodded. Even though he and Ronny were in no way blood relatives, it always made him feel better somehow when Ronny referred to him in this manner.

"Let me get you some clothes. I got some sweats you can put on."

Justin watched him rummaging around on the floor, through the piles of clothes scattered there, looking for something suitable. Ronny's frame was lean and hard, the upper part of him covered in red, green, and black tattoos, a crazy mixture of Chinese letters, stars, dragons, and tribal symbols that all somehow seemed to work together. He was ten years older than sixteen-year-old Justin, and the fact that Ronny chose to hang around with him made him feel proud, like he was cool.

Except for tonight. They had never veered into territory this violent before. Sure, they had yelled at the fags on Halsted and Clark, even pitched a few beer cans their way, but that was the extent of it. And sure, their activities hadn't always been strictly legal but had never gone much further than smoking a little weed and maybe lifting a lighter or two off the counter at 7-Eleven while the clerk's back was turned, reaching for smokes. But they had never done anything like tonight. It still seemed like a dream.

Or a nightmare.

Ronny was coming toward him with a long-sleeved T-shirt and balled-up gray sweats under one arm.

"You think those guys are gonna be okay, don't you?"

Ronny handed him the clothes, and Justin began pulling them on. Ronny lit another cigarette and blew the smoke toward the ceiling. "You worried about the sweethearts?"

"Well, maybe a little. Wouldn't want them to be dead or nothin' like that, you know?"

"They're queers, man, remember? Those guys are like cockroaches. You can't wipe 'em out. When I was a kid, my old man told me AIDS was gonna do that...just get rid of 'em all, but you see how they beat that."

Justin wasn't sure how that was logical, or even in the realm of sanity, but he kept his thoughts to himself.

Ronny grinned. "Still, we put a good hurt on both of them. They're not gonna be doing much suckin' or fuckin' in the near future." Ronny barked out a short laugh. "Or talkin'." He shook his head. "But they'll be okay. Don't worry about it, little man." He reached out and ruffled Justin's reddish brown hair. "When are we gonna get this buzzed? Like mine?"

Justin's stomach churned. "Dunno."

"I am going to smoke a bowl and get some sleep, man. You in?"

Justin followed Ronny out of the bathroom and sat next to him on the stained sheets of his bed, sinking down into the mattress, watching as Ronny pulled a bag of bud from beneath his bed. He wished he could go home tonight, but his mother, Patty, had a date and had told him that she would appreciate "a little privacy" if Justin wouldn't mind "having a sleepover" at one of his friends'.

Justin had had a lot of sleepovers during his short life.

And a lot of them lately had been with Ronny, which was cool, except the place was filthy, stank, and had cockroaches.

"Here you go," Ronny croaked, breathless, and held out the metal one-hitter to him.

That was one good thing about Ronny and staying here: he always had good weed, and if you smoked enough of it, you forgot all about what a pigsty you were in.

Justin took the one-hitter, fired it up, and drew in deeply. Tonight there was a lot he wanted to forget.

*

Even with several hits clouding his brain, Justin found sleep elusive. He only felt groggy and sick, and the oblivion he sought stayed stubbornly just out of reach. He lay beside Ronny, who slept on his back, one arm flung over his forehead, snoring loudly. He wondered how the guy could have done what he just did and then go home and sleep, as if nothing had happened.

Images kept coming back to him. He would see the terrified look on the younger guy's face, the pleading in his eyes just before Ronny brought down the bat on his head. Justin didn't know if he could ever get that out of his mind, the sickening crunch of bone as the bat made impact. He saw the other guy, the older one, decked out in leather, stumbling behind his car to try to get to his friend. He was whimpering, and the terror stamped on his features was real. Luis was laughing, but Justin just couldn't see the humor in what they were doing. It was sick. He just hoped the guys were able to crawl away, to get the help they would undoubtedly need.

So he lay there, restless, after spending hours of tossing, turning, and glancing at the little digital clock on Ronny's nightstand, surprised to see that only minutes had passed since the last time he had looked. He just wanted to go home, if there was such a place. But he knew his mother, Patty, wouldn't like it if he showed up too early, wouldn't want there to be an uncomfortable meet and greet across their scarred breakfast table.

Now the light was peeking in from the spaces around the sheet Ronny had hung over his sole window. Justin looked again at the clock. It was going on seven. He turned on his side, drawing his knees up closer to his chest. The movement sent Ronny onto his side, and then he was lying up against Justin's back. One sleepy arm fell across Justin's chest, and he stiffened. He could feel Ronny's dick, hard, against his ass. He must be having some dream! He wanted to slide from the bed but didn't want to wake Ronny, didn't want to face his queries about why he was getting up so early.

Ronny snuggled closer in his sleep, and his hand brushed across Justin's stomach, then dropped farther south. He cupped Justin's crotch and then let out a big snore.

Justin jumped from the bed. His heart was beating fast.

Ronny opened bleary and bloodshot eyes and looked up at him.

"What the fuck?" Justin asked.

"Huh?"

Justin gave out a little laugh, but there was no mirth in it. "You were grabbin' my dick, man."

Ronny rolled over on his back and groped on the bedside table for his smokes, lit one up, and blew the smoke toward the ceiling. "What the fuck are you talkin' about, man?"

Justin began to feel sheepish. "In your sleep, uh, your hand grabbed at my dick." Justin felt himself begin to tremble again, so he reached down and pulled on the sweats and T-shirt Ronny had given him the night before. He stared at his friend.

"So what? You think I'm going queer for you or somethin'?"

Justin shook his head. "Naw. It was just weird, is all."

Ronny propped himself up on one elbow. "'Cause if you think I'm queer, I ask you to please think about last night, dude. That should give you all the evidence you need that I am straight as they come." He took a drag and blew out the smoke angrily. "I was asleep, end of story."

"Okay," Justin whispered, as much to himself as to Ronny. "I'm gonna book. The coast is probably clear at my ma's by now. I'll get the clothes and throw 'em in a dumpster on my way home. I'll make sure to throw them in one that's nowhere near here."

"You do that." Ronny snuffed out his cigarette and rolled back over on his side. Justin waited until he was snoring again. It didn't take long.

Justin moved toward the kitchenette and found a black plastic garbage bag under the sink, then went into the bathroom and lifted the jeans and T-shirts they had thrown into the bathtub the night before. He stuffed them into the bag, trying not to look at the garments as he did so. He snatched his South Park T-shirt from the porcelain and placed it atop the pile of balled-up clothes in the bag. As he did so, he caught sight of a little blob of pinkish matter on the leg of one of the jeans.

And finally, it happened. Everything came up, and he turned just in time to hurl into the toilet, his eyes watering as he heaved on and on, until there was nothing left inside.

Nothing but remorse.

He tied the bag and heard Ronny call out, "Lightweight!" He realized he probably just thought Justin was hungover. God, didn't he understand what they had done?

He hurried toward the door.

Chapter Two

Sounds, bursts of light, people moving about, came to him slowly. The pain in his head was immense. Donald tried to open his eyes, but they would only widen to slits, as if some invisible force were holding the lids down. Behind his eyes, though, an immense, demonic pain was rushing around, applying scorching heat to the tender area inside his eyes, making his temples throb. He tried to swallow, but there was no spit in his mouth. All he could see was pale yellow light, geometric blurs. The air smelled of isopropyl alcohol. Somewhere, someone was talking, a metallic squawk of a voice.

But what was it saying?

He tried to shift a little, to move his eyelids just a tiny bit farther up, but even that small amount of movement caused horrible pain to scuttle through him, and he slumped back down. What was beneath him? Something soft? A bed? A pillow? He didn't dare try to turn his head to look. But he thought he felt scratchy linens pressing against the back of his neck.

Finally, almost involuntarily, a groan issued forth from his lips, followed by a whimper. The noise prompted a response from someone in the room with him. He listened as footsteps rushed across a floor. A woman's voice, frantic. "Donald?"

He groaned again. Once more, the world went black.

*

The next time he awakened, he was able to open his eyes. The pain was still there in full force, and the bright overhead light invading his retinas caused the piercing hurt to go into overdrive. But he let his eyelids flutter, allowing the light in in tolerable amounts until he was at last able to see, even though his eyes were crusted with gunk.

He needed to see.

Someone wiped at his eyes with a damp tissue. He blinked and looked up into the face of his sister, Grace. Her dyed blonde hair was tied back into a ponytail, and, unusual for her, she was wearing no makeup. Her plain fifty-seven-year-old face blinked back at him, creased with worry, horror, and concern. Her eyes were bright with tears, and one dropped on his face as she stared down at him, her mouth in a little traumatized *O*.

He tried to lift an arm toward her sad, terrified face, and the pain rocketed through him like a jolt of electricity. He cried out.

"Donald? Donald? Can you hear me, honey? Don't move. Just lie still." She put a hand to his forehead. The hand felt cool, dry. She stroked his face and smoothed back his hair. "Just try and lie still. You're gonna be okay." She leaned close to his face, and he could smell the coconut shampoo she favored. "You're gonna be okay. I promise. But you can't get too excited, sweetheart." She bit her lower lip, and he could see his sister was trying with all her might to hold back tears. Grace was never too good at that. She could collapse into sobs from a Hallmark commercial, so he knew her restraint must have been taking Herculean effort on her part. The thought almost made him want to laugh, but already he had enough sense to know that a spasm of laughter would send only pain, and no joy, right through him.

For a while, the siblings simply stared at one another. Grace leaned close, her light touch on Donald's forehead, a quivering smile on her lips.

Where was he? What had happened? Something horrible... Donald knew that something life changing and traumatic had occurred, but he didn't know what, not yet. But Donald could feel it out there, waiting, almost like an unwelcome visitor perched on a chair, just outside his line of sight. He wasn't sure he wanted to know, yet another part of him desperately needed to be brought up to speed, to discover what had brought him here, a place that was clarifying itself now as a hospital room.

Had there been a car accident? Had he been injured on his way to work? A terrorist attack? He knew it was none of these, knew instinctively that the truth was standing in the wings, ready to reveal itself in all its horror.

And he didn't know if he was ready.

So he looked up at Grace and tried, without much success, to grin, because a smile would have been way too much work, and managed to croak, "Water. Thirsty."

Grace moved out of his vision for just a moment and then was leaning close once more, pressing a flexible straw to his lips. The first sip hurt his throat, but he sucked down all the water in the plastic glass, in spite of the wincing pain. It was the coolest, best beverage he had ever tasted.

Grace smiled. "You want some more?"

Donald shook his head very slightly, very slowly. Grace replaced the water glass on a table next to the bed and stood above him, wringing her hands and trying to smile. "You've been through a lot, little brother."

Donald blinked, unsure of his capacity to form words. Finally, he croaked, "What? What happened?"

Grace glanced nervously toward the door, as if someone were standing in the corridor, waiting to come to her rescue, Donald supposed. He had enough presence of mind to realize Grace had some very bad news for him, and he also knew that his sister wasn't the stalwart type who could deliver it without breaking down herself. She shook her head and ran a trembling hand through his hair again. "Let's not worry about that right now, huh? You just woke up."

Donald stared at her. He was too exhausted to argue, too worn out to press the issue. Or maybe he just didn't want to hear what had happened. Even though he could remember nothing about what brought him here, to this hospital, part of him dreaded what the actual truth was. Maybe it would be okay to stave it off, to wait just a little while before the big, mean world came crashing in again. He nodded.

Grace placed her hand on his chest. "You're gonna be all right. You've been out for a couple days." She smiled. "And I've been here the whole time." She rolled her eyes. "I must look like a fright. But even though they told me there was nothing I could do and I should go home and get some rest, I just couldn't leave you here."

"Thanks." Donald reached up and placed his hand over his sister's. It hurt, but he wanted her to know how much he appreciated her being there.

"Are you hungry?"

At the mention of food, his stomach did a slow-motion flip-flop, and nausea welled up in the back of his throat. The very idea of eating something at the moment held no appeal. He shook his head and finally closed his eyes. "Tired," he whispered, releasing his grip on Grace's hand. "So tired." In fact, he had never felt more tired in his whole life, never mind that he had just been asleep for two days.

He closed his eyes and drifted off, Grace's comforting hand still on his chest.

*

When he awakened, Grace was gone. The poor woman! She had spent two days there with him? God, she deserved a break. Although if he knew Grace, he knew she would not have headed home to her apartment in Lincoln Square, but she was probably just down in the cafeteria, getting some coffee. It was good to have her, his sister. They had always been close.

He started wondering again what could have happened to him. The event stood in a dark corner of his mind, waiting for him to shine some light on it. He still didn't know if he wanted to. He realized that executing such an exposure would mean there would be no turning back. No more blissful ignorance. No more oblivion.

There were footsteps outside, someone nearing his room. In spite of the pain it caused, Donald sat up a bit straighter, leaning against the pillows and wondering how awful he must look. Vanity never seemed to die! It was probably just Grace, back from a coffee run. Maybe she brought him food? He thought he could finally eat a little something, especially if it was a sweet: a cinnamon roll maybe. One thing he could never resist was sweets.

What had happened to him all rushed back when the footsteps stopped outside his room and a familiar face swept in, smiling. The horrible night outside the Brig, the attack, all of it came flooding back, almost making him dizzy.

Mark!

It couldn't have been as bad as he feared. Mark looked fine, not one of his blond hairs out of place, his color vibrant. He wore his favorite: a purple Northwestern University sweatshirt, jeans, and a pair of Asics running shoes. He looked so good it immediately made Donald feel a little better.

"Jesus! You're okay! You're okay!" Donald grinned. "Man, just seeing you is working on me like the finest Vicodin." Donald laughed, and Mark joined him in his laughter as he drew close to the bed. "That's right, come on over here and give Papi a kiss."

Mark's lips were cool on his, and Donald attributed that to the fact he was probably running a temp from all of his injuries. But it was so good to see Mark, to put an arm on his strong shoulders and draw him close. He thought Mark should have been in the same condition, or worse, but here he was, looking just fine. Not even a scratch marred that handsome face he was so in love with.

"I gotta tell you, honey, you're working like a balm on me."

"Now, don't get too excited. You still need to rest." Mark pulled away and made Donald lie back farther by pressing gently on his chest. Mark fussed with his blanket, better tucking him in. "Just relax."

Donald closed his eyes for a moment, smiling. When he opened them, Mark stood above him, shaking his head. "You know what, Papi? You are going to come out of this just fine."

"Well, I should. I may not be as young as you, but you seem to be no worse for the wear. I can't fucking believe it."

Mark didn't respond. He just stood, staring down at Donald, his smile almost beatific.

"So where ya been? You see Grace?"

Mark's blue-eyed gaze went to the window. Then he looked back at his man. He shook his head. "No, haven't seen her."

The two men were silent for a moment. Then Mark reached down and squeezed Donald's hand. "Honey, I can't stay too long." The touch was like an electric jolt, and for an instant, Donald had a vision of the night sky, crowded with stars.

"What? The doctors tell you that? You tell them you can stay as long as you damn well please. You have just as much right to be here as my sister, and she's been here for the past two days."

"It's nothing like that. I just wanted to make sure you were okay." He paused for a moment, as though he was thinking. "And to tell you that, no matter what, we'll always be together. Love never dies." And with that, Mark turned and started out the door.

Donald got up on one elbow to call him back, and that was when he started screaming.

The back of Mark's head was a bloody, open dent. He could see shattered bone and brain matter.

Donald slumped down, staring at the ceiling and screaming.

*

Grace shook him. "Donald! Donald!"

And he awakened, staring up into the terrified face of his sister, not remembering where he was or who he was or what had just happened. He felt hot, his face clammy with sweat. The screams made his throat feel raw.

Grace leaned down and hugged him as best she could. "Oh, sweetheart, you were having a bad dream. That's all. Just a nightmare. Dr. McGowan said this would happen. It's from the trauma."

Donald pushed his sister away, and she stared down at him, surprised. "No! It wasn't a nightmare. Not quite." He took in a great, quivering breath. "It was Mark."

"Mark?"

"He was here."

And Grace's hand flew to her mouth, her eyes bright with fear. She slowly shook her head from side to side. She looked away from him, toward the window. When she looked back, her eyes were damp with tears.

"Oh no, honey, no. Mark wasn't here. You were only dreaming."

Donald sighed. "Now don't tell me what I just saw. He was here, plain as day, just as real as you standing next to the bed." He grabbed his sister's hand. "But Grace, he was hurt. Someone needs to look at his head."

Grace's lower lip quivered, and he saw it coming, a torrent of tears. She lowered her head to his chest and sobbed, great choking sobs unbroken for what seemed like several minutes. Donald stroked her hair.

What was going on?

When she was able to pull herself together, when her breath was ragged and quivering but calmer, Grace raised herself up and grabbed a tissue from the nightstand and blew her nose. She breathed in several times, exhaled slowly, and then turned back to her brother.

"Honey, we need to talk. There's something I have to tell you."

Donald shrunk into the bed, the pillow. He knew what was coming and yet didn't want to hear it. His physical aches and pains faded into the background, dull aches more welcome to him than the searing pain he just knew, instinctively, his sister was about to deliver. Part of him wanted to close his eyes, to find an oblivious spot in slumber, to never wake again.

And part of him just wanted to get it over with.

He stared at Grace like she was his executioner, like she was a jury with a guilty verdict, like she was the phone call in the middle of the night. He didn't even know if he had blinked.

Grace pulled up a chair next to the bed and took Donald's hand in hers. Her sobs had slowed to a few sniffles, and he could tell she was trying, with every ounce of will she possessed, to pull herself together. He knew she had to, knew she wanted to be strong for her little brother. He also knew, without thinking much about it, that this moment was killing her.

"Well? What is it? Sometimes there's no better way of saying something than just saying it." Donald knew the words were strong, but under the covers, he was trembling, knowing that Grace's next few words would shatter him. He tried to swallow and found, once again, he had no spit in his mouth. He thought for a second about asking Grace for water, but that would just be prolonging things. He was sure there was worse suffering in store than simple thirst. Thirst could be slaked. Whatever was on its way, he feared, was something that could never be corrected.

Grace scooted the chair as close to the bed as she could, until its arms were pressing against the mattress. She stared at a spot over Donald's head, then looked back into his eyes. She took a deep breath, the deep breath of preparation. She squeezed his hand. "Honey, there's bad news."

Donald nodded, the tears beginning to well up in his eyes but not falling, not yet. In his mind, he heard himself ask, "It's Mark, isn't it?" But he couldn't seem to summon the breath to say the words, nor could he remember how to shape his mouth and maneuver his tongue to get them out. He stared mutely at Grace, numbly anticipating the blow she was about to deliver.

Grace closed her eyes for a minute. When she opened them, the tears began to fall again, but this time she didn't sob. Her voice, broken and raw, betrayed her. But she was a brave little trouper and got through it. "It's Mark, Donald." She looked away, and her shoulders hitched once. "Shit! This is so hard."

Donald nodded. He wanted to help her; he really did. But he just couldn't seem to remember how to talk.

"Okay. You guys were out Saturday night, and you were attacked. Mark took a bad blow to the head with a blunt object, among other things. By the time the police got to the street where you guys were, you were unconscious, and Mark..." Her words trailed off, and her gaze returned to that spot above Donald's head. She looked back at him. "And Mark was already dead." She reached out an anguished hand to touch his face and stopped just short, the hand trembling. At last, she dropped it to her side and cocked her head. He knew she hated herself for the words she had just spoken. He knew she was feeling like she had just delivered a physical injury to him. In a way, she had.

Even though he knew the words were coming, they hit him with such force he wondered if he would pass out. Everything inside him went still. It was as if his heart stopped beating, his pulse stopped pounding. It was like everything just shut down. He expected to feel grief, horror, immense sorrow.

Instead, he felt nothing, other than the fact that one's emotions always had the capacity to surprise. He just felt dead inside, as if there were nothing left for him to do but draw in air and expel it, whether he wanted to or not. The trembling beneath the covers stopped. He wasn't even sure his head hurt anymore.

"Are you okay?" Grace whispered. She shook her head. "What a dumbass question! I'm sorry. Of course you're not okay. Oh, sweetheart, my dear little baby brother, I am so sorry. I can tell you that they said he probably didn't suffer, that he pretty much, um, passed quickly." She turned her head away from him and said in a dull voice, "I should just shut up."

Again, Donald wanted to offer her some words of consolation, to help her out of this hole of grief and sorrow in which she found herself, but there were no words.

Brother and sister sat for a long, long time that afternoon in Donald's hospital room, and neither spoke. Never once did Grace let go of Donald's hand. They sat quietly together until rays of late afternoon sun spread themselves across Donald's blanket.

Finally, Donald found some words. "I think I'd like to be alone for a while. Would you mind, Grace?"

Her lower lip was trembling as she regarded him. Her eyes were red. "Are you sure?" she whimpered.

Donald nodded and released her hand at last. He watched Grace get up and silently walk from the room.

Chapter Three

The staff at St. Joseph's had packed for him. Donald was too tired to worry about what the hospital staff thought about the ensemble he was wearing when he had been admitted three days ago. He didn't wonder if the nurses had snickered as they packed up the leather chaps, bar vest, and biker jacket. He wasn't curious about what they thought of his size twelve Harley-Davidson boots or his biker cap. The wallet with a chain, the white T-shirt (now stained the rust of old, dried blood), leather armband, and spiked cock rings were really the last things on his mind right then. Let them wonder. Let them snicker. No one could ever hurt him again as badly as he had been hurt just for being gay. So if the licensed practical nurse, a stoic black woman with cornrows and teddy bear print scrubs, would have a story to tell to her coworkers and her family when she got home, so be it.

He was beyond being a curiosity. Funny how being beaten and left for dead had a way of putting things into perspective. Funny how having the love of one's life die at the hands of some homophobic thugs made things like giggles and raised eyebrows trivial.

Now he sat in a wheelchair (although he didn't need it, but it was hospital policy), waiting. Earlier, Grace had brought him a pair of Levi's, his beat-up but comfortable leather Nike tennis shoes, and a dark-blue knit Henley.

His worn denim jacket would ward off the chill the gray skies outside his window promised.

Grace was taking him home. He wondered if he should revise that to Grace was taking him back to his condo. The concept of home no longer applied, not without Mark. Home had certain connotations, and those had been erased by brutality and hate. No, Grace was taking him to a condo: several walls, furniture to sit and sleep on, a bathroom and kitchen to attend to life's necessities, those pesky requirements that had no respect for his grief or the darkness clouding his mind.

Grace had begged him to come and stay in her upper story two-flat in Lincoln Square. She had reminded him that she could take care of him, that he wouldn't have to be alone. When he met her entreaties with stony silence, simply shaking his head, she threw up her hands. "Then do it for me, your big sister. If you won't come back to my place for just a few days, then be selfless and do it for me. Let me have the pleasure of taking care of my little brother. Give me no reason to worry, okay?" And then she had collapsed into tears.

Donald had been moved by her desire to help. Grace had an almost physical need to nurture and to see him through the immediate future, a future fraught with loss, grief, and physical pain.

But he had a prescription for Vicodin that would ease the pain of bruises and cuts. And he didn't know if anyone—not even his sister, who loved him more than she loved anybody—could ease the pain of losing Mark.

In the end, he had said, "Honey, I just want to be back in my own place. Those things of Mark's? The way he painted the kitchen yellow? The sage-green bath towels he bought? The framed photos of us? I want all those things around me. I need my time alone with my memories." He had looked at his sister, knowing his next words would be jarring and just a tad manipulative, but he said them anyway. "They're all I have left."

That had shut down Grace's campaign. Speaking of Grace, he could hear her cheerful voice outside the room, talking to one of the nurses. In moments, she was in front of him, smiling. She looked better than she had in days, finally having gone home to shower and change. Her blonde hair was pulled back into a ponytail, and her blue eyes sparkled. She had taken the time to put on some lipstick, mascara, and blush and had outfitted herself much like her brother in jeans, sweater, and running shoes. She looked ten years younger than when she had left him the night before.

Donald was glad that at least someone had found some solace in sleep.

He wanted to smile back at her, he really did, but it seemed the muscles in his face had forgotten the complex pattern they needed in order to create a smile, so he just looked up at her.

"You ready to blow this joint?"

He wanted to caution his sister to can the attitude of false good cheer but knew that would be mean. So he just nodded and let the LPN take the handles of his wheelchair.

What would the world outside be like without Mark in it? Would it be different, in deference to the loss?

"I stopped by Ann Sather and picked up some cinnamon rolls," Grace chirped. Once upon a time, they had been one of Donald's favorite calorie-laden treats, but the idea of consuming one caused only an acidic nausea to rise up in his gut and splash against the back of his throat.

He forced himself to recall how to put on a half-convincing grin and looked up at his sister. "Great," he mumbled. "Thanks, sweetheart."

Before he knew it, they were at the glass doors that would lead outside. Donald took a deep breath and glanced up at the LPN. "I can take it from here." He winced a little but otherwise was able to stand. Grace hurried to take his arm, and the pair headed outside.

*

Once in the car, Donald found he wasn't as keen on getting back to his condo as he thought he was. The memories waiting—Mark's running shoes beside the bed, his vitamins in the medicine cabinet, the flannel pajama bottoms he liked to wear when they watched TV, the organic bread he had bought in the refrigerator—all of these things would be painful reminders that Mark would never return to claim any of them.

"How about a drive down to the lakefront?" he asked his big sister, staring straight out through the windshield at the gray day. He could feel her gaze on him and could imagine her expression of curiosity.

"Uh...okay. But I thought you were so gung ho about getting home."

"I am. But I've been cooped up in a hospital for the past several days, and I just want to see something natural. Besides, it looks gorgeous from here." The pair was traveling north up Lake Shore Drive, and Donald could see the lake from the car. It reflected the gray sky, and its water appeared metallic, pewter maybe. Waves crashed against the boulders and concrete barriers along the shoreline, sending up splashes of spray.

The mood of the water matched Donald's own interior: cold and turbulent. He wished he felt well enough to just ask Grace to drop him off at the lakeside park so he could walk along the water's edge, getting damp from its icy, airborne droplets. At least then he could feel something.

Donald longed to feel something. He had yet to cry.

Grace drove to a parking lot that was near the water's edge, put the car in park, and shut off the ignition. "Well, here we are." Donald looked at his sister, watching her as she scanned the horizon of infinite gray water. He wondered if she was worried about the big slate blue, almost black, clouds on that same horizon, promising imminent rain or maybe even snow if it was cold enough. After a while, she turned to her brother. "How about one of those cinnamon rolls? Are you hungry?"

"Not now. I just want to sit here...quietly, if you don't mind." Donald's skin prickled with the comment. However gentle he made his voice, he knew Grace would be hurt by it. She would see it as her kindness being rebuffed; she would see his request for silence a shutting down of emotions. Grace was a great believer in communication, in talking things out. It had always been her way.

But Donald just wanted to be alone. Quiet. Silent.

So he could remember.

*

He had found Mark, fifteen years his junior and with the face of an angel but the mind of a demon, at the Brig, the leather bar they had patronized "that" night. But this was last winter, March, and it was bitterly cold. The bar was a Chicago institution with a strict leather dress code and lots of macho posturing. A Harley hung from the ceiling. Tom of Finland posters adorned the walls. Hard-core porno played on monitors hanging from the ceiling. A St. Andrews cross was set up in one corner. And then, of course, there was the infamous back room, where anything could happen. Donald knew the latter for a fact, since once upon a time, he had been a habitué of that back room, instigator, hunter, and hunted.

The Brig was not exactly celebrated as a place where love ignited and blossomed. It was known more for multiple, faceless partners in the crowded back room, where a full-length urinal ran along the length of one wall and one could indulge oneself with many partners in an evening, all of them unrecognizable should you pass them on the street the next morning. The idea of romance and a long-term relationship by the Brig's standards was a one-night stand.

Donald had fully expected, that night in March, to enter the bar, grab a shot of Jack and a Budweiser, down them, and head to the back room for a quick release. Oh sure, it wasn't pretty, and it certainly wasn't romantic, but it was efficient, and he could go home feeling that his evening was complete. His night had begun innocently enough with dinner with his friend Mary on Devon Street at their favorite Indian hole in the wall (they shared samosas and chicken tikka masala) and then a play at The Steppenwolf.

He could have, maybe should have, gone home after that, but once he dropped Mary off at her condo in Evanston, he found he was still wide awake and hungry for a different kind of companionship than his good friend could possibly offer.

But life often had a way of surprising you. Life often was deliberate and patient, waiting until just the right moment, when hope, such as it was, was extinguished, to throw a big, surprising present right in your lap.

And that present was Mark. Donald hadn't even glanced around the bar for potential suitors. He wasn't looking to make idle chitchat, to buy someone a beer, to go to some walk-up in Rogers Park where passion would rule for an hour at best, only to be eclipsed by an awkward exchange of numbers and excuses Donald would make about having to get up early in the morning and needing to head home. No, Donald was on his determined way to the back room, half downed beer gripped in his fist. He knew he could be in and out of there within minutes and home in his comfy bed in Edgewater fifteen minutes after that. The routine was becoming habitual, and Donald wondered, in darker moments, if he wasn't stunting himself emotionally with such behavior.

But dark thoughts like these were not foremost in Donald's mind as he neared the arch that would lead into the back room. The thoughts he was having (a warm mouth just waiting for him in the shadows) were rudely interrupted by the appearance of a stranger, blocking his path. The guy was young, blond, and smiling, dressed all wrong for the Brig. (His leather biker jacket was the only thing that had probably allowed him in the door on a Saturday night.) He had the kind of innocent face one might call cherubic: pale-blue eyes, creamy white skin, cheeks that were noticeably rosy even in the dim, functional light of the bar. His hair was a riot of curls, very Shirley Temple. Under the biker jacket, he wore a pair of Levi's and a dark cotton crewneck sweater with a white T-shirt underneath. Christ, the kid was even wearing Asics! The guy on the door must be asleep at the wheel tonight.

Donald almost couldn't believe the kid's smile was for him. He tried to brush by him. But then the kid said, "Don't I know you?"

Donald regarded him with a wary eye. Donald was six-two, with salt and pepper hair and a full beard to match. He had stayed in good shape and still filled out a form-fitting T-shirt well. The wrinkles around his green eyes and the bushy eyebrows above them only served to make him more appealing...especially to kids like this one, who, he knew, wanted to get around to calling him "Daddy" sooner or later.

He gave the kid a smile and shook his head. "Don't think so." He tried to brush by him again. Even though the kid was cute and the fact that he had approached him opened the door to possibility, Donald just wanted to get in, get off, and get out. He wished it weren't so, but Donald couldn't hide from himself, not after thirty years or so of hanging out in just such places as the Brig.

"Sure. You work construction...downtown. At Wacker and Michigan?"

Donald rolled his eyes. Was he supposed to be flattered? He supposed he looked the part, but he hadn't done any job even remotely physical since he had landed a summer job in a steel mill when he was in college. The truth was, Donald made his living as the director of marketing for a professional association downtown, not far from the corner the kid had just mentioned. If the kid had seen him at that intersection, he would have been wearing khakis and an Oxford button-down, not flannel, denim, tool belt, and hard hat. He placed his hand on the *kid's shoulder, and a little jolt went through him, unexpected but delightful. The kid felt solid beneath his cotton and leather, a real man's body, broad-shouldered, belying the Shirley Temple hair and the angelic face. It gave Donald pause. He met the kid's blue-eyed gaze and grinned. "Yeah, I drive a fork lift down dere." Donald could do a good Chicago south-sider accent. He burst into laughter. He couldn't maintain the ruse, not even for a few seconds. "Actually, I do work near Michigan and Wacker. But in a high-rise that was finished long ago. And the most physical labor I do is adjusting a mouse pad just so."*

The kid winked. "I probably could have guessed that, but I knew I needed a good opening line fast when I saw you walk in." He shrugged and took a swig from his beer. "The best I could come up with." He took another swallow and looked up at Donald. "I'm ready for another one. How 'bout you?"

And so it began. Before Donald could even respond in the affirmative, Mark had taken note of what brand of beer he drank and had nimbly made his way through the crowd, ordered, and returned with two fresh, sweating brown bottles. Donald hadn't even had a chance to think about answering the siren call of temptation issuing forth from the back room, just opposite from where he stood. In any event, when Mark pressed the beer into his hand and pressed close to him, Donald suddenly abandoned any thought of the back room. Tonight was going to be different. And no one was more surprised about the turn of events than Donald himself.

*

Donald's eyes were closed, his head lolling back against the headrest. He thought a perfect capper to this memory would be a lone tear, trickling, no, coursing, down his cheek. But the tears still eluded him. He felt a great nostalgia for that night when he and Mark had met, the magic of their union, how they had gone on to talk until the bar closed at five a.m., and how they had come home and fallen asleep in each other's arms, which was almost better than the sex they had when they awakened around noon. But where more recent events were concerned, Donald felt only numbness, a bland blankness of emotions that made him wonder if something was wrong with him. If perhaps the beating had somehow stolen his heart. Shouldn't he have cried by now?

Mark had never left after that first night, not really. There were a couple of weeks of back and forth from place to place, but it seemed like too much effort when both knew all they wanted was to be with the other, so they surrendered to their impulses. (And Donald would say they ignored common sense.) Mark broke his lease and moved in with Donald before March was up.

That was only six months ago, yet it seemed they had spent a lifetime together. How could one particular place in time, one single relationship, seem at once never ending and all too brief?

Donald opened his eyes and was surprised to see his sister, her back against the driver's side door, facing him and studying him.

"I almost thought you'd fallen asleep."

"Maybe I did. These painkillers make me go in and out so that I hardly notice."

"But you weren't?"

Donald shook his head and sat up straighter, wincing at the pain that screamed out in his ribs from the movement. He gave a pasty-faced smile to his sister. "Speaking of painkillers, I think I'm about due for some. Do you wanna get me home now?"

"Sure. Anything you want to talk about? You looked very deep in thought there for a while."

"Nah. Not right now. I just want to get home, take a couple Vicodins, hop in bed, and hopefully sleep for about twelve hours."

"That would be good for you." Grace started the car up and backed out of the parking space.

It was fewer than ten minutes before she was pulling up in front of Donald's Edgewater condo. He looked up at the building and felt nothing, no sense of homecoming or welcome. Anyone could have lived there.

Grace turned to him, smiling brightly. "You want me to come up? I can fix you something to eat, straighten up a little. I don't mind." Donald detected a small note of alarm in his sister's voice.

"Gracie..." He put his hand on her shoulder. "You don't have to be afraid of leaving me alone. I'll be okay."

She gave him a wan smile. "I know. I know you will. But I would like to help, to keep you company for a bit. Even if I just sit and watch TV while you sleep, it will make me feel better." She grabbed his face. "Do it for your big sister."

Donald gently pulled away. "Really, honey, I appreciate it. But I just want to be alone. How about we get together for dinner tomorrow after the wake? Maybe you could make me up a pot of Mom's vegetable soup? I'll need some comfort food." Donald deliberately kept mention of Mark's wake light; he didn't want to get into a whole discussion about that right now.

Grace smiled, more fully this time. Donald felt manipulative, but he knew that giving his sister a task would end her insistence on coming up to the condo. He just couldn't anticipate his reaction when he opened the door to that now empty space, and he really wanted to be by himself with those feelings, whatever they were.

"Well, if you're sure. Let me get your stuff." Grace put on her emergency flashers because she was in front of a fire hydrant and hopped from the car to get his small bag. She removed it from her trunk and set it on the ground near his front door. She then turned to him, arms outstretched.

"Be gentle," Donald warned, thinking about his bruised ribs.

"Bet it's been a while since you uttered those words." They both laughed. Grace gave him a brief hug, and then she was off, looking at him in the rearview mirror and waving. Donald waved back, then turned to the door and groped in his pocket for his keys.

As he approached the door, he saw someone through the glass. He closed his eyes and whimpered.

There was no doubt. Mark was ascending the stairs. His curly blond hair, the way his ass rose and fell in his faded Levi's... He had watched that same ascension with something akin to joy many times in the past. Now Donald placed his head on the doorframe, breathless.

He looked back, and the interior stairs were empty. His heart thudded. Seeing Mark was not like having a vision. There was nothing wispy or ephemeral about him, like Donald might imagine would be the case with a ghost. He seemed as real and solid as when he was alive. Suddenly, Donald didn't want to be alone, didn't want to have to face that hallway by himself. He turned to the street to see if it was too late to call Grace back, but her car was gone. Part of him said to call her on her cell; she would be only too happy to come back.

The other part just sighed and, with a trembling hand, fitted his front door key to the lock.

Chapter Four

Donald stared at the casket and squeezed Grace's hand. They were sitting on folding chairs at Reese's Funeral Home, where Mark was being waked. The casket was closed, allowing Donald to think hopefully that Mark was not really inside the bronze-finished steel box. Sure, it was all an elaborate ruse; Mark had faked his own death and was really still alive. Mark had links with mobsters from the south side that Donald never could have imagined, and the fag bashing was not done by hate-filled boys, but special agents for the witness protection program.

When Donald had seen Mark on the condo's outer stairs, he had not imagined it. He was really there, picking up a few last belongings before heading out to his new home and new identity.

Sure, that was why Donald couldn't cry. That's why he felt so completely numb sitting here in this hushed, tastefully done neutrally colored room. Deep down, he knew Mark was still alive, knew it on a subconscious level. He felt silly for having put on the charcoal gray suit with its delicate pinstripes, the starched white shirt, and the red silk rep-striped tie. The lace-up black Cole Haan dress shoes hurt his feet.

He looked around. The place was crowded. He never realized Mark had so many friends and family members. He and Mark had sort of cocooned themselves, as lovers often do in the early months, against the outside world.

Donald would have said they were still in their honeymoon phase. He hadn't even seen Grace as much as he used to once Mark came along.

Was Mark in the crowd right now, wearing a clever disguise? He would be eager to hear the loving words those left behind uttered, the fond memories and funny recollections. Would he be feeling much the same sense of loss that Donald was feeling? Perhaps he was one of the guys gathered near the front door. They certainly looked enough like Mark: big boned, ruddy complexions, and the curly blond hair that had so turned Donald's head.

Grace brought him out of his reverie and wishful thinking. "Check out the guys by the door up there," she said softly. "Those have to be Mark's brothers. They look exactly like him."

Of course. Mark had two brothers, Phil and Steven, both older, but not by much. Donald had seen pictures of them but had yet to meet them. He had yet to meet any of Mark's family, in fact, and that had been a sore spot in their relationship. But Donald, the older, supposedly wiser member of the couple should have understood Mark's trepidation. It would have meant bringing home his first boyfriend.

"Yeah. Quite a resemblance." Donald drew his lips into a tight line. He wished they hadn't come to the funeral home, to the wake that had been delayed for reasons he didn't quite understand. He looked at his sister, whose eyes were rimmed in red. She had pulled her hair into a bun and wore a simple black dress, heels, and a strand of pearls that had once belonged to their mother. Grace had done enough crying for the both of them in their short time at the funeral parlor. Apparently she had no problems believing it truly was Mark in the casket.

"You know what? I was thinking. What if that box up there is empty? What if Mark isn't really in there? What if he's still alive?"

Grace's mouth dropped open, and her face took on an expression of stricken fear. She looked nervously around her. Donald supposed it was to see if anyone on adjoining folding chairs had heard his remark. She smiled, but it was an uncertain smile that bore more of a relationship to a grimace than an expression of joy.

"What are you talking about?" Grace cocked her head and put her hand to Donald's face.

He moved away. Her hand dropped. "What are you doing? Checking for fever?"

"No, of course not. But, sweetheart, what you said, that's crazy. You do know that, right?" Her brows furrowed, and she leaned close enough that he could smell cinnamon, the Dentyne she had tucked into her mouth.

Donald shook his head and sighed. "It's just wishful thinking. Maybe trying to understand why I have yet to cry over this."

Grace squeezed his hand. "Oh, baby brother, that's easy. You're still in shock. You haven't accepted things yet. It's understandable."

Donald stared again at the casket, his gaze roaming over all the mourners, the little groups of them gathered in clusters, all speaking in hushed, serious tones, as if they wanted their conversation to match the muted wallpaper, ecru walls, plush carpet, and the overly heavy drapery.

What did any of this have to do with Mark?

He turned to his sister. "I know Mark is not in that box."

She cocked her head and frowned.

He waved her away. "Listen. He's not in that box. He's not in this room. I'm not crazy. Sure, wishful thinking made me entertain—for like, five seconds—that Mark isn't really dead, but I know he is. But I also know Mark isn't in that box. Not Mark. Mark's shell. Mark's body. Maybe. Those things might be there. But Mark is no longer with us. So he can't be in that box. He's not in this room either. He wouldn't be caught dead..." Donald sputtered out a mournful laugh at his unintentional quip. "At a place like this. Mark was full of humor and life. If he were here, he'd be cracking jokes in a corner, trying to make people laugh. He'd be trying to turn this wake into a party, just like his Irish ancestors probably did at one time."

Grace put a hand on her brother's chest. Donald could see she was relieved. "You're so right." She started to say something else and stopped. Donald had seen, peripherally, the movement he supposed had caught his sister's eye. One of Mark's brothers was heading their way.

Donald marveled again at how much the man looked like Mark, albeit an older variation on the same theme. He had the same wild blond curls, although his were more tamed by his shorter haircut, the same broad shoulders, although this man sported a gut Mark didn't have, and the same cherubic face. He was heading toward them with purpose, a smile lighting up his features.

Donald swallowed, his mouth suddenly dry, and tried to smile back. He didn't know if he was ready to finally meet some of Mark's family. He supposed he could mouth the same words that had been mouthed at funerals since time immemorial—sorry for your loss, such a tragedy. He could only hope the sympathy would be returned.

The man stood before them, smiling. Grace started to say, "We're so sorry about your brother—" But the man cut her off and turned his attention to Donald.

He continued to smile, but his words were tinged with acid. "You the boyfriend?"

Donald's mouth grew a little dryer. He nodded, suddenly unable to put his brain and tongue together to form speech.

"I just wanted to say how happy I am to lay eyes on you. How happy we all are—here in this room—to finally see you." He cocked his head, grin undiminished, blue eyes (so like Mark's!) twinkling. "See, I wanted to thank you." The smile faltered for an instant, and a sob went through the man's body, like a tremor. His eyes welled with tears. Then the emotion vanished, replaced once more by that hateful, terrible smile. Donald thought it would have been so much better if he were frowning, furious, yelling at the top of his lungs. "See, I wanted to say thanks for making my little brother a fag."

"Oh, now—" Grace whimpered, but the man put up a warning hand near her face to cut her off.

"Thank you very much, sir. Before he met you, my brother was normal, just one of the guys. He played touch football with us; he did normal things. He even had a girlfriend. Thanks to you, he's dead. Thanks to you, he was so badly beaten that we delayed the funeral so they could work on him, make him presentable so we could have a last look at him." He glanced over at the closed casket. "You can see how well *that* worked out." The man smiled more brightly and nodded, as if he and everyone around him agreed with what he was saying, as if he were speaking the voice of reason. And even though his voice was soft, the intensity with which he spoke caused the other people talking around them to go silent. Donald's face felt hot as he realized people were eavesdropping. He wondered if they felt pity or hatred for him, wondered if there was any ground between the two extremes.

"Yeah, you 'turned' him. Isn't that what you pansies like to do? Look at you. You were old enough to be my brother's father! Why couldn't you have just left him alone?" He turned away for a moment, and when he turned back, the smile was gone, and tears were rolling down his face. His mouth was drawn into a tight line. "None of us would be here now if it weren't for you, you perverted son of a bitch."

Donald's face felt even more heat, as if it were on fire. He was so stunned by the man's words, his mind had gone blank. He could think of no rational way to respond. The whole funeral parlor had now gone silent. He realized people were staring at him and Grace.

And he realized he didn't belong here.

Another of Mark's brothers, the eldest, Donald imagined, with a bald pate, came over and took the man who had just bashed Donald verbally by the arm. "C'mon now, man, this isn't right. Let's just go outside and cool off." The other man cast a glance back at Donald, and Donald was grateful to see that there was sympathy in his gaze. He mouthed the word "sorry" over his brother's shoulder and continued to pull him away.

Grace and Donald sat in stunned silence for only a few minutes. Grace took his hand. "I think we should go. You want to say goodbye?" she gestured with her head, stiffly, toward the coffin at the front of the room.

Donald managed to gather some spit in his mouth, enough to say, "No. I'm not saying goodbye."

Grace spoke softly, her voice infused with kindness. "Then let's just go."

Dear old Grace, Donald thought, bless her heart for holding it together when she could have easily let everything spin out of control. *My rock.*

Donald followed his sister out of the funeral home, feeling again the heat in his face as conversations went silent as they passed, as gazes bore, like lasers, into his back.

Outside, the pair of Mark's brothers stood stiffly next to one another, smoking cigarettes. Neither was speaking. They simply stared forward, two strangers who happened to be occupying the same place at nearly the same time. Donald could feel the tension coming off them, though.

"Just a minute," he said to Grace. He felt himself begin to tremble as he walked away from his sister and her comforting closeness. But he couldn't leave things as they were. He neared the brothers and caught the gaze of the one who had spoken so cruelly to him inside. The man glared at Donald, ready for a fight.

Donald cleared his throat and said, in a soft voice, "I'm really sorry you lost Mark. But I lost him too. And when you're calmer, maybe you'll realize that it wasn't me who killed him, or the fact that we loved each other, but it was attitudes like yours." Donald swallowed. "I hope, for Mark's memory, you can come to see that."

Donald didn't wait for the man to respond. He simply turned, took Grace's hand, and walked away.

*

After Grace dropped him off, once more begging to come upstairs with him, Donald slipped out of his suit coat and flipped on the gas fireplace. Grace had tried to shame him, reminding him that they had planned to have dinner together after the wake. "I even made the vegetable soup you wanted! It's on the floor in the back." Donald had felt bad about his sister, but his need for solitude overrode it.

He was about to turn on some lights, because it was already dark outside, but the flickering illumination of the flame suited his mood perfectly. Besides, what would he do with the light? Read? He hadn't picked up a book since the attack, even though, in his former life, he was always reading something: a new novel, a memoir, a biography, and, since Mark, even cookbooks. Watching TV seemed equally out of the question. Sitcoms and reality shows were even more trivial than they once had been, and the little he had stared at the tube had found him in a state of mind where it was difficult to concentrate on even something really simple, like *House Hunters* on HGTV. And after his experience at the funeral home, his concentration was shot. He still felt shaken, trying to get the image of Mark's brother's smiling face out of his head.

"So what are you going to do, sit here alone in the dark like a dog?"

The voice came from behind him, and it caused Donald to tense. He dug his nails into the leather of the couch, forcing his back hard against the cushion. What? Now he was hearing voices? Or maybe someone had broken in? But if it were a burglar, would he ask such a question?

"Hey, I asked you a question, mister. It wasn't rhetorical."

Donald's throat clenched, and a lump formed then, something about the size of a golf ball. He recognized the voice. He would not look back. He could not look back. It was almost as if he were frozen or paralyzed into this position, doomed to stare at a too-steadily flickering flame above some ceramic logs forever.

"Oh, I get it. This is the silent treatment, right? You know, you always were just a teensy bit passive-aggressive." The voice paused, and Donald felt a tremor, cold, course through him.

The voice was Mark's. Unmistakable. Rough edged, too deep for his blond hair and angelic face. Donald had once told him he sounded like Brenda Vaccaro, and Mark hadn't recognized the actress's name. He was too young.

Donald didn't want to look for two reasons. One, Mark would be standing right behind him.

And two, Mark would *not* be standing right behind him.

Donald wasn't sure which possibility was more terrifying.

"Aren't you going to say anything?"

Donald gnawed on his lower lip, surprised when he broke through the skin and was rewarded with the metallic taste of his own blood. He drew his shoulders up close to his ears as he heard sneakered feet slide across hardwood, the floor creaking in all the familiar places. He could now feel Mark standing right behind him.

"Well, Papi? What's the matter, cat got your tongue?" Mark laughed, and the comforting sound was like a balm to him. There was no strangeness in it, no terror, nothing paranormal. The sound was like the fire before him, only inside, warming him and illuminating him from within, for the first time since the attack.

"No, that fuckin' cat has not got my tongue. I'm just a little pissed at you." Donald drew in some breath. "Is that aggressive-aggressive enough for you?"

"Why?"

Donald felt the tension slip from him as he felt Mark draw nearer. "You left me."

"I'm here now."

Mark's hand reached down and kneaded his shoulder. Donald closed his eyes at the comfort of the big hand massaging, so familiar and soothing. He didn't know if this was real or some kind of fantastic hallucination, but he didn't want it to end. Donald was afraid that if he turned his head or tried to touch the hand on his shoulder, Mark would vanish like a stray wisp of smoke...and he would be alone again.

So he sat still, grateful when Mark's other hand landed on his other shoulder and got down to the business of giving him a good back rub. Mark was always so good at it, and Donald had once considered telling him he should go professional. Only he never mentioned it to Mark; he wanted to keep Mark and all of his talents to himself. Donald let his head loll back on the sofa cushion, eyes closed. He didn't want to think, to question.

"That feels great, honey. You always knew how to loosen up my muscles." Donald, without thinking, reached up and covered Mark's hand with his own. The touch was electric. Mark's skin was cool, but other than that, felt just as solid and normal as it ever had. Donald squeezed the hand and let out a little cry.

But then, almost simultaneous with the touch, Donald felt a jolt pass through him. A wave of nausea roiled within him, and he struggled to keep down what little he'd eaten. He felt a sharp, stabbing pain in his lower back, and his face broke out in a terrified sweat. His mind conjured up an image, unbidden and unwanted: Mark's face, looking at him, his eyes filled with terror, pleading with him for help. Behind him a shadowy figure moved, pulling Mark up and off his feet. Mark opened his mouth to scream.

Donald's eyes snapped open, and he was alone in a room that suddenly felt emptier, colder than it had before, in spite of the dancing flames above the ceramic logs in the fireplace. He lowered his arms; they had been upraised to answer Mark's plaintive gaze. The silence roared in his ears. Donald reached up once more, touching his own shoulders, wondering if Mark's hands had ever actually been there, really there. Or was it just something he wanted so bad his imagination conjured it up?

Why didn't I allow myself to look up at him? I would have loved just one more look.

Donald rose from the couch and paced the room, searching for evidence that Mark had been there. But his condo, a bachelor pad once more, looked unchanged. The place needed a good cleaning. The floors were dusty (and no, there were no ghostly footprints), clothes were strewn atop chairs, dishes were piled in the sink.

Donald sighed. His sister was right. He needed to get out more, to try to at least pretend he was still alive. Maybe if he pretended hard enough, the pretense would take on a reality of its own and life would go back to normal.

Right. Right now, that possibility seemed as remote as his next vacation being on Mars.

He stood in the middle of the room, trying with eyes clenched tight to rekindle the feel of Mark's hands on his shoulders. It had been real. It had been real. Until he had touched him...

"You want to watch the touching, Papi."

Donald looked around him, doubting again his own senses, but he *had* heard Mark speak, hadn't he? His voice was as clear as it ever was when he was alive.

Except when Mark was alive, Donald could see him when he spoke, and now the emptiness of the condo only mocked him and his isolation. What did he mean, anyway? "You want to watch the touching?" Was he warning him? Donald thought about how his touch brought up a painful image. Was Mark telling him not to touch him?

Donald shook his head and tried to laugh but failed. This was all too *Sixth Sense*, too *X-Files* for him. He crossed the room and picked up the phone, called Grace. When she answered, Donald asked her if she had any of the vegetable soup left and would she mind bringing it over.

Chapter Five

"Come on, they're waiting for us." Grace smiled at Donald, and he knew she was putting on her most kindly face, knew she didn't want him to think she was pushing him even though that's exactly what she was doing.

The two of them were in a parking lot in Donald's Prius. Grace had driven them down to the Chicago police precinct at Belmont and Western, where they had made an appointment to come in and look at mug shots.

Donald stared out the car's window. Finally autumn had dropped the curtain on its relentlessly cheery, blue-skied Indian summer days and had reverted to the kind of weather Donald now preferred: dark, dreary skies with a constant drizzle in the air. It was the kind of day where it was impossible to get warm, where the chill crept into your bones.

It seemed appropriate for his state of mind.

"I don't know if I can do this, sis. Maybe we could come back another day? Suddenly, I'm really tired." Donald didn't look at Grace as he spoke. Instead, he watched the smear of rain on the passenger window and thought about how it blurred the grim shape of the police station outside.

As he knew she would, Grace placed a hand on his shoulder. "Look at me."

He turned. Grace looked pretty today, her blonde hair down and curled around her face. She had put on lipstick, blush, mascara, and eyeliner. Her crisp white blouse, jeans, and black leather jacket all worked together to make her look tough and feminine at the same time. Under different circumstances, he would have teased her about hoping to meet up with a sexy cop, but he didn't seem to have the energy for teasing today.

Grace said, "They're expecting us, Donald."

He cut her off before she could continue, grabbing his cell phone off the dashboard and holding it out to her. "All you have to do is call them and tell them we've had something come up and we can't make it today. Schedule it for another time."

Grace regarded him, her frowning lips compressed into a thin line. Finally, she said, "And will another time be easier?"

Donald set down the cell phone. "I guess not." He turned and stared out the window again. A flash of lightning illuminated the slate blue sky and the low-hanging clouds. It was the kind of day that promised snow. Donald thought, *bring it on*. He turned back to his sister. "It's just that I'm afraid..."

"Of course you are. Of course you'd be afraid."

"No, wait! I'm not sure you get it. I'm afraid of two things: one, that I won't see or recognize any of the guys who did this to us, and two..." Donald drew in a shaky breath. "And two, I will." He leaned close to his sister. "What if I see one or all of them again, Grace? I don't know if I could bear it!" He knew his voice went up, a little shrill, on "bear it," and he didn't care. He was entitled to a little hysteria, wasn't he?

Grace placed her hand over his. "Donald, if you recognize one of them, that could lead to them catching the assholes who did this to you and Mark. Isn't that what you want?"

"I don't know, Grace. I honestly don't know. There's something that has me genuinely worried."

"What?"

"What happens if I can look at some guy's mug shot and say 'Yeah, he's the one'? What happens then? They bring him in. Maybe I have to come back and look at a lineup. Bingo again. Then what? A trial? Me getting up on the witness stand to testify, to relive the whole nightmare all over again, this time in front of a crowd of strangers and some defense lawyer who's going to try and make Mark and me look bad because we were out at a leather bar that night and strolling around Chicago when all the decent folks were home in bed? What good will it do?"

Grace took Donald's chin gently in her hand and turned it so he faced her. "What good will it do? Do you really need me to answer that? The good it will do is maybe it will get these guys off the street... The good it will do is maybe it will prevent what happened to you and Mark from happening to someone else." She dropped her hand, lowered the window, and lit a cigarette. She blew smoke out the window as rain pattered on the car's interior. "Isn't that enough good?"

Donald grinned in spite of himself. "Ah, my Gracie. You should have been an attorney, or at least in sales. You are a persuasive one. And when did you start smoking again?"

Grace threw the half smoked Marlboro out the window and closed it again. She smiled. "I didn't. I haven't." She looked over at Donald. "Let's go in and get this over, okay? I'll be with you every step of the way."

Donald felt nausea rise up in him and tasted bile at the back of his throat. "Thanks, sis."

And they got out of the car.

*

Grace and Donald were left alone in a room that was entirely what they expected.

"Jesus Christ," Grace whispered, once a uniformed male officer left them alone in the room. "It's just like an episode of *Law & Order*."

"Shhh," Donald said, casting wary glances over his shoulder at the large mirror along one wall. But Grace was right. The room was pretty much exactly what one would imagine for a police station interrogation room. It was surprising only in the fact that it was so unsurprising, Donald thought, and then wondered if that made any sense.

The room was small and square, maybe eleven by eleven. There were gray-painted cinderblock walls and no windows. The only furniture was a laminate table and three wooden chairs. The floor was green tile, industrial, scuffed. Donald wondered how many victims had sat in this room, how many thieves, killers, rapists. He wondered if they would bring him and his sister tepid, weak coffee and if two cops would come in, one to play the bad, one the good.

But they were not suspects. They were here to look at mug shots of some young men who had been involved in "similar activity" in the past. When the detective called earlier in the day (Donald couldn't remember his name but thought it was something predictably Irish, like Byrne), he had told Donald they had gone through and put together a few shots based on his descriptions of the men he had given them while he was in the hospital and the fact that these guys had all been arrested for what the detective called "hate crimes" in the past.

The funny thing was Donald had no memory of being interviewed at the hospital and certainly no recollection of giving anyone a description of who had attacked them on that awful night. Everything about that night was hazy. He didn't know how much help it would be looking through mug shots. He imagined himself staring into the face of one of his attackers and feeling no recognition. He wasn't sure if that was a curse or a blessing.

He turned to his sister and shrugged. "Again, I don't know what good this is gonna do. I don't know if I'd recognize any of 'em if they came up and spat in my face, let alone look at a mug shot and see them."

Grace's brow furrowed. "Just relax, Donald. Don't try too hard. You're right. Nothing might come of this, especially if you're trying to force it. But you never know. Maybe one of those asshole's pictures will be in the stack, and once you see it, you'll know. You'll know."

"But how? At best, that night is a blur."

Grace leaned close. "It's there, little brother." She tapped on his forehead and then looked over his shoulder at the cinder block wall, then back at him. "I was there in the ER, when they brought you in, holding your bloody hand and beside myself. You don't remember that, do you?"

Donald tried to access the memory but got nowhere. "I don't remember that."

"And you don't remember that you were conscious and you talked to a pair of detectives, a man and a woman, and gave them descriptions of the three guys who attacked you."

"I did not!"

"You did." Grace slowly shook her head. "Your mind is protecting you now, hiding things away that could hurt, like I put pins in a pincushion, if you can follow the analogy." Grace took a breath and glanced at the closed door behind her. "Where the hell are they, anyway?" She turned back to him. "You told them there were three guys, all young, probably teenagers, early twenties. You mentioned a souped-up car, one of those muscle cars, they call them. The guys were white. One wore a baseball cap; another had a bandana wrapped around his head. Maybe one was Latino? It was hard for you to remember much detail because it was dark and it happened so fast."

"I said all that?"

"You did. And that's why I think it's a good idea that you take a look at the mug shots, because I think those memories are there, and if the right guy is shown to you, it could trigger the memory, and you'll just know." She smiled. "You know?"

Before Donald could answer, the door opened and a uniformed police officer entered, carrying a stack of photos. She was broad-shouldered, heavyset, blonde, and had a "don't-mess-with-me" manner about her that probably served her well on the street. In spite of the uniform, the gun, and the cuffs, there was still something sweet about her face, which was rosy-cheeked and blue-eyed. She hadn't seen thirty yet, Donald thought.

"I'm Officer McKee. I'm going to be helping you out here this afternoon." She pulled out a chair, sat down, and crossed her legs. The mug shot prints she laid facedown on the table, where they immediately became blindingly conspicuous. Donald chastised himself for expecting her to turn the chair around backward and straddle it while she talked to them. He couldn't help but think of how his mother would have referred to the officer as a "tomboy," then wondered why he was thinking such things at all.

Grace eyed the door. "I thought the detectives would be meeting with us."

McKee nodded. "Usually, we don't do it that way, ma'am. We like to keep things simple and want to be sure there's no undue influence on your brother here. I am not connected with the case, so my body language, et cetera, isn't going to give any clues to your brother, subconscious or otherwise."

Grace nodded.

McKee continued, "What we're gonna do is look at the pictures one by one. Now, the important thing to remember is that you shouldn't conclude that because we're showing you these pictures someone involved in the crime is portrayed in one of them. This may lead to something, and then again, it might not. I will be keeping note of your reactions, Mr. Griffiths." She slid the photos across the table. "Take a look. Turn them over one at a time. Turn the one you were looking at facedown after you're done. If you see someone who looks familiar, set that one aside. We can shuffle and go through the photos as many times as you need."

Donald stared at the stack before him wondering if, like a monster under the bed, a young face was in the stack waiting to leap out at him and bring the awful nightmare of the night he lost Mark back to life in his memory. Was this really such a good thing? Maybe not remembering was the wisest course of action. Maybe if he could make it to his next birthday, and the one after that, and so on, without remembering, he would be okay.

"I don't think I'm going to remember anything," he said softly.

Grace spoke up. "Take a look, Donald. I'm right here. Remember, we want to catch these guys so it doesn't happen to someone else."

"Right." Donald placed his hand on the stack and let it lay there for a beat, then turned the first mug shot over.

*

Donald sat in the car, hands over his face. Grace kneaded his shoulders. He knew she was trying to find just the right words to comfort him.

"It's okay. Just because you didn't recognize any of the mug shots doesn't mean a thing. They could *have* mug shots of the culprits and the police just didn't ferret them out to show you. They might never have been arrested, and so there wouldn't *be* any mug shots."

Donald let his hands drop to his lap. "And I might have been staring right at them and not realized it."

"Like I said in there, I don't think that would happen. I believe if you saw one of the animals who did this to you, you'd have a flash of recognition."

"I don't care what you believe."

"Donald!"

"I'm sorry. It's just that I'm all mixed up. You know? I mean, I want to put all this behind me somehow, some way, if that's even possible. And I'd like to think these 'animals,' as you call them, getting put behind bars might give me a little closure. It's all well and good to think about finding them to protect other people out there from their hate, but right now I only have room to think of myself. Is that terrible?"

"No."

"But if there's a chance I can't even recognize them, that I have some sort of mental block, I don't see how they'll ever get caught. And does that mean I'm stuck in this hell, this limbo, forever?"

Grace smiled and said, "Even a lapsed Catholic like you should know that limbo and hell are not the same places."

Donald growled. "Leave it to you to split hairs at a time like this."

"Forget it, Donald. I was just trying to lighten things up a bit."

"Oh, that's great. Let's find the humor in getting fag bashed." Donald looked over at his sister's stunned face, her mouth hanging open, and immediately felt a hot flush of shame rise to his face. "I'm sorry, honey. I'm just not myself these days."

"I know." She ran a hand through his hair. "I understand." She started up the car and tuned the radio to WXRT. An old Counting Crows song, "Round Here," was playing. Its plaintive melody just added to the sadness in the car. Grace snapped the radio off. "How about we go grab a bite to eat? I can just head up Western to Devon, and we can be at Hema's Kitchen in no time."

Donald knew she was just trying to please him by suggesting one of his favorite Indian restaurants to take his mind off his heartache, but the idea of food, even his favorite kind, was not appealing right now.

He sighed. "Could I take a rain check? I don't much feeling like going out to eat. I'd just like to go home."

Grace switched the wipers on. "No prob. It's a perfect day for a rain check." Grace put the car in reverse, backed up, and headed out onto Chicago's busy streets.

*

The next morning, Donald still felt like a failure as he sat in front of the TV in his condo, wearing only a robe and boxer shorts. A cup of coffee, gone tepid, and a box of untouched Entenmann's chocolate doughnuts were on the coffee table before him. He had muted the sound but could see a young couple in Portland, Oregon, looking at master suites and designer kitchens...another HGTV show about happy people finding a home. He didn't want to hear their comments on room sizes and how the yard needed to be fenced for their dog.

He didn't want to think of happy couples nesting. But the movement, the flickering screen, helped divert his attention away from the time at the police station, gave him no reason to question why he couldn't do something as simple as remember the thugs who had beaten him so badly his ribs still ached and who had stolen his Mark away from him. His Mark...so young and so beautiful. It wasn't fair that all the happy years ahead of them had been snatched away in what? A few minutes' time? Snatched away with the casual cruelty of hate by people whose idea of fun was dealing out disaster.

And now he was here, in their old home, the condo Donald had bought alone but which Mark had insisted, in his quiet way, on making theirs. It was early morning, and the brilliant late autumn light filtered in through the wooden blinds Mark had picked out. Donald could look around the little one-bedroom condo and see the entire landscape of two men who had loved one another and not the abode of a bachelor. There was the comfy leather couch Mark had found in the Howard Brown thrift store. There was something sweet about the small tear in the leather that Mark had tried to close with duct tape and then conceal with brown Magic Marker. It was ugly and beautiful, all at once, because it was so like Mark, welcoming and completely without pretense. And there was the lamp Mark had found thrown out in an alley in

Lakeview. Sort of a Grecian statue motif, the base was a half-naked youth holding his hand aloft as if he were holding up the light bulb socket. It didn't look half bad once Mark had cleaned it up and topped it with a spiffy new black shade. The kitchen held all sorts of things Donald, never much of a cook, had never thought he needed: Wusthof knives, All-Clad pots and pans, a food mill, something called a Microplane, and another gadget Donald snickered at when Mark told him it was a "reamer."

Yes, the place was full of memories. There was even some of Mark's hair in the bathroom sink, tighty-whities still in the hamper, a pair of Asics in the living room, one overturned, waiting for their master to return. Donald hadn't the heart to remove any of these things.

So why couldn't he cry?

He had yet to shed a single tear. He had thought, when he first came back home from the hospital, that the return would surely bring on an onslaught. But he moved through the two days since the wake in a kind of haze, a zombie. He might as well be dead himself, for all he felt for the world, for all the engagement he had with it. He had no interest in returning to his job and wasn't sure when he would. He had accrued more than four weeks of vacation time and was seriously thinking of taking them all. The busy autumn days outside, the beach a few blocks away, the shops on Broadway, the Vietnamese restaurants he loved just up the street...none of these held any interest for him anymore. He even felt annoyed by these things, these places, continuing with the hustle and bustle of life when his own world had shattered into little pieces.

Grace and other friends had brought him food, and it piled up in the refrigerator, untouched. His sleep was a kind of stupor, heavy and dreamless, from which he did not want to wake. He hadn't showered or shaved in days and knew he was beginning to smell.

He got up and went into the bathroom, pissed. His urine was dark yellow, and Donald thought how the color was a sign he was not hydrating himself enough. What did it matter? He flushed and looked at himself in the mirror above the bathroom sink and laughed. He looked like an old man. "You are not even someone Mark would look at twice," he told his reflection.

A sunny day like this would be one he and Mark would have treasured. Mark would have headed out early for a run along the lakefront and come home to wake him with the smell of coffee brewing and bacon roasting in the oven. They would have lingered over the *Tribune*. Maybe taken a shower together that would have ended with both of them soaking the sheets of the bed with water and, soon enough, sweat.

Donald took up his place on the couch once more and stared out the window, again wondering how the world could continue so blithely after such a catastrophe. The traffic moved, drivers honking their horns in annoyance. A group of teenagers walked by, talk loud and raucous, laughing. Didn't they realize they should be mourning and not pretending that everything was okay? Didn't they know it was disrespectful to go on acting like nothing had happened? He shook his head, wondering if he could ever be part of this world again.

Eat. He had to eat something; it didn't matter what. Like the old man he thought he looked like, Donald slowly reached out and snagged a doughnut from the box. He consumed it, grimly and with no pleasure, washing its cloying sweetness down with cold coffee.

The sound of someone buzzing him from downstairs made him jump and gasp. The metallic bark and buzz was so loud and unexpected, it sent a jolt through him. Who could it be now? He didn't want any more sympathy and casseroles. He had told Grace he would see her for dinner later that week. She understood that this was his way of saying "Leave me alone for a few days; I need my space." But Grace wasn't always amenable to propriety, especially where caring for him was concerned. It was probably she, he thought, throwing the box of doughnuts into the trash and hurrying to the little intercom box on the wall.

"Yep." He leaned close to the box.

A man's voice came through. Not Grace. "Hi. You don't know me, but I'm your new neighbor." The man paused. Donald supposed the man downstairs had the amusing idea that this was a two-way conversation. He thought wrong. Donald considered briefly just walking away from the box. "And? Is there something I can help you with?" Never was an offer of help loaded with so much reluctance. Donald almost found it amusing. Almost.

The voice came through, a little awkward, with a forced cheeriness Donald found annoying. "Well, I just wanted to introduce myself. I'm Walter, up in 4B? Right above you?"

There was a pause, and again Donald considered just walking away from the intercom, shutting himself up in his bedroom, and not responding if Walter rang again. But he stood there, frozen. Finally, he pressed the button to speak. "Hey, Walter. It's Donald."

He paused with his finger on the Listen button. Finally, "Hey, Don. Could you come down here a sec?"

And a chilly finger of fear ran up and down his spine. He had pretty much shut himself away from the world since the incident and suddenly had the thought that the people who had harmed him and killed Mark were still out there, walking around. Who was to say they weren't downstairs to tie up loose ends and to make sure there were no witnesses to their murder?

Donald pressed the Talk button again. "No, I'm afraid I can't. I'm not well. Now, please, I need to rest."

Donald leaned against the wall, breathing hard, a light sheen of sweat breaking out on his face, chilling him even more. He was waiting for another buzz, but none came, and after a few moments, he walked away. He crossed the living room and peered out through the blinds overlooking the street. Downstairs was a man about his own age standing near the door. He had a shaved head and wore a pair of dark jeans and a windbreaker. He was holding onto a leash attached to a very unruly German shepherd mix that was barking furiously at a poodle in a Saab parked up the street. There was also a U-Haul parked in the loading zone.

Donald put it all together. The poor guy was probably moving in and maybe needed some help, someone perhaps to keep an eye on the dog while he lugged boxes and furniture inside to the elevator. Donald let the blind fall back into place. He couldn't have helped him if he wanted to; he was still too sore from being fag bashed.

"Last one." Mark let out a sigh and set the last of the moving boxes down on the floor. He leaned back against the wall, panting. All day, the two of them had struggled up and down the stairs with packing boxes, pieces of furniture, and odds and ends that wouldn't fit into boxes, like lamps and plants. Now the living room looked like a very unsuccessful thrift store: crammed with both Donald and Mark's belongings.

Donald eyed Mark and gave him a smile. "It's official. The bachelor pad is a bachelor pad no more. Now we're nesting." He could barely contain his happiness. His sister, Grace, some of his friends from work, and even a few of his bar friends from the Brig had all advised him against this, saying it was too soon, telling him that if it was right, the wait would only make their eventually living together even sweeter.

They were all wrong. Donald knew he, himself, would have advised against a couple cementing their relationship so soon after meeting by moving in, but when things were right, they were right.

He crossed the room and gathered Mark up in his arms, pulling him close and nuzzled Mark's neck. His sweat was sweet, with a slightly acrid under taste that only served to turn him on more. He moved up to cover Mark's lips with his own and explored Mark's mouth with his tongue.

Breaking away, Donald stared into Mark's blue eyes. "We're already sweaty; we're already panting. How about we hit the bedroom and see how much more we can take?"

"Why bother with the bedroom? What's wrong with right here?" Mark pulled the T-shirt over his head, revealing his muscled torso, pumped up from all the heavy lifting he had done that day. He pushed his jeans down around his ankles, exposing his lean runner's thighs and his cock, jutting out in front of him. "I can't wait, Papi." And he sunk down to the welcome mat just inside the front door. "Come on..." he urged.

Outside, the bark of his new neighbor's German shepherd mix brought Donald out of his reverie. Donald looked out to see the dog tied up to the streetlight just beyond the front door and yelping mournfully as his owner disappeared inside with another armload of belongings. Mark would have loved the dog. His family had had two German shepherds, and from their first week together, he had bugged Donald about getting a puppy. Just three weeks ago, he had worn him down enough to take a look at a breeder in Des Plaines who had a litter of puppies for sale. There were pictures and more on the Internet, and Donald had reluctantly agreed that they could ride out to the western suburb and take a look. "But that's all, just a look. I'm not promising anything here." And Mark had smiled, and Donald knew why. Mark understood that if he could get Donald in the same room with the puppies, he would not be able to refuse him when he asked to bring one home.

He was right.

Donald remembered that today was the day they had scheduled to go look at the litter, now eight weeks old. He imagined them in the Prius, headed west on Golf Road toward a litter of puppies, with thoughts of expanding their family on his mind. He saw how restless Mark would be, practically unable to sit back in his seat with anticipation. He saw and understood how it was he, Donald, who would really get the pleasure from this trip, giving Mark this wondrous gift of new life.

Finally, finally, Donald staggered back to the couch, collapsed on it, covered his face, and wept.

Chapter Six

"Did that hurt?" Justin touched the helix piercing in his uncle Walter's ear.

Walter reached up and touched the place where his nephew's hand had been and grinned. "Well, the needle went through cartilage, so what do you think?"

"It hurt."

"Yeah. A bit. But it was worth it. Drives the guys crazy." Walter leaned in close to his sixteen-year-old nephew and gave him his best Groucho Marx eyebrow wiggle.

Justin put up his hand. "You know I don't like to hear about that shit." Justin spun around on the barstool and then looked up at his uncle, who was busy at the counter in front of him, chopping onions and garlic. "Let's talk about something else."

Uncle Walter's hands moved in a blur as he chopped the garlic, getting it finer and finer with each movement. He had told Justin that the finer the garlic, the stronger the taste, and that was okay by him. Justin's uncle was forever teaching him about cooking. Uncle Walter said it was the single most important skill a human being could have, because all life and nurturing centered on it. Justin knew that a simple task like making chili for his nephew in his new apartment was pretty close to his uncle's idea of heaven. Justin also knew that his uncle loved him like his own son. Hell, he had told him the same thing enough times while gripping him embarrassingly in a sloppy bear hug, with Justin protesting all the while and pushing him away. "Cut it out! You know I'm too old for that shit!" Justin would think, but didn't say, that the physical contact with a gay man made him just a bit on edge. But he knew his uncle really did love him as the son he'd probably never have. And in his more quiet moments, when he was away from people like his friend Ronny and away from the weed and the alcohol he drank on the not-so sly, he appreciated having Uncle Walter in his life more than he could ever say. His mother, Patty, sure as fuck left a lot to be desired when filling the void of parent. It was hard for Justin to believe that she was Uncle Walter's sister. About the only thing they seemed to have in common was their lust for men.

But Justin preferred not to think about that. The thought made his stomach turn.

Uncle Walter put the onions and garlic into a big pot on the stove. Earlier, he had put bacon grease and butter in the pot, and when the vegetables hit the hot oil, they sizzled and immediately began sending up a scent that made Justin's mouth water. Walter rubbed his hands on the front of his jeans and smiled at Justin. "You know what, kid? I like having you over. It's nice."

"Yeah, it is."

"I sometimes wish it could be more permanent, you know?"

Justin rolled his eyes. "Uncle! I got a mom. I don't need another one."

Walter cast his gaze downward, and Justin wondered if he had said the wrong thing. "I know," his uncle said quietly. Then he looked up with a big fake-looking smile on his face. "And how is my dear sister?"

"Doin' good. She just got on in the cafeteria at Senn High School."

"Good for her. Although I gotta hope they don't have her cooking anything."

To make up for his earlier remark about already having a mother, Justin hastened to add, "Hey, Uncle, nobody could compare to you. She wouldn't even try. Nah, I think they've got her loading dishes into this big industrial dishwasher. Real glamorous." Justin guffawed.

Walter wagged a finger at him. "Hey. It's honest work. And it puts food on the table—such as it is—for you and her." He began breaking up ground turkey into the pot. "I don't have much more goin' on myself. A barista at Starbucks sounds more exotic than it is, and it's probably a lot less than a guy my age should have accomplished."

"I think you're doing great. Like you said, honest work."

Walter gave a stir to the pot. Hank, his German shepherd mix, sniffed up at the stove, tangling himself in his master's legs. "Shoo, Hank. You just had your supper." Walter shoved cans of tomatoes and kidney beans toward Justin, along with a can opener. "Get these opened for me, will ya? So what's your mom doin' tonight?" Walter wiped his hands on a dish towel hanging from the refrigerator door handle.

Justin set down the can of beans he was opening. He stared down at the laminate-looks-just-like-granite counter and said softly, "Who knows? Who cares?"

"Ah, Justin, don't be like that."

Justin shook his head, a head he had shaved close only yesterday, in imitation of his uncle. "Why not? She'd say the same about me. I doubt if she even knows I'm over here. I doubt if it's even crossed her mind to wonder where I am tonight."

"She knows. I texted her."

"That's not the point." Justin finished opening the cans and shoved them toward his uncle, who tipped them into the pot of now simmering onions, garlic, and ground turkey. "She's got a new man." Justin scratched his head. "What's this make? The third new man in what? Three months?" Justin laughed. "At least there aren't quite as many men around since she started going to NA. I guess that's a good sign."

"Damn right. It took a lot for your mom to make that step."

"Yeah, we'll see how long it lasts."

Walter lowered the flame under the pot and went around the counter to sit on a stool next to Justin. "Listen, I don't want you talking like that. She's still your mother. She's still my sister." Walter let out a big breath.

Justin knew what was coming. Uncle Walter had been having similar "talks" with him since he was in, like, third grade.

"I know it's tough on you, kid. I know it's been hard growing up around all the booze, and the men, and the drugs, sometimes. And I know that my sister probably wasn't always the most attentive mother."

Justin snorted.

"Hear me out. But I do know she's always loved you. She just got herself tangled up in things that were stronger than she was." Uncle Walter leaned in close enough to Justin that Justin could smell the garlic on his breath, forcing him to lean back. "If I didn't know that Patty loved you with all her heart, I would have tried getting you away from her. But I also know, in spite of everything, that would have killed her." He rubbed his hand over Justin's stubbly head. "Enough of this serious shit! My chili's going to suffer if I don't get back to it."

Justin just had one more thing to say on the topic of his mother. He couldn't help it. "I know. I know everything you said is true. I just wish she could stop with all the men. Just for a little. Give it a break, you know? There's not one of them worth anything."

"Oh, you know your sister and me... We just can't keep the men away."

"I told you, I don't want to hear it." Justin gave a mock shiver. "It's gross. And besides, shouldn't that be the other way around?"

Walter laughed. "You probably have a point." He stood up and gave the pot a stir. "There's a cute one downstairs. I see him looking down from his window sometimes, all brooding and butch."

Justin covered his ears. Walter rolled his eyes and started shoving aside spice jars in the cabinet next to the stove, pulling out cumin, chili powder, and cayenne pepper. "Damn," he whispered. "I'm all out of bay leaf. Can't make chili without it."

Walter thought for a moment, then grinned. He lowered the gas under the pot to barely an ember glow. "I know what I'll do. I'm going to run downstairs and introduce myself and see if Mr. Brooding and Butch has some bay leaf in his spice rack."

Justin rolled his eyes. "You probably have a big jar of it. I can see right through you."

"Think what you want. I won't be long." He began heading toward the bathroom, then stopped and turned to Justin. "You wanna tag along?"

Just to surprise his uncle, Justin said, "Sure." Justin got up and hung back in the little bathroom while his uncle splashed some water on his face and surveyed himself in the mirror. Justin could practically hear him thinking: *I don't look too bad for forty-seven*. His uncle's stubbly face, hazel eyes, shaved head, butterfly tattoo on his neck, and the piercings (the helix in his ear and the small stud in his nose) did make him look younger and like something of a tough guy. Justin also knew the tough guy illusion was shattered the moment Uncle Walter opened his mouth and started talking about recipes for piecrust or what Heidi Klum wore on last week's *Project Runway*. Aside from men, fashion and food were two of his passions.

Walter turned and pulled his black T-shirt away from his flat stomach and gave it a once-over. "Not too bad," he mumbled. "For once, I managed not to get any tomato sauce on it...yet." He turned to Justin. "Ready? I just hope he's home." He began leading Justin toward the front door and talking over his shoulder. "Even if he's out of bay leaf, I'd still like to meet him. I've been looking for an excuse for the last couple weeks."

"I told you. I don't want to hear it."

"Okay. Okay."

"Let's just go get whatever you need and get back. I'm hungry. It's goin' on eight o'clock. A guy could starve."

They headed down the stairs, and Justin listened as Uncle Walter described his new neighbor, wishing he wouldn't talk about another guy in such glowing terms. "I've been looking for an excuse to meet Mr. B & B—that's brooding and butch, in case you forgot—for the two weeks since I moved in. But the guy never seems to go out, so my carefully planned trips out to the dumpster or the mailbox have gotten me nowhere."

"How do you know this guy is even a homo?"

Walter stopped on the bottom step and turned to his nephew. "Now, you know I don't like terms like that." He continued on down the hall, Justin trailing behind and wishing he had just stayed in Uncle Walter's apartment with Hank. He didn't want to see the pair make eyes at each other or some shit like that. Walter stopped at what Justin presumed was the guy's door. "I have an ace up my sleeve, anyway. I've seen him out...at the Brig, a little establishment your uncle occasionally frequents." He laughed. "I know. You don't want to hear it."

No, Justin didn't want to hear it. Wasn't the Brig where those two guys came out of that...that night a few weeks ago? Justin felt a cold sweat break out on his face at just the mention of it. His stomach churned. He had heard one of the guys had died. Did that make him a murderer even if it was Ronny wielding the bat? Justin *had* participated, after all. He was what they called an accessory, right? He didn't want to think about the Brig or anyplace like that. He didn't even want to think about that night and had pretty much avoided Ronny since then, even though Ronny had texted and called him several times, trying to tempt him with beer and weed into joining him for an evening, as he put it, of "good, wholesome, fun."

Justin was about to tell his uncle he was going to run back upstairs, trying to think of a lame excuse like he thought the chili should be getting more heat or something, but just as he opened his mouth, he heard a voice from behind the door in front of which they had stopped.

His uncle looked back at him, a finger to his lips.

There was quick, furious whispering going on inside the condo. At first Justin couldn't make out much of what was being said, but from the tenor and tone, it sounded desperate and pleading. He wondered if his uncle should just send him to the convenience store over on Thorndale for some bay leaf. Obviously, the dude had company.

Walter cocked his head a little closer to the door, and Justin prayed someone didn't swing the door open suddenly, leaving his uncle, flabbergasted, to tumble inside the condo, like he was part of some bad situation comedy.

"Can't you just stay a little longer? Can't you please?"

Those words were clear enough. It was because whoever was saying them stopped with the whispering and just said them out loud, with a defeated tone. Justin felt heat rise to his face, embarrassed, finally, that he was hearing this. Again, he pondered whether he shouldn't just grab his uncle by the arm and pull him back upstairs, telling him he'd run out and get the spice.

But his uncle was already knocking on the door.

For several seconds it was very still in the condo. Then the door opened, and Justin felt something inside him drop, like his insides all plunged south. His heart started hammering. His throat closed up. He wanted to cry and throw up and wasn't sure which would come first and how he would hold back either...or *explain* either to his uncle...or to the man standing before them.

It was him. One of the guys they had beat up two weeks ago. There was no doubt in Justin's mind, and as if to confirm it, there was a cut on the man's forehead. There was an old bruise, faded to a sickly yellow, on his neck. He was the same guy, standing right here before him! The dude lived downstairs from his uncle! Oh God, what was going to happen now? Justin stared and knew his mouth hung open. He tried to rationalize that this was too coincidental, that this could not possibly be the guy they had attacked. But it was. He had the same salt and pepper hair, the same beard, the same broad shoulders and narrow waist. Justin remembered how powerful he looked that night, and he had been afraid that if he fought them, they'd be no match for him. At least not without the baseball bat Ronny had so thoughtfully put in the trunk of his car.

The man's face looked stricken, his eyes bright with fresh tears. He wore a tatty flannel shirt and old sweats. His feet were bare. His stricken expression, though, quickly turned to one of annoyance. He looked Walter up and down with distaste. Justin assumed he hadn't even noticed him, standing just behind his uncle. At least not yet. What would he do when he saw him? Go ballistic? Call the cops?

He had every right.

"Do I know you?" the man said to his uncle, none too politely. Justin moved farther back behind him, not caring how weird it looked. He felt himself begin to tremble, and something acidic and alive had awakened in his gut and was moving around down there. He wanted to just run...but something, an absurd sense of propriety perhaps, held him rooted to the carpeted floor.

Walter, completely oblivious, extended his hand and gave his most winning smile. "Hi. I'm Walter Wakefield. I live upstairs from you." And then he stepped aside, revealing Justin. "This is my nephew, Justin."

Justin felt a dizzying jolt pass through him when he came face-to-face with the man and wondered if this was what one felt just before passing out. He knew—from that night everything went down—they'd never get away with it.

The other man took Walter's hand and shook it, but only perfunctorily; there was visibly no strength in his grip. "Donald." He glanced toward Justin and gave a little halfhearted wave. There was no recognition on his face. Could it be? It *had* been dark, and he *had* been hit in the head as well. And Justin *had* just shaved off all his hair. *Jesus Fucking Christ, could I be standing here right in front of the dude, and he doesn't even know who I am?* The thought did nothing to dispel the physical distress he felt, nor his urge to just turn and run. He didn't return the wave but simply stared at the man.

But the neighbor had already passed his attention from Justin back to his uncle. He said nothing more, and to fill in the dead air, Walter began talking.

"My nephew and I were upstairs whipping up a pot of chili. Cold night, you know? Anyway, just went through my spice shelves and discovered I'm all out of bay leaf and wondered if you might have any I could borrow?"

Donald sighed and turned from the door, mumbling, "Let me check."

Since Donald left the door open when he walked away from him, Walter took it as an invitation and followed Donald into his condo. Justin had no choice but to stay close to his uncle. Inside, it was dark, and there was the smell of rotting food in the air, alleviated somewhat by a roaring gas fire in the fireplace. The apartment, with the same layout as Uncle Walter's upstairs, was a mess (unlike Walter's): clothes strewn all over the place, dirty dishes in the kitchen sink. Through the open bathroom door, Justin could see damp towels piled on the floor.

Justin felt a pang rend his heart. The guy probably was still trying to recover, to pick up the pieces after what they had done to him. *Maybe I can just turn and run? Get the fuck out of here. I'll think of some way to explain it to Uncle. I just can...not...be here right now.* In spite of his thoughts, Justin stayed put, standing close to his uncle.

And then it hit Justin, and it made his skin prickle with the weirdness of it. There was no one else in the apartment. These places were small one-bedrooms, and with no doors closed, Justin could see into every room from where he was standing.

So who had the guy been talking to? There was no radio or TV on to account for the voice they had just heard. Justin bit his lip hard enough to taste his own blood and quickly shoved away the answer that came logically and immediately to him. He tried to swallow but had no spit. He turned his head and saw a framed picture on top of the entertainment unit in the living room...and shut his eyes. When he opened them again, he avoided looking in that direction.

The photo was the older man and a younger blond guy. The older man stood behind the blond with an arm wrapped around his chest. Both of them were smiling, and they were outside somewhere, with lots of greenery around.

The blond guy was the one they had murdered.

"I don't feel so good all of a sudden, Uncle."

"What?" Walter seemed annoyed with him. "What's the matter?"

"Just feel really sick."

His uncle looked hard at him for the first time since their little trip down the stairs. He put a hand to Justin's face. "You're all sweaty. Go ahead back up. I'll be right there." His eyebrows came together with concern, concern of which Justin suddenly didn't feel worthy.

Before Justin could make his exit, the man came back from the kitchen, holding out a glass jar from Whole Foods. "Bay leaf, right? You're in luck." He pressed the jar into Donald's hand, saying, "Keep it."

Walter waved the gesture away and unscrewed the lid. "I only need a couple." He extracted two of the dried leaves from the jar and handed it back to Donald. "Well, thanks."

"No problem. Enjoy your time with your nephew." He looked at Justin again, and Justin was sure he would pass out right here. But he didn't. And again, the man showed no sign of recognition.

"Thanks." Walter shifted his weight from one foot to the other. "Um, if you're not doing anything, maybe you might want to join us? There's plenty. I make a mean bowl of chili."

Justin's stomach flipped.

"No. I don't think so."

"Another time, then." Walter turned away and started out the door. Justin was positive his uncle was still half hoping the man might at least say, "Sure." But the only response Walter got was the door being closed behind his back.

"Cold fish," Walter mumbled, heading for the stairs.

"Yeah."

"You okay? You look white as a sheet."

They headed up the stairs, and Justin feared this simple exertion might cause his pounding heart to explode, or at least cause him to vomit right in the stairwell.

He tried to smile through the queasiness and gasped, "Just came over me all of a sudden, man."

He followed his uncle back inside the apartment.

"Hope you're not coming down with something."

*

Somehow, Justin managed to get through the rest of the evening with his uncle. Somehow, he managed to eat a bowl of chili and not vomit when his uncle pressed shredded Cheddar, chopped avocados, and sour cream on him. Somehow, he managed to make small talk about his mom and what was up at school. Somehow, he was able to sit still and listen to Uncle Walter bitch about his job and his lack of anyone special in his life.

But the whole time, Justin was replaying that night in his mind: seeing the guy from downstairs bent over in front of his car looking for his keys and hearing the jeers Luis and Ronny threw his way. He recalled how scared the guy was, how scared both of them were.

And it made Justin feel sick.

When the blood and the violence of that night weren't replaying on Technicolor loop in his memory, Justin was wondering what would happen next. Yeah, maybe the dude hadn't recognized him tonight, but what about the next time? Should he just stop coming over to Uncle Walter's? He couldn't do that. For Christ's sake, Uncle Walter was about the only stability he had in his life.

Maybe he could change his appearance even more, try to let the peach fuzz grow out a bit on his upper lip. Get a tattoo on his face. (He'd seen guys do that, shit like tears and stars.) Maybe if he looked different enough, the guy would never recognize him, no matter how many times their paths crossed.

And then, in his darkest moments, and this was when it was hard to give his uncle even the most fake-looking smile, he wondered what Uncle Walter would think if he knew what he'd done.

Yeah, Justin thought the whole gay thing was pretty gross. He didn't get how two guys could possibly do that to each other! With his uncle, he could just shove away any thoughts of him being with another guy and try to block it out when he made any comments that reminded Justin that his uncle was built "that way," as his mother referred to her brother's homosexuality. Uncle Walter didn't really *seem* gay; he didn't have any effeminate mannerisms; he wasn't swishy. Other than liking to cook, he was a pretty regular guy.

The point was Justin managed to pull it off. He got through the evening pretending he was just a little under the weather and going through the motions of eating, talking, and even laughing, like a regular human being.

And then that bloody attack would rise up again and make Justin wonder all over just what kind of human being he was.

He had to get out of there. He was down for spending the night at his uncle's and knew Walter had even rented a Godzilla (one of Justin's favorite monsters) movie from Blockbuster and had made a batch of brownies for later.

It all seemed too wholesome for someone involved in a murder.

"Hey, Unc, would you be too horribly offended if I took off?"

Walter looked at him, and the smile he had worn moments before vanished. Disappointment was plainly stamped across his features. "What are you talkin' about, man?"

Think, Justin, think. "I, uh, just got some stuff I wanna do tonight. I might hook up with my bud Ronny in a bit. He has a car and all." Justin tried to give him a winning smile but knew it probably came out looking more like a grimace.

"Yeah, but I got the Godzilla flick and got the couch all made up. I was planning on taking you to breakfast at Ann Sather in the morning."

Walter looked away from him, and it tore Justin up inside to hurt his uncle like this, when he knew Walter had tried so hard to make a nice evening for the two of them.

"C'mon, you don't want to babysit a teenager on Saturday night, do ya?" Justin felt a trickle of sweat roll down his back. He needed his uncle to release him or he was going to say or do something mean, just so he could get the hell out of there and breathe again. He felt dizzy, and the chili was acidic and tickling the back of his throat.

"I don't look at a night with you like that, Justin. You know that."

"I know. I know. It's just, you know, being a little under the weather and all that..."

"All the more reason you should stay here."

"Man, I really want to go!" Justin didn't mean to shout, but he felt he was going to explode if he had to stay there with his uncle even five more minutes.

The hurt look on Walter's face was immediate. "Then do what you have to. Just do me a favor and come back here...and don't make it too late. Okay? I know your ma thinks you're with me, and I don't want to lie to her."

"Patty doesn't give a fuck."

Walter sighed, and Justin could see he had tipped the scales in his own favor, such as they were. Walter put up two defenseless hands. "Just go. And be careful."

He got up from the little breakfast bar where they had had dinner and began rinsing plates in the sink. Justin knew his uncle was making a point of not looking at him. He hoped he wasn't crying.

Shit.

Justin hurried out the door.

The cold air outside made him feel a little better. At least he didn't feel like the walls were closing in on him or that he would throw up or pass out. The traffic whizzing by, the people on the streets, the bright lights lining the streets, all helped make him feel anonymous. He started walking toward the lake. Maybe he would sit on the beach and look at the waves roll in, see if he could see any stars. Maybe then he could stop thinking about what he'd done.

As he headed down Thorndale toward the water, he groped in his jacket for his cell. He didn't know if he was doing the right thing, but hell, how was a sixteen-year-old kid supposed to know what was the right thing? Especially with what he came from?

He flipped open the phone and began texting a message to Ronny: *We need to talk.*

Chapter Seven

The apartment was closing in on Donald. Like some great yawning and dark mouth, it was just waiting to snap shut, to envelop him in depression and despair. All around him were reminders of Mark, of the promising start they had made on a life together. His clothes, the pictures of Mark, photos of the two of them together, Mark's pots and pans and knife set in the kitchen, the faint smell of his shampoo still clinging stubbornly to a pillowcase Donald couldn't bring himself to wash, all of these things conspired to keep Donald a prisoner in his own cell of grief.

And then there were those times Mark himself had appeared to him. Those times were bittersweet, ratcheting up the terror and the loss and, at the same time, paradoxically giving him comfort, making him want to never leave his—their—home. What if he was gone when Mark appeared again? How would Mark find him?

In his more rational moments, Donald wondered, ironically, if he was losing his mind. If Mark's appearance was just a glorified form of wishful thinking. Dead was dead, right? Mark wasn't coming back.

But what if he was? What if all the stuff he had read about ghosts was true, especially about spirits clinging to this plane because of unfinished business? Maybe Mark was trying to tell him something. Maybe his appearances, vague, ethereal, and comforting as they were, pointed a finger in some direction, were sending a message Donald needed to receive before Mark could truly rest.

Thoughts like these were making his head pound. He stood and wandered to the window, where outside night had fallen and the bright lights of Chicago beckoned. It was Saturday night. Before Mark, Saturday nights meant one thing: sex. It meant taking what he referred to in his younger days as a disco nap and then armoring himself in leather and denim, heading out into the night to prowl, to connect in the most basic and base ways. None of that had ever been very satisfying, but that long period before he met Mark did have its high points and its moments, however transitory, of satisfaction, even if it was the satisfaction found only in something as common as an orgasm.

Even as he was feeling guilty, as though he were somehow cheating, Donald was—finally—heading for the shower. Maybe getting back on the horse, so to speak, would be the first step on the road back to some kind of normal life. Maybe going back in the Brig, terrifying as the prospect was with its new memories and bloody red flags, would help him push away this awful black wall of despair threatening to crush him. Perhaps seeing some of his old buddies would allow him to forget, even for a few minutes, the terrible destruction that had ripped his life apart. A few beers and maybe a shot or two of Jack Daniel's certainly couldn't hurt in the quest for a little oblivion.

He was entitled to a little of that, wasn't he? Oblivion wasn't necessarily a betrayal, was it? Life was for the living and all that.

Donald stripped off the smelly clothes and placed them in the hamper. He regarded himself in the mirror over the sink and thought that, even though he had foregone all but the most necessary food and trips to the gym, he looked good: his tall frame still packed with muscle and dusted with coarse salt and pepper hair. His dick hung thick and meaty between his legs, and he couldn't recall the last time he had even jerked off.

Had the last time he had come been with Mark?

Stop thinking like that now. Donald reached into the shower, turning the faucet to get the water good and hot, and checked to make sure there was plenty of soap and shampoo.

Sex for Donald had always been a kind of escape. He was good at it and, even at age fifty, was a sought-after partner, especially in the leather bars he frequented. Maybe a good lay (or even two) would help take the pain he had been living with—physical, emotional, and intellectual—down a notch or two.

What could be the harm in that?

While the water warmed, Donald stepped into the bedroom, dug in his closet, and filled the bed with faded and ripped Levi's, a leather bar vest, form-fitting white T, spiked armband, and leather bandana. He stooped and pulled out his combat boots from beneath the bed.

As he headed toward the shower, he thought he was like an actor preparing to step into character. And the truth was, it really wasn't much different than that.

But maybe if he pretended hard enough, the pretense, after a while, would become reality. It would be a diminished reality to be sure, for he could never completely lose that yawning void Mark had left in his wake, but maybe this new reality could become one with which he could *live.*

Donald stepped into the shower, looking forward to the hot sprays and suds that would hopefully begin to wash away weeks of accumulated grief and torpor.

*

Standing outside the Brig, Donald questioned whether he could go inside. He had stood now for a full five minutes, watching other Saturday night revelers, all dressed in uniforms of leather, Levi's, and latex, head into the Brig through the modified eighteen-wheeler flatbed that was its entrance.

He couldn't help but remember the last time he had gone through that portal.

Perhaps he should just hail a cab and head down to Halsted. He didn't have to go to this bar. There were other leather establishments in the city. But this was *his* hangout. If he went somewhere else, he would be letting *them* control him. Their actions would be changing the course of his life. Hadn't they already changed it enough?

But getting over this hurdle, Donald believed, was important. He took a deep breath, and the cold night air stung his lungs and was, in its own odd way, invigorating. *There's no time like now. Just put one foot in front of the other. They have painkillers in there in brown glass bottles that will make it easier. Look at it as a kind of spiritual detox.* Donald grinned at his own train of thought and stepped up on the flatbed and went inside.

Things were just the same as he remembered. Somehow, he expected his old haunt to have changed, in deference to his loss. But it appeared on this late Saturday night that his particular loss had been forgotten. Men were drinking and laughing in pairs and groups. Others leaned against walls, beer bottles clenched firmly in their fists, watching and waiting. They were like wallflowers at a high school dance, praying someone would notice and extend a hand. Ice clinked, and a techno beat played beneath the conversation. Once upon a time, the air would have been filled with cigar and cigarette smoke, but Chicago had stamped that out, and so the air was clear and somehow took away from the atmosphere, the appearance of raunchy, hard-drinking men so many of these guys wanted to project.

Donald stepped up to the bar. A gorgeous young man, clad only in a harness and strategically ripped jeans, came up to him. He had a perfect build, and his torso was covered with tattoos, mostly of flames. His shaved head and pierced nose made him look devilish. Donald felt a not entirely unwelcome pang of lust issue from somewhere south of his belt and then chastised himself for it.

"Sir, what can I get you?"

"Uh, Budweiser." The guy started away, but before he got out of reach, Donald grabbed his arm. "And put a shot of Jack down beside it."

"Yes, sir."

After three more beers and two more shots of Jack, Donald was no longer thinking about Mark, no longer replaying the events of *that* night in his mind, reliving the terror and the helplessness. No, now he was thinking more of keeping his balance and, if anyone did speak to him, keeping his words sure and unslurred.

He was just a little drunk.

And it felt good. It felt good to be free of his sorrow, even if the alcohol had just thrown a blurry veil over him, numbing and not really erasing. He looked around the bar, hoping to see a familiar face, but the anonymity of a big city like Chicago was working against him. He had remarked, more than once, how you could go into a bar in Chicago and not run into anyone you knew.

Tonight the place was filled with fresh new faces. Some of the faces, grizzled but youthful, were tempting. But Donald didn't know if he had the fortitude to go up to any of them and make small talk. He was unsure if the old conversational gambits and opening lines would work anymore. In the face of his grief, such come-ons seemed silly, shallow, and beneath him.

Yet his groin tingled, and he knew that his objective in coming out tonight was not to get drunk, although that was serving its purpose, but to get laid.

His gaze scanned the men going through the door into the back room. The back room, with its lights on, was probably little more than a filthy large closet, with a slop sink in one corner. But in the dark, it became a place of mystery, of wanton desire unleashed. The darkness and the press of bodies, the smell in the air, all made it possible to lower and often even cast aside one's inhibitions. It was liberating, anonymous, and sad all at once. Once upon a time, before Mark, Donald had found the back room to be a very efficient way of meeting his needs. Often, he could be in and out in a matter of minutes, his seed shot into a willing and anonymous orifice. The transaction left a lot to be desired when it came to actually meeting and connecting on a meaningful level with other human beings, but it served its purpose. No one got hurt, right?

Except, even back in the days before Mark, Donald couldn't help but feel just a little empty and depressed after he had availed himself of the willing men standing or kneeling in the shadows, as if he had eagerly opened a colorfully wrapped box to find nothing inside but dust.

Even as he was thinking these very rational and logical thoughts, and even as they were telling him it was probably time to go outside and hail a cab and head home to the relative safety and warmth of his bed, his combat-booted feet were heading across the bar toward the door that led into the back room.

He knew what would happen, knew that there would be more than one willing mouth or ass awaiting him, and knew that, in the end, though his balls would be emptied, he wouldn't really be satisfied.

But he did it anyway—crossed into the shadows. Why did he do it? Because he knew it was the one place where Mark would not be. And he needed to go to that place.

The crush of bodies in the back room made it hard for Donald to move. It was hot back there, and before he was even in the small confined space for a minute, several hands had grabbed at his crotch. The dizzy exhilaration of beer and whiskey propelled him forward. A nagging sense of claustrophobia pulled him toward the exit...and the war raged on. But the lust for physical contact was winning.

He stood near a wall, the urinal at his side. It was so dark he could barely make out faces. Nearby, a tall, skinny guy in a white T-shirt was getting sucked off by a dark shape on his knees before him. There were slurping sounds and, to Donald's amusement, every so often the sound of gagging. Donald could feel the suckee's gaze on him, inviting him to join in the fun, but Donald wasn't quite ready. He stared resolutely forward, as if he was unaware of the other man's pointed stare.

Finally a different man, this one presenting a strong and well-built silhouette, neared him. Donald couldn't make out any definite features in the dim but could tell the man had broad shoulders and a thin waist. His head was shaved. That was about all Donald could discern before the guy dropped to his knees in immediate supplication.

Donald was tempted to edge by the guy and wriggle his way through the crowd, get out where he could breathe again and move his arms. But instead, he took a swig of the beer in his hand and did not look down as the man groped at the buttons on his Levi's, fumbling and finally freeing his cock, which had already hardened. Donald was certain the man was grateful as his cock, already leaking precome, slapped him in the face.

The man took Donald into his mouth, and the swirling wet warmth gave Donald even more a sensation of oblivion. He closed his eyes and let the man work, his head moving restlessly up and down the shaft of his cock, breathing deep and taking it all the way down to the root, moving back up to pause and take it into his hand, staring at Donald's cock like it was an object of worship, which Donald supposed it was. The man tongued his balls for a while, then moved back to sucking, his tongue swirling around the shaft, teeth nibbling just beneath the corona. Donald kept his eyes shut tight, surrendering. Sometimes, he thought, it was just easier to do nothing, to simply let things happen.

Donald wanted to come and could even imagine the juices roiling in his balls, preparing for release, yet something kept him from going over the edge. It wasn't so much that a crowd had formed around the two of them, watching. That part made the whole scene even raunchier and more exciting. It wasn't that the feel of the man's stubbled head beneath his fingers commanded his senses, making him want more. And it wasn't that his faceless partner was good at what he was doing—the man was a cocksucking virtuoso. Donald shuddered to think how many other dicks had been inside the guy's mouth— tonight alone.

But he didn't know why he couldn't go that last yard and cross the finish line, so to speak.

He reached down to grip his lover-of-the-moment beneath his armpits, and pulled him to a standing position. The guy tried to kiss him, but Donald wasn't ready for that. He jerked his head back and away from the guy, thinking how, as his face neared Donald's own, it was somehow familiar.

He didn't want to look at that face, didn't want to place it. "Turn around, fucker," he growled into the man's ear.

And the man complied. He fumbled with his jeans, lowering them to his knees, and bent over, bracing himself on the urinal's porcelain, open and waiting. Donald thought for a moment of his sister, Grace, and how shocked she would be at what passed for romance in a leather bar on Saturday night.

Then he found a condom in his vest pocket, tore it open with his teeth, and rolled it down the length of his shaft. He paused, his dick poised at the man's crack, asking himself if this was what he really wanted to do. If this was how he wanted his first fuck after losing Mark to be. He squeezed his eyes together and banished the thought. When he opened them again, the man was looking behind him, trying to catch Donald's gaze and whispering urgently, "Come on, man."

And Donald didn't disappoint. He used his hand to guide himself to the guy's crack and then pushed. When the guy moved his hips to back against him, Donald shoved his entire length inside.

The man gasped but didn't move away. Instead, both of his hands moved back and gripped Donald's thighs firmly, to pull him in deeper. Donald thought of nothing as he gathered up the man's T-shirt in his hand and, using the fabric like horse reins, began pounding into the man's ass, hard and ruthless, with no heed for whether he might be hurting him.

And from the sounds the other man was making, Donald knew there was little need to worry that he was hurting him. The guy met his every thrust with a backward push, drawing him in deeper and deeper, as if Donald couldn't get his cock buried enough, as though hard as Donald might pound, the man wished for it to be still harder.

The sex turned hot, aerobic. Donald realized that most of the activity in the back room had stopped. A circle of onlookers had continued to grow around them, many of them rapidly massaging their own cocks and some succeeding at what Donald couldn't bring himself to do. Come drizzled to the floor, pale white globs in the darkness. Poppers were passed back and forth. The show was going full steam now. Donald and his lover-of-the-moment had become like a machine, working in perfect synchronicity, thrusts and groans being delivered with abandon. Donald pushed up his partner's T-shirt to expose his back, to allow the sweat to drip from his brow onto the man's pale skin. Donald could see the broad expanse of flesh was decorated with tattoos but could not make out the particulars of any one design.

Someone forced a bottle of poppers into Donald's hand. He took a hit on the foul-smelling liquid inside, and his head exploded with heat, rushing down to fill him, to cause his skin to tingle and his heart to race. At almost the same moment, another man slipped from the watching crowd to get on his knees and take the man Donald was fucking into his mouth.

The combined view of his bottom getting sucked and the rush of the poppers finally took Donald soaring over the brink. He groaned loudly and bucked his hips, burying himself so deeply inside his partner that his ass and Donald's groin were melded together, almost one flesh.

The orgasm was violent and seemed to go on for minutes. Donald writhed, the pleasure so intense and all encompassing as to be nearly unbearable, almost painful. He held himself deeply inside his partner as he felt the spurts ebb and slow. And then he took a deep breath and pulled himself out. The condom, looking like a pale sock, hung off the end of his rapidly deflating dick. He tore it off and flung it to the floor, where a pair of grabbing hands immediately snatched it up. Donald didn't want to think about the condom's fate or what use it would now be put to. There was a smattering of applause, and Donald felt himself blush.

He looked back briefly at his partner, who was still turned away, gripping the porcelain and breathing heavy. Just barely, Donald could see a pool of come on the floor at his feet.

Oblivion. He had achieved it.

And now he wanted nothing more than to get out of there. The walls were pressing in, and Donald did not appreciate the shoulder squeezes and strangers whispering words and phrases in his ear, like "Fuckin' hot," "Way to go, man," and "Can I be next?"

Donald did not pause at the bar for another drink. He did not stop in the bathroom to wash off and take a piss. He headed straight for the exit, craving the cold night air like an addict craves a drug, needing it desperately.

He hurried through the door, ignoring the doorman's call to him to have a good night, and headed across the truck's flatbed. He had eyes only for the sodium-vapor lit sidewalk before him.

Outside the bar, Donald breathed in the cold night air as if it could cleanse him. He checked to make sure he had zipped up, that his wallet was still in his hip pocket, and that he still retained the keys to his apartment.

He looked north and south on Clark Street, hoping to see a yellow cab coming his way, its overhead illuminated, letting him know it was empty. He had a brief flash that chilled him and almost made him stumble, of a muscle car coming down the street.

But the avenue, for the moment, was empty. Donald shivered and hoped this would not be a night where he would have to wait long for a cab. Usually, on Saturday nights, cabs were plentiful, and he was confident that he wouldn't have to worry about standing out here, defenseless, while carloads of thugs cruised by, preternaturally tuned in to what he had just done and wanting to punish him for it.

As these thoughts were rushing through his mind and his respiration was returning to normal, Donald felt someone standing behind him. *No, please, I don't need anyone to talk to me just now. I need to get home. Please move along. There's nothing to see here.*

The telepathy wasn't working. The figure behind him stayed put, and Donald had the sense that whoever was back there was waiting for him to turn and acknowledge his presence.

Donald was tempted to be stubborn, to continue the ruse of being intensely absorbed in watching for a cab—or even a bus. At this moment, Donald would have gladly hopped on a Number Twenty-two, even if it was going in the wrong direction. But he couldn't...and, since no mode of public transportation was coming to his rescue, he turned.

He realized two things at once: first, the man standing behind him was the guy he had just mercilessly fucked in the back room, and second, he was his upstairs neighbor. Donald did not remember his name.

The guy was kind of cute, in a post-punk, sloppy, ruggedly handsome sort of way. The sheepish grin spreading across his face, Donald couldn't help but notice, made him look even more appealing.

But Donald did not smile back.

"Hi," the other guy said.

"Hi," Donald returned too quickly, his gaze moving back to Clark Street, as if a cab could slip by him undetected.

"You remember me? I'm your neighbor, Walter."

"Sure," Donald said. "Upstairs."

"Right. Thanks for the bay leaf."

"No prob."

"I was hoping to get acquainted, but that was more than I dreamed about." Walter paused, thinking. "Well, maybe that's not quite the truth. I mean about the dreaming." He barked out a little embarrassed laugh.

Donald didn't have the heart to stay quite so tight-lipped. "Yeah, it was pretty hot."

The other man extended his hand to Donald. "Just as a reminder, I live upstairs from you, and I'm a bottom." Walter laughed. "And I have a flair for stating the obvious."

Donald allowed himself to smile, although he was still preoccupied with willing a taxi to come into view. "You don't have to remind me, Walter." Donald turned back to the street, scanning, watching cars pass.

"Um, you heading home?"

"Yeah. I was just wondering where the hell a cab might be. If I had driven over, there'd be probably about a dozen of them that would have passed by now, but Murphy's Law is one I have come to realize I must live by."

"That's good." Walter chuckled and moved his toe to shift some gravel on the sidewalk, then looked up at Donald. "I don't have a car. Since we're going to the same place, do you want to split that cab when it does finally come along?"

Donald most definitely did not want to split a cab, but what could he possibly say without coming across as rude and the world's biggest asshole? Aside from the fact that he had just fucked the guy, it was just common courtesy. The fact that they lived in the same building only made the proposal make even more sense. So Donald, in a demonstration of what was, for him, at this point in his life, largesse, shrugged and said, "Suit yourself."

Walter smiled broadly and seemed more like he had heard Donald say something like, "I'd love to have you with me for the ride home."

Before Donald had a chance to think of an excuse to get away (he was already contemplating an urgent need to use the bathroom inside or to have just one more beer after all), the cab, as if it had been waiting for just this moment, rolled down Clark Street, the white light on its roof shining like a beacon of welcome.

"That wasn't too bad of a wait." Walter stepped forward and extended his arm, and the cab glided to the curb.

Walter let Donald get in before him, then slid in next to him. Too close, Donald thought, but again, what could he say? He stared out the window.

"I must be your good luck charm," Walter said.

"Right."

The cab sped away from the curb.

*

In front of their building, Walter caught Donald's gaze and said, "You wanna come up for a nightcap? I've got beer, wine, a little of the harder stuff if you want..."

Donald groped in his pocket for the fare. He shook his head. "Maybe some other time. I'm really beat."

Walter grinned. "I bet you are."

Donald let the reference to their sex pass without comment or smile. He handed the cabbie a ten and told him to keep the change.

"Hey, I didn't mean for you to pay for the cab! Let me give you half."

Donald slid out with Walter behind him, bringing out his wallet and still protesting that he couldn't let Donald pay. Donald put his hand on his shoulder and looked him in the eye. "It's okay. You can get it next time. How 'bout that?"

Donald didn't have to be psychic to know that the promise of a next time was all the motivation Walter needed to smile. "Oh, okay. Thanks, man. You sure you don't want to come up for a drink? Help you wind down..."

Donald watched the cab pull away from the curb. The street was quiet, too quiet, and suddenly Donald felt vulnerable and exposed. "I'm sure. But thank you very much."

"Here, let me get the door." Walter produced his key, and Donald trailed him, wishing there were some way he could just enter his own building alone.

*

The sudden weight on the bed awakened Donald. He felt as though he were swimming up from great depths. The alcohol he had consumed clouded his brain. Finally, his eyelids fluttered open. His mouth and throat were dry. The room, with curtains and blinds drawn, was pitch-black, so Donald opened his eyes to a darkness so thick he almost felt like he could reach out and touch it. But this realization was tempered by the feeling that someone had sat down, or perhaps lain down, on his bed.

In another life, this would have terrified Donald and sent him scrambling for the lamp on the bedside table. In another life, the unexpected presence of someone else in a dark room in the middle of the night would have set his heart to pounding, his blood pressure to rising, and his adrenal glands to working overtime. Sweat would have popped out on his face, trickled down his back. He would have wondered, once, how he might surreptitiously snatch the phone and dial 911 before the intruder grabbed the instrument from his hand and placed a gloved hand over his mouth.

But this was in another life...a time before three wayward youths had decided they would make Donald and the only man he had really loved completely and without reservation, cruel sport to enliven a dull and drunken Saturday night. That was before his world was shattered.

Now the presence weighing down the bed was a comfort. No, it did not reassemble his shattered world, but it came close.

Donald knew the presence on the bed was Mark. For one, he could smell him, that particular aroma that was unique only to his partner, a mix of sweat and Old Spice shower gel. He wondered if Mark knew of his whereabouts earlier...and what he had done. A heated wave of shame rose to his face.

But in spite of the guilt and in spite of wondering if it was even possible to betray the dead, he felt grateful Mark was there with him...once again.

He had little else to live for.

He relaxed back in the pillows, feeling no fear, only contentment. Donald knew better than to turn on a light. Other times, he had learned that the light often chased Mark away. The first time Mark had come to him, he had switched on the light and found the bedroom empty. But in subsequent times, he had not been so stupid and kept the room dark, the way Mark seemed to like it now.

"Mark?" Donald whispered into the darkness. "Honey, are you there?" His voice was hoarse from need. It had been days, perhaps even a week, since Mark had come to him, and he needed to feel him near. Without his touch, even in this limited way, Donald feared he would go insane.

He knew others would think he'd already reached that destination.

He felt a hand grasp his ankle, and he smiled. "Oh," Donald said simply, his eyes brimming with tears and a warm blush rushing to his cheeks. He felt Mark stretch out beside him. "I've missed you."

Donald felt Mark's hair brush against his face and could picture those golden curls in his mind's eye.

At one time, Donald had been the more dominant one in their relationship. But since this change, he had been forced to learn to be submissive. Mark's presence was a fragile thing, and, like the light, any eagerness on

Donald's part could frighten him away, so that Donald was again left alone. He had learned to lie patiently and to wait. Sometimes it would take a long time. Sometimes he would have to be satisfied to simply feel his man stretched out beside him.

And other times...

Even though the room was pitch-dark, he closed his eyes when he felt Mark lean over him and kiss him. He parted his lips to allow Mark's tongue to enter his mouth and reveled in the sweet, clean taste of him, the little wintergreen taste beneath his saliva of Trident gum, Mark's favorite. He did not allow himself to lay his hand on the back of Mark's neck to draw him closer, as he would have liked to do, but met Mark's mouth with his own, hungrily, mashing his lips into Mark's and sucking his tongue.

It was all so real, so sweet.

And then it was not. What happened when he touched Mark began to rise up again, images from that night. They were always disjointed, as if someone had taken a film of the attack, cut it up, and spliced it back together haphazardly. There was Mark, lying on the ground, bloody and unconscious. Now, bent over to reach for his keys, Donald could see a pair of combat boots and dark jeans. There, the quick ascent of an aluminum baseball bat. All of this was accompanied by a dizzying sense of nausea Donald was sure was not brought on by his consumption of alcohol earlier in the evening.

He jerked away from Mark, both wanting to flee and desperate to revel in the nearness of him.

He lay in the dark, panting, and could feel Mark lying silently beside him. He turned and could see Mark's profile in the darkness, the strong nose, the mass of curly hair upon the pillow.

Donald did not dare touch him again.

But he could touch himself. Tears stinging the corners of his eyes, he reached down and grabbed himself, stroking roughly, never moving his eyes away from Mark. In this way, perhaps he could erase what he had done earlier that night. In this way, perhaps he could be with Mark once more.

Mark turned to him, and his blue-eyed gaze met Donald's. He smiled, unbearably sexy. And Donald so wanted to reach out and stroke his face, pull Mark on top of him, but knew the mixed blessing that would be.

Instead, he let himself dissolve into Mark's very real and hungry stare.

It took only minutes, and Donald cried out, writhing and bucking as he shot, remembering every single time this had happened before it all came crashing to a violent close.

And Donald was alone.

Now the gray light of dawn was filtering into the room, making vague shapes of clothes-littered furniture. Donald propped himself up on his elbows and searched the half-light for Mark, hoping to see him at the foot of the bed or maybe emerging from the adjoining bathroom. But he was gone.

Donald reached down and touched the sticky mess that was all over his stomach and chest. He scooped up some of his own come and brought it to his lips, wondering if he'd ever taste Mark's again...wondering if he could ever hope for more.

He rose and opened his blinds. The light was golden, the sun just peeking over the tops of the buildings to the east. He snatched at a corner of the sheet and wiped the now crawly semen off himself and sat down on the floor.

"Why don't you ever stay?" he wondered aloud.

The silence in the room mocked him. Donald got up and headed for the shower.

Chapter Eight

"Here come the fags," Ronny sang out, to the tune of "Here Comes the Bride." He snickered and sank down lower in the driver's seat of his Duster.

Justin shuddered as he watched his uncle and another man emerge from a cab and head toward the door. Uncle Walter wore black jeans and his biker jacket, on the back of which he had painted the red Chinese symbol for inspiration. The other man Justin recognized with horror as their victim. For just a moment, he had that dizzying sensation again and worried that he would faint. How would he ever explain it to Ronny? That man was dressed in jeans and a leather jacket, too, a leather bandana hiding his salt and pepper hair. Justin couldn't help but wonder what he would think if he knew two of his attackers were sitting not a hundred feet away from them.

Ronny took a drag off his cigarette and flung it out the half-open window. "Jesus Christ, do these guys ever find time to do anything else than fuck around with each other? I mean—"

"Dunno." Justin was close to trembling, for fear that Ronny, too, would recognize the man they had beaten, or worse, his uncle. Justin had introduced the pair only a few weeks ago, of course not mentioning his uncle was a homo. But Justin knew he probably wouldn't recognize them. Unless it was looking into a mirror, Ronny didn't seem to take much of an impression away from looking at other people.

"We should throw a little scare into them," Ronny said as the cab pulled away.

"What? Right here? This is where my uncle lives, dude! Remember?"

"So, you think he's gonna look out his window and see us?" Ronny laughed, rolling his eyes.

"Maybe. Who the fuck knows?" Justin stared out the window, praying his uncle and the guy from downstairs would get inside soon, before Ronny did something stupid. "Nah, but it just wouldn't be cool. It's too busy around here. And besides, they're lookin' for us. You know that dude died, right?" This wasn't the first time Justin had brought up the fact that they had murdered someone, but the momentousness of the information never seemed to faze Ronny.

Ronny pulled a one-hitter from the glove box and brought it to his lips. The flare of the lighter illuminated his face briefly. He held the smoke in, finally exhaled, and passed the little metal pipe to Justin, who took it gratefully. He suddenly needed the oblivion it would bring. And it might help him sleep, a prospect that seemed nearly impossible these days without pharmaceutical intervention.

He noticed Ronny had his hand poised on the door handle. *Please, Ronny, no...* He watched as his uncle and the guy talked in front of the building, wishing, wishing, wishing they would just get inside before it was too late. *Hurry. Just get the fuck inside, guys.*

What would happen if Ronny insisted they go after them, give them a little taste of what he called medicine? Over and over again, he said he didn't care that the other guy had died, usually capping the sentiment with the prediction that the guy who died probably would have succumbed to AIDS anyway. "This way, we just saved him some time. Quick and painless."

Justin did not share his friend's philosophy or his outlook that their victim's demise was painless. He had seen otherwise with his very own eyes.

Just as Ronny opened the door a crack, the men turned and went inside. An unavoidable whoosh of relief flew out from Justin's lungs.

"Shit." Ronny closed the door. "And I was up for a little fun."

"Me too." Justin smiled sickly in the darkness, whispered fevered thanks to any God, anywhere, who would listen.

Justin took another hit from the little pipe and handed it back. "Cashed," he said, holding his breath.

Ronny shook his head, produced a baggie of weed from the glove box, and began restuffing the pipe. Justin hoped Ronny had a big fresh supply. He wanted to be really stoned when he got into his uncle's apartment. He hoped Uncle Walter would be in bed by the time Justin climbed up the stairs, but even if he wasn't, his uncle was pretty tolerant of red eyes and a distant stare. Walter was no stranger to the enchantment of weed.

Ronny hit the pipe once more and passed it to Justin, who once again took it with great inner gratitude.

"Say," Ronny said, expelling a plume of smoke through the cracked open window. "Does your uncle know his new apartment is in a den of faggots?"

Still holding in his hit, Justin grunted, "Doubt it." He exhaled and said, "The north side, man; it's pretty hard to find a gay-free zone, you know?"

Ronny nodded, and Justin thought he could see a flicker of rage cross his friend's features, even in the darkness. But Justin immediately forgot the anger, immediately forgot even the jeopardy his uncle had been in only minutes ago. The pot was beginning to weave its soothing wisps through his brain, making him feel both lethargic and light-headed. *Good*.

"I should get upstairs. My uncle will freak when he sees how late I'm getting in."

"Okay, dude. But you should warn him to watch his back." Ronny laughed too hard at his own joke. Justin tried to manage a chuckle but came up empty.

"What's with you?"

"Just tired, man. Too much of this." He held up the pipe and then handed it back to Ronny. "This and the six beers. I need to crash."

"You sure you don't want to crash at my place?" Ronny asked in a voice that Justin interpreted, even through the marijuana haze, as hopeful.

"I'd like to. But I promised Uncle I'd come back tonight." He didn't want to argue the point. He had not slept at Ronny's since "that" night. It seemed too weird now.

Ronny stared out the windshield. "Suit yourself, dude. See you tomorrow?"

"Sure." Justin hurried from the car, racing across the street. He felt his face go hot as he caught, in his peripheral vision, a Chicago police car coming slowly down the street. Were they watching them? Tailing them, like he saw in the movies? Just waiting for a wrong move, maybe? Had they left something, some DNA shit or the like, at the scene?

Calm down, Jus, that's just the weed talkin'. Get inside. Almost simultaneously, the cop car and Ronny's Duster were gone from the street, in different directions.

*

Much to his chagrin, Justin found Uncle Walter still up as he fumbled with his key outside the door. He must have heard him out there, because he swung the door open and stood, grinning down at him. In the background, Justin could hear the Godzilla movie his uncle had rented playing.

"Have a good night?" Walter stepped back, opening the door wider.

"It was okay." Justin brushed by him, trying not to meet his gaze. He knew his eyes would be wrecked, a dead giveaway. In spite of his uncle's past use, Justin knew he was living the clean life now.

But apparently more than his eyes were a giveaway, because his uncle took a good whiff as Justin brushed by him. "Uh-huh. From the smell of you, I'd say you managed to have some fun, huh?" Walter laughed, but Justin could hear an edge of concern, maybe even disapproval, in his voice.

Justin felt the high drain out of him and longed for it to come back, throw a cloud over him once more. He never knew himself to feel so stone-cold sober after toking up and wondered if it was because his nerves were jangling. Justin threw his jacket on a barstool and plopped down on the couch, feigning intense interest in the movie.

Walter sat down beside him. "So what did you guys do tonight?" He punched Justin's shoulder. "Other than down beers and smoke pot?"

Justin turned his head slowly to regard his uncle, who was grinning. "That's about it, you know? Same old, same old. Cruised around, got bored, cruised around some more."

"You guys have too much time on your hands."

Justin leaned forward and grabbed the remote control and began studying it, as if he had never seen it before. "What did you do tonight?" He already had a pretty good idea, but he was curious as to how his uncle would respond.

"Well, since I lost my company here..." Walter gave Justin a pointed stare. "I went out and had a few beers myself."

"Oh?"

"Yeah, at a little place not far from here called the Brig. Ever hear of it?"

"Uh...no." Justin flashed on sitting outside the bar, watching guys emerge, waiting for just the right ones, waiting for the perfect window of opportunity, when it was late enough that the street would be relatively empty. His stomach churned. He wondered if his face was turning white. He tried to smile. "Have a good time?"

His uncle looked wistful. "Oh yeah."

They were quiet for several minutes, watching Godzilla rampaging through the streets of Tokyo. Uncle Walter spoke. "I thought you'd have some crack about not wanting to hear it."

Justin smiled. "I'm just glad you had a good time."

"I met our downstairs neighbor."

Justin felt a jolt pass through him. Was it getting hot in here? He felt a trickle of sweat run down his back. "Yeah, right. I was there, too, remember?"

"I didn't mean when we borrowed bay leaf from him, moron. I met him at the Brig."

"Was he any nicer?"

"A lot." His uncle again took on that wistful stare, and Justin had a pretty good idea of why, and it contributed to the growing nausea within him.

"I gotta get some sleep, Uncle. You mind?"

"I'm not stopping you."

"Yeah, you kind of are. You're sitting in the middle of my bed."

"Well, excuse me! I'll just clear out." Walter stood and looked down at him for a moment. Justin wondered if he was hoping he would relent and ask him to stay and finish the movie. But Justin had neither the energy nor the heart to make his uncle happy. So he just said, "Thanks," picked up the remote, and banished Godzilla to darkness.

Uncle Walter hurried from the room. "Don't forget: cinnamon rolls, eggs, Swedish pancakes...the works in the morning at Ann Sather."

"Great," Justin whispered, snatching the blanket, pillows, and sheet his uncle had left on a chair opposite the couch. He felt bile splash the back of his throat and wished he had asked Ronny if he could take a bud with him when he left.

Chapter Nine

Morning came much too early for Justin. He had failed to close the living room blinds before falling into an uneasy sleep the night before, and now the sun, rising up over Lake Michigan, came pouring in like an unwelcome invader, much too cheerful and bright for his mood and the lethargy that had crept into his limbs during night's passage, making him feel like an old man. He turned toward the back of the couch, pulling the pillow over his head and hoping sleep would come to his rescue once more.

But it didn't.

Wearily, he sat up, letting the covers fall off him. He stared at the golden light as if was an affront and wished he had a smoke but knew Uncle Walter would have a shit fit if he lit up in his house, hell, if he even knew Justin was polluting his sixteen-year-old lungs.

He sank back in the cushions and threw his feet on the coffee table. He didn't need cigarettes anyway. He wasn't yet hooked on them the way his mother was, or Ronny. Those two needed the cancer sticks to survive; they were like oxygen for them. Justin could go for quite a while—days, weeks—without even thinking about having a cigarette.

No, what he needed was to forget. The beer helped. The weed helped. But nothing really successfully banished the memories of that night from his mind. Even his uncle Walter was a constant reminder of what he had done, the carnage he had wreaked. And when he did finally close his eyes and sleep washed over him, his dreams recreated scenes from that night: the blood, the screams, the guy reaching out just before Ronny bashed his head in.

He wished he could talk to someone about what he had done. Maybe someone else would understand how he just got caught up in things and they just spun out of control. He never thought either of those guys would be hurt seriously. They had done the fag-bashing routine before, many times, but it had always stayed pretty safe: name-calling from cars, maybe roughing the guys up a bit and scaring them, but never anything that would leave scars or leave someone *dead*. He had expected more of the same that night in October that seemed so long ago now and, oddly, that seemed like only yesterday. He hadn't known about the baseball bat Ronny had in his car. By the time he had seen it in Ronny's hands, things were already careening out of control. Justin hated himself as much for his silence as his complicity. He didn't want to seem like a *boy*, you know? He was so flattered that Ronny, at twenty-six, wanted to be his friend.

But to not screw up a friendship to save a life? Man, that was *sick*.

But things that night just went so fast! It was like the name-calling and getting out of the car was like the part of a roller coaster ride where you're being pulled slowly uphill. The downward plunge was wicked, death defying, and over in seconds. Yeah, it was like that. The whole scene hadn't taken more than a minute or two, but when he replayed it in his mind, everything seemed to go into slow motion, giving him plenty of time to try to talk Ronny and that dude Luis out of what they were doing.

Yet he hadn't even tried.

And now he worried that Ronny would want to do it again, now that he had a taste for it. Would Justin be strong enough to stop him, or at least walk away? He just didn't know. He was—what do you call it?—an accessory now. If he risked Ronny's anger or disapproval, his older buddy might be only too willing to seek revenge, maybe even turning the law on him, Justin, no matter how self-destructive that could be to Ronny.

And what if Ronny did get caught? Justin had watched enough *Law & Order* to know how things worked in those interrogation rooms. Deals were cut, and they usually involved someone squealing on someone else. Ronny, he knew, didn't have the character to take the fall for Justin, no matter how much he seemed to like him. In exchange for a lighter sentence or whatever, he would be only too happy to implicate Justin, to tell his interrogators, in fact, that Justin was the ringleader...and that Justin was the one wielding the bat.

It would always just be Ronny's word against his.

He was stuck.

And in spite of it all, he still had this weird kind of affection for Ronny. It wasn't anything sexual. He was square with himself on that score; he did not go in for that shit in any way, shape, or form. Yet Ronny made him feel that someone cared about him, made him feel like a man, maybe even a bit of a badass. Uncle Walter gave him some of that, but he was blood, and something about Ronny's feelings for him made Justin feel special. Chosen, somehow.

"Sleep well?"

He hadn't even heard Uncle Walter come in behind him, and he literally jumped and gasped. "Jesus, Uncle! You scared the shit out of me!"

Walter chuckled. "Sorry about that."

Justin knew he was anything but. He had probably sneaked up on him to get just this effect. Screw him. He wasn't in the mood.

He turned to see Uncle Walter standing in the kitchen area behind him, leaning on the bar that separated the two spaces. He was clad in sweatpants and an old Clash T-shirt. "You want the shower first, or do you want me to go? Your choice."

Justin didn't have to think long. Maybe some suds and hot water would help to wash away the lack of energy and the crushing guilt he just couldn't seem to get over. Maybe not. But it was worth a try.

"I'll go first." He pulled on his T-shirt and got up from the couch. "You make coffee."

"Yes, sir!" His uncle laughed, and Justin wondered, heading toward the shower, if his uncle was really so out of it not to realize the torment his nephew was in. Didn't the dude have eyes?

*

Outside, the air was cold, and it made Justin feel a little better. The wind whipping off the lake and his body's shivering reaction gave him something else to think about as he walked beside his uncle over to Ann Sather's, the Swedish restaurant at the corner of Clark and Foster.

Uncle Walter was wearing the jacket he had on the night before at the Brig, and Justin wondered if the leather made the pair of them seem like a gay couple, then banished the thought as silly and paranoid. And in this neighborhood, filled with lesbians and gay men, the appearance of homosexuality on a Sunday morning was hardly anything to worry about.

Justin wished he could think of something to talk to his uncle about, but the harder he pressed his mind to come up with conversational gambits, the more blank it became. Uncle Walter, as usual, seemed oblivious to his inner turmoil and focused on getting to Ann Sather's and the cinnamon rolls for which the Chicago institution was famous.

One of the reasons Justin could think of nothing to say was the fact there was something nagging at him that he wondered if he shouldn't bring up with his uncle. His fear that his uncle might be in danger, especially if he continued to get to know his downstairs neighbor better, was a real concern in Justin's mind. Not only was he afraid that the man might one day recognize Justin, but he was also afraid that Uncle Walter's association with him might make him more of a target, especially if Ronny ever realized who the other man was he had been with the night before.

Ronny was all about no witnesses, and the fact the cops were probably looking for them, now that one of their victims was six feet under, might make him eager to see that Uncle Walter's neighbor did no more talking about what happened that night. He could see Ronny thinking of getting rid of the guy as getting rid of any link they might have to the murder, even if doing so was adding another killing to the list.

The whole thing was crazy. Justin just wanted to go home, crawl in his bed, and pull the covers over his head. Earlier that morning, he had even considered running away, but to where? And what would a sixteen-year-old do for money?

He shuddered to think.

They were just about to turn a corner onto Clark Street when Justin heard a low familiar rumble, the roar of a souped-up engine and the growl of a modified muffler. *No, it can't be. That would just be too fuckin' coincidental.* But it made a kind of sense that Ronny might come to call on this chilly November morning, to see if Justin wanted to hang out, so it wouldn't be so surprising if the bass of the engine was heralding the arrival of his friend.

The roar of the car grew closer, and Justin didn't want to look, even if looking would mean confirmation that it was another car making the racket and not Ronny. The fear that it *would* be Ronny was enough to keep Justin's gaze focused desperately on the sidewalk.

The car was finally idling just behind them, and Justin could tell it had slowed down. *No. Please, no.*

"Man, I'm hungry. Let's hurry up." Ann Sather's sign was within view; the door was but a few steps away.

Uncle Walter smiled at him and picked up the pace. But it was too late. Why had Uncle Walter worn the same jacket as last night? Maybe if he had worn something different, Ronny wouldn't put two and two together and realize that Justin's uncle was a fag, a sin worse than almost anything in Ronny's mind.

Nervously, Justin looked over and had his worst fears confirmed. It was Ronny's Duster, slowing to double-park. He was leaning over and grinning, rolling down the passenger window.

Justin just stared. He knew his mouth hung open and knew Uncle Walter was wondering what was up.

For a brief, panicked moment, Justin and Ronny's eyes met, and Justin could see Ronny was just about to call out a greeting when the smile vanished from his face, and he stared at Justin, then at Uncle Walter, then back again. It took fewer than ten seconds, but the look on Ronny's face was all the confirmation he needed to know that Ronny recognized his uncle. Ronny cocked his head, his eyebrows coming together.

Justin was about to say something, to call out an inane greeting, anything to break this horrible tension, but then Ronny did something that was worse than if he had called something out, even something as spine-stiffening as "Hey! What are you doin' with that fag?"

But Ronny said nothing. He quickly rolled up the window and shot back into traffic, the engine roaring as he sped away. Other brunch-goers turned to look.

Uncle Walter seemed both amused and baffled. "What was that all about? You know that guy?"

Justin couldn't force his tongue to do the necessary maneuvers to form speech and so didn't respond to his uncle. He merely stood staring after the fast-retreating car.

"What's with you?" Uncle Walter put a hand on his shoulder. "You're white as a ghost."

Justin tried gamely to smile. "Nothin'. I just must be really hungry. Can we get inside and order?"

"Sure."

The pair continued inside and had arrived early enough that they didn't have to wait for a table. Justin was quiet, unable to utter more words than to order one scrambled egg and a piece of limpa toast.

"I thought you were hungry."

"This is fine." Justin stared at the table, stiffening when he heard the little trill of his cell phone in his jacket pocket informing him he had a text message. He sat, frozen, at the table, his stomach churning as Uncle Walter stuffed bites of cinnamon roll into his mouth. He shifted the sweet to one cheek and asked, "Aren't you gonna get that?"

Justin tried to swallow but found he had no spit. Wordlessly, he flipped open the clamshell. Ronny had written: "What the fuck is going on?"

Justin didn't know how he'd manage to even eat one bite of his small breakfast.

Chapter Ten

Donald didn't expect the Brig to be so busy on a Sunday night, but the place was packed with guys looking for one last bit of excitement before the workweek began. Donald's gaze roamed over the crowd, and he actually saw a couple of guys he knew. Both were guys he had tricked with before he met Mark, and he quickly looked away from their faces, not wanting to be recognized, not wanting to talk to anyone.

What was he doing here anyway? He knew: more oblivion. He hoped Mark didn't see this as a betrayal, but it seemed like the only balm to his pain was sex. For those brief, intense moments, he could forget about what had happened to them. He could put on a back burner the ache in his ribs, the scabs on his head, and the crushing reminder that he had lost everything that mattered to him. In that back room, it was dark and anonymous, just the kind of place Donald needed to be right now, even though he knew, deep down, that the connections he made there would only fill him with more emptiness. But while they were taking place, his mind and his body went somewhere else, reacting biologically to the feel of warmth, wetness, and tightness around his cock.

Would this be his future, then? Burying his pain in sex, becoming a man who no longer felt beyond the tactile? Donald shoved this line of thinking down into a dark cavern in his brain, with a weak promise to examine it more closely in the light of day.

He glanced furtively at the bartender, tonight a man about his own age, wearing leather bib overalls and no shirt. His hair was buzzed, and he was painfully thin. Exposing his chest and protruding ribs did him no favors. His cheeks were sunken. He had probably been at his vocation for years.

Donald wondered, slipping through the crowd, if he would one day soon end up looking like this man. He didn't want to make eye contact because he didn't want to order any alcohol. Tomorrow he would return to work for the first time in six weeks, and he wanted to be at least somewhat fresh, his mind unclouded by alcohol fumes and vapors.

Like home base, the portal to the back room, dark and at the same time welcoming, rose up before him. Donald slipped inside, and it was like moving into another world. Silhouettes moved in the darkness. There was the smell of beer, the sounds of slurping, muffled groans. Someone dropped a beer bottle, and it crashed and shattered on the cement floor. No one laughed, and the activity going on back there continued uninterrupted.

Donald situated himself beneath a barred window that looked out only on blackness and waited. Soon enough, someone was on his knees before him, tugging at the buttons of his 501s. Donald closed his eyes, eager for the warmth of an anonymous mouth to surround him. He didn't care what his partner looked like, only what he could bring.

Lips and tongue encircled him, and Donald threw back his head, wanting the moment, the pure physical sensations, to last and, at the same time, to be over quickly. The man was an expert at cocksucking, and he took Donald deep into his throat, squeezing, then releasing. He moved up and puckered his lips, then let the head of Donald's cock break through. It was like fucking an ass. Donald grabbed hold of the man's baseball-cap-clad head and thrust savagely into his mouth, not stopping the bucking of his hips until he felt the tremors go through him.

Wanting to at least give the guy the option to pull away, he whispered, "Oh, man, here it comes. You want it?"

The man vigorously nodded, swallowing him deeper as Donald shot into his throat.

The man moved away quickly and didn't even look back at Donald, searching, Donald supposed, for his next means of sustenance. Donald surveyed the room with new eyes and thought about how shit like this was going on every night here, sometimes more crowded, sometimes less.

He had once been happy he had escaped this scene. He had not expected to find himself back here so quickly.

And then he saw him, standing across the room but visible even in the darkness: Mark. His face was in shadow, but his build, the outline of his blond curls, were unmistakable. Mark cocked his head, staring.

And Donald—face burning—rushed from the room, pushing those who barred his way aside. He was like a swimmer kicking upward out of deep water, hurtling to the surface for air.

He continued straight on and out the door.

Outside, the air was frigid. But it wasn't the cold winds heading down from the north that were making Donald tremble.

He stuffed his hands in his pockets, staring down at the sidewalk, and started the long walk home.

*

Justin didn't know why he let Ronny talk him into it. He didn't really even know why he saw Ronny anymore. Wasn't there some way out of this web in which he had ensnared himself? He especially didn't know why he let Ronny convince him to come out this Sunday night. He had unfinished homework, his mother was around for a change, and his apartment, for one brief moment, felt snug and secure, like a home, with the sleet tapping on the windows. Patty, his mom, had made Campbell's tomato soup and grilled cheese, gourmet efforts for her. The cold night and his mother's pathetic maternal attempts made Justin feel like he was at home, a concept he wasn't exactly accustomed to feeling.

But when Ronny had called a little over an hour ago, he could barely resist the impulse to just let voice mail take the call. He even lingered, staring down at the caller ID screen for several seconds before pressing the talk button. He needed to know what Ronny would say about seeing him...and his uncle that morning.

And at first, Ronny had said nothing. He picked him up in front of his mother's apartment and had a joint already burning. Perhaps the weed had caused Ronny to forget about seeing him with his uncle—his gay uncle—earlier that day. At least that's what Justin hoped. He didn't know what he would say should Ronny confront him, asking questions about Uncle Walter.

But once they had started driving and finished the joint, Ronny regarded him out of the corner of his eye. "So what's up, dude?"

Justin stiffened, recognizing a loaded question when he heard one. Still, he could enjoy a few more minutes of nonconfrontation by playing dumb. "Not much." He slid down in the seat, wondering why the pot wasn't performing its usual magic on him. He was tired of feeling tense, yet it seemed nothing, drugs included, could obliterate the feeling.

"Come on, man." Ronny swung the wheel, and they were headed down a one-way side street. All around them were two- and three-flat apartment buildings, yellow lights glowing in windows. Justin assumed that inside these havens of light, people were doing normal things: watching TV, getting ready for the workweek, talking, fighting, making love. Would he never reenter this world, innocent and devoid of murder? Could he just say to Ronny "Let me out here" at the next corner and then just never see him again? Would that be so hard?

But his complicity bound him to his older friend, just as securely as if they were handcuffed together at the wrist.

"You know what I mean. I saw you this morning with your uncle. What's his name, Walter?"

"Yeah, so?" The compulsion to jump out of the car was stronger.

"That was the same homo we saw last night. I didn't put two and two together until I saw the two of you this morning. That faggy leather jacket he was wearing was the tip-off."

Justin sighed. "Yeah, Ronny, my uncle is a fag. What can I do about it? He treats me okay. What he does in private on his own time is his own business, okay? It's none of mine. It's none of yours."

"And you like hanging out with him?" The incredulity came through loud and clear.

"Look, I got no choice. Sometimes, my mom sends me over there, and that's about the only place I can go. It's really not an issue. It's not like being gay is all he talks about. We have dinner, we play games, we watch movies. He's a good guy."

Ronny shook his head. "Un-fucking-believable." He drove in silence for several minutes. "He ever try anything funny with you? Ever walk in on you in the shower or shit like that?"

"No! I told you, it's not an issue with us." Justin didn't know what else he could say. He sank down farther into his seat, staring at the darkness gathered on the floorboards. He just wanted to go home.

"Well, my young buddy, I just hope I don't have to worry about you. I hope he isn't setting some kind of weird example for you to follow."

"It isn't like that."

They didn't say anything for a while. They were now in Andersonville once more, and Justin knew the Brig wasn't far away, a couple of blocks over, in fact. He didn't like it that Ronny seemed to be heading back to their old— and literal—stomping grounds. "Hey," he said, trying to put some lightness in his tone, as if the matter of his uncle and gay people had been talked out. "You up for playing some games at the arcade? On Belmont?"

Ronny stared out the window. "Nah, I'm more in the mood to cruise by that fag bar and see what we can see."

Justin's stomach flip-flopped. "Ah, I don't know..."

"Sure you do. What, you don't want to? Got some kind of allegiance now to your uncle or something?"

Justin wanted to say yes to the question but didn't dare. Ronny was ten years older than he, and there really wasn't any way he could argue with him. He just hoped there were no gay men walking down one of the many side streets—dark and treelined—alone. One thing Justin did know: he couldn't go through with another bashing. He didn't even know if he had the breath or the nerve for name-calling. "Why don't we just go back to your place? Get high? That's some great shit you've got, and we could pick up some munchies and watch porn. Sound good?" Ronny and Justin had spent many evenings like the one he had just described, and although the porn part of it kind of creeped him out, Justin was up for any alternative that didn't involve cruising by the Brig.

"That what you do with your uncle? Does he have some of that bareback shit?" Ronny seemed, to Justin, just a tad bit too interested. He wasn't going to dignify his question with much of a response.

"Forget it."

It took only moments before they were slowly passing in front of the Brig. There were other gay bars on that section of Clark Street, and even on a Sunday night, there were clumps of guys gathered, walking up and down the street.

"You know what that is?" Ronny pointed to the doorway of a dirty building that looked as if it had seen better days. There was a little neon rainbow flag above the door. Aside from that, there were no other identifiers.

"No. Should I?"

"It's a fuckin' bathhouse, man."

Justin looked at Ronny blankly.

"You know what they do in there? They take off their clothes and fuck and suck everybody else. Nobody even cares who they're doin' it with as long as they get the cock and the come."

Ronny stared at the entrance. Justin thought he looked wistful.

"How do you know?"

Ronny didn't say anything, and Justin could tell he was bristling at the question. Ronny's mouth became set in a line. Finally, he said, "I hear things, man. It's no secret. If you were older, you'd know." He turned to circle around the block. "It's sick, dude. The diseases and shit they pass around in there..." he trailed off, shaking his head.

Justin didn't know whether to believe his friend or not.

Ronny slowed the car. They were on a quiet side street now. "Look, man, there's one now. Away from the herd. I bet he just got done fudge packin' at the bar or that bathhouse."

Justin looked over and saw a lone man walking quickly through the darkness. He wore a leather jacket and had a baseball cap pulled low over his face. It was hard to make out much detail about his face because he was staring with determination at the sidewalk.

Ronny slowed the car so they were driving alongside the man. Justin felt nauseous, trying to quell a nearly irresistible urge to reach over with his foot and hit the accelerator.

"Roll down your window," Ronny whispered, snickering.

"Aw, c'mon, man."

"Seriously, dude, roll it down."

Justin tried to swallow and discovered he had no spit. "Come on, Ronny, let's just go back to your place."

"Fuck you." Ronny punched the brake hard enough to send Justin careening toward the dash. Ronny threw the car in park and leaned over his friend to roll down the window. "Hey, sweetheart," he yelled. "Lookin' for some more cock to suck?" Ronny guffawed. The man stopped and stared at them.

"Don't do this," Justin said under his breath. Ronny didn't seem to hear.

"Get enough come yet?"

The man shook his head and turned away from them, walking more briskly now. Ronny made the car move slowly forward, steering with one hand as he matched the car's pace to the man on the sidewalk's quickening gait.

And Justin could see it ahead: a fire hydrant and a big fat space for Ronny to pull the car over, which he did. The street was deserted; it was late and it was cold. No way was Justin going to take part in this. Not again.

"Maybe just a little tap on the noggin will set him *straight*." Ronny chuckled and reached into the backseat, where Justin knew he had a baseball bat. He wondered if it was—and knew it probably was—the same one from before. Was there still hair and blood caked to its steely surface? Why hadn't they gotten rid of it along with the clothes?

Justin grabbed his friend's arm. He tried to look firm but knew, even in the car's dark interior, his face must be white, slicked with sweat. It felt like his heart would hammer right through his rib cage. But he somehow orchestrated tongue and breath to say, "No. Don't do this. What if we get caught, man? What if somebody comes along? Gets your plate number? I fuckin' told you... They're probably lookin' for us after what happened with the other guy."

"You're a chickenshit. Stay here in the fuckin' car if that's what you want." Ronny grabbed the bat from the backseat, and before Justin could do anything further to prevent him, exited the car.

Justin watched as he followed the guy down the street. The window was still down, and he could hear the kissing sounds Ronny made as he followed the man, who was now breaking into a run. *Please, God, don't let this happen again.*

Ronny was out of control.

He watched as Ronny decreased the distance between himself and the man, even though the man was now running at breakneck pace, casting horrified looks over his shoulder. And Ronny was closing in. It would take only seconds before he caught up and raised the bat and brought it down on the guy's head. Justin recalled with horror the sound of the bat as it made contact with a human skull. He hiccupped out a breath and realized he was sobbing.

"Hey, gay boy! I got a real big dick for you right here."

Justin closed his eyes; he didn't want to see. He promised himself he would get out of the car and catch a ride home on the L. This was it. He wasn't going to see Ronny anymore. If he didn't like it, he'd tell him he was going to the cops.

But that plan wasn't necessary. Even without opening his eyes, he could sense the presence of another vehicle pulling slowly up beside the Duster. In slow motion, barely breathing, Justin opened his eyes and looked out the driver's side window. A blue and white Chicago police car had pulled up beside the car. Justin's heart—he swore—stopped beating for just a second.

The officer in the passenger seat was motioning for Justin to roll down the window. Where was Ronny now? Would this be it? Would this be where he would be taken in? Justin was afraid, once again, he would faint. Funny how he had never had cause to faint before in his young life, and now, all of a sudden, he was finding all sorts of good reasons to pass out.

But the delivery of such oblivion was elusive.

He rolled down the window.

"You need to move the vehicle, sir. That's a fire hydrant you're blocking."

The cop seemed friendly enough. His words didn't seem to go beyond anything other than run-of-the-mill police procedure. Justin gulped and said, "I'm just waiting for my buddy to get back. He'll move the car right away."

"Where is he?"

"Just down the street. Um, he has to pick somethin' up from a friend."

"Tell you what. We'll circle around, and if you're still here when we come back again, we'll have to cite your friend. And it's not a cheap ticket."

"Fair enough, Officer."

The police car drove away.

As soon as it turned the corner, Ronny startled him by hopping in the car and flinging the bat into the backseat. "Fuck, dude! That was close." Ronny was actually laughing. "Can you believe that shit?"

Justin shook his head.

"It was that fag fucker's lucky night."

"Yeah. Lucky."

Ronny pulled away from the curb. As he turned to head north, presumably to his studio on Morse, Justin said a little mental prayer of gratitude that the close brush was enough to quell his friend's murderous instincts for at least this night.

But what would happen the next time?

Justin brushed the tears from his eyes. "Come on. Let's go get high. At your place."

Chapter Eleven

Donald glanced over at the clock on his nightstand. It was 4:15 a.m. What was it about the middle of the night that caused time to pass more slowly, especially when sleep was an elusive bastard, always just a few steps out of reach? He had tried lying on his back and on both sides, but still sleep would not come. He thought he had last looked at the clock more than an hour ago, yet in reality, it had only been seven minutes.

He kept imagining another presence in the room. Wishful thinking. Since he had seen Mark standing in the back room at the Brig, he was certain his lover would appear to him again at home, even if it were only to scold him for his irresponsibility and infidelity. A branch tapping against the living room became, in Donald's mind, the creak of a footstep at the bedroom's threshold. A toilet flushing in the apartment upstairs had to be the liquid glide of a more spectral Mark, just before he settled on the bed.

But Donald was alone. He looked again at the clock— 4:17 a.m. Staring at the clock like this was getting him nowhere. It surely was not helping him sleep, and it did not make the time pass any faster. He lay awake, eyes wide open in the dark, nerves tingling.

The blowjob at the Brig had offered no satisfaction. Donald had assumed the physical release would be enough to allow him to sleep. Earlier in the day, he had called his workplace to tell them he'd be in the next morning. How would he face a full corporate day on no sleep? How would his mind function? Worries like these kept him tossing and turning. Usually, when he had been with Mark and they had made love at bedtime, it sent Donald into a contented, restful slumber.

Well, of course, you idiot. What you did tonight bears about as much resemblance to the sex you and Mark had as an elephant to an ant. Mark was a buffet. The encounter in the back room was crumbs, tasteless and dry as ashes.

He sat up in bed, letting sheet and comforter fall from his chest. The room, to his sleep-deprived eyes, no longer looked all that dark. It just seemed there was gray light filling the space, making the furniture and piles of clothes accumulated on the floor and the rocker in the corner nothing more than vague shapes—identifiable, yet somehow threatening. *Stop it; you're just being stupid now.*

Swinging his legs over the side of the bed, Donald rubbed at his burning eyes. *Since this is getting me nowhere, I might as well get up and do something.* He thought he would check his email, see with what new entreaties his sister, Grace, was trying to tempt him. He had been a horrible brother these last few weeks, avoiding all of her calls, so that at last she sent him overly bright and cheerful emails, promising home-cooked meals, weekend trips to Door County, antique shopping on Belmont Avenue. Donald had ignored most of them, sending them to the trash with the click of a mouse. He knew this was no way to treat his sister, who, after all, had only love and concern for him.

But when he powered up his Mac, he ignored his Gmail account and went directly to Craigslist, clicking on the "men seeking men" category. He told himself he only wanted to see what other kind of nutcases were up in the middle of the night posting messages to strangers to come over and have sex with them. There could also be the added benefit of some interesting photos to sort through. Donald had always been surprised at the boldness of some of the posters, putting naked and even face shots out there for almost anyone in the world to see, coworkers, straight friends, even Mom. Who knew who was looking at what on the Internet?

Donald scanned the orderly rows of blue-linked messages with their obscene, pathetic, and occasionally intriguing come-ons. Guys looking for three-ways and more-ways. Guys looking to PnP. Guys looking for husbands. Guys looking for head. Guys looking to bottom for black guys, Puerto Ricans, Middle Eastern gentlemen, little people. Guys with big cocks and small cocks. Guys with deep throats and ready holes. Guys looking to bareback. Guys looking to play safe. Guys looking for Mr. Right and Mr. Right now.

The list of requests, organized by date and time of posting, went on for an infinite number of pages. After a while, even the photos of muscular young studs with enormous cocks and pictures of other oversized members penetrating mouths and assholes became boring, having all the excitement of looking at medical textbook photos.

And still Donald was not tired. He refreshed the page to see what new messages appeared, and one caught his eye: "Horny in Edgewater." *Hmm, it's in the neighborhood, and who knows, maybe a second release would be just the ticket to slumberland.* He clicked on the link to open the ad, disappointed there was no photo attached.

"Good-looking in-shape guy in Edgewater, shaved head, nice endowment with hot ass and throat, looking for a little company. Anyone still up and looking for the same?" the ad read.

Donald hesitated, his finger poised above the email link that would allow him to send a message to Horny-in-Edgewater through Craigslist's anonymous messaging system.

Should I really do this? Shouldn't I just crawl back in bed? Even if I don't sleep, I can at least rest. And maybe a few hours of rest will allow me to get through my first workday in six weeks with at least a semblance of normalcy. And who knows? Maybe if I just give up on sleep, really give up on it, and lie down, the contrary bastard will knock me out, just for spite.

His thoughts all sounded very logical to him. In spite of the logic, he hit the link on Horny-in-Edgewater's ad that would take him into his email program and heedlessly typed: "Still up and horny, just like you. Also in Edgewater. Hit me back." He hesitated for only about a fraction of a second before sending his message off into cyberspace. Odds were, with this kind of thing, he'd never even hear anything back.

But almost as soon as he'd sent off his query, the little gong on his email told him he had a new message.

The message had only one word, a question, and it was from Horny-in-Edgewater: "Stats?"

Donald typed in his height and weight, the color of his eyes, the length and circumference of his dick, and the assurance that Horny-in-Edgewater would not be disappointed. He debated over whether he should attach a photo to the email and even browsed through the photos he had collected of himself (some for this very purpose, once upon a time) and opted not to. Let the guy take the dimensions he had given and do with them what he would. Donald wasn't even sure he wanted to actually get dressed and leave the apartment for some early-morning assignation.

But the stats must have been to Horny-in-Edgewater's liking, because he immediately responded. "Sounds hot. It's too late and I'm too impatient to play a game of email correspondence. Why don't you just come on over and we'll take it from there?" Donald noted that the guy also had not included a picture of himself and wondered if he was playing tit for tat or if he had something to hide. Or maybe, Donald told himself, the guy was simply being upfront about his lack of patience and simply did not want to waste time.

But if I show up at his door and one or the both of us is not pleased with what's waiting for us, wouldn't that too be a waste of time? He glanced up at the clock in the upper right hand corner of the computer. It was now 5:00 a.m. Dawn was a mere couple of hours away, yet in the still and the dark, it seemed an eternity. To Donald, it was like he and Horny-in-Edgewater were the only people awake in the whole city of millions. He also noted how he did not feel tired in the least, and if the guy lived close enough, he really had little to lose. *Nothing ventured, nothing gained. And maybe one more orgasm will be just enough to allow me an hour or hour and a half of restful slumber.* So he wrote back, agreeing with everything the guy had said and closing with, "So where am I going?"

When the address came back a minute or so later, Donald laughed and then really began to question how fallible decisions like this, made in the midst of insomnia and on the brink of dawn, really were.

The address was for his own building. And the apartment number was the one directly above his own. *Jesus, it's my new neighbor. What's his name? Would it really be so smart to start something up with someone so close by*? Donald knew he should just log out of his email, close Firefox, and go back to bed. But another voice urged: *What's the harm? He's right upstairs. You don't even have to get dressed...no shoes, no coat. You could be there in less than a minute's time. And it's not really "starting something up." This is no more the beginning of anything than the frantic, intense few minutes we recently shared in the back room at the Brig. And the guy* was *good.* Donald typed that he would be there as soon as possible. Little did the guy know that as soon as possible meant only long enough for Donald to throw on his jeans and a T-shirt. He hoped he'd be ready for him.

In fewer than ten minutes, Donald was upstairs and hesitating outside his neighbor's door, the one that was exactly like his own, save for a different number. He could still go back. He had yet to knock. He could tell the guy he needed to crash and he would take a rain check. It was all true.

Donald balled his hand into a fist and rapped on the door.

When "Horny" opened the door, he laughed. "Oh my God, it's you." He cocked his shaved head and gave Donald a wicked grin that Donald had to admit, even in his current state of mind, he found very fetching.

"In the flesh." Donald smiled and thought again briefly of Grace and how she would pale if she knew the kind of shenanigans gay men got up to in their spare time. "Disappointed?"

"Not at *all*. Come on in, Donald." The man stepped back to allow Donald in.

Donald brushed by him and was embarrassed he still couldn't remember the guy's name. Fortunately, there was a secretary desk in the entry, and on it was a stack of mail. Donald took a quick, surreptitious glance and was rewarded and reminded: Walter.

Walter looked good. He was clad in a pair of blue and green plaid boxers and nothing else. His body, in the warm light of a single lamp in the living room, was good: hard and lean with several tattoos. His chest was hairless and well defined. He looked manly and taut. Donald didn't want to make small talk, didn't know if he could bear it, so he reached out and pulled Walter hard against him, pressing his bearded face to Walter's grizzled one in a full-on tongue kiss that was passionate, deep, probing, and which lasted long enough to leave them gasping and for both of them to feel erections pressing against the other's stomach.

Donald growled and pulled away long enough to gasp, "Bedroom?"

Walter took his hand, interlacing their fingers—the gesture seemed oddly tender—and led him toward the right. Donald already knew the way, since the layout of this apartment was the same as his own. He was grateful all the blood had rushed from his brain to his dick. All his inhibitions and second thoughts vanished, replaced with a ferocious hunger. He liked that hunger; it hid so much.

The room was dim. There was a TV on one of the dressers, and a porno was playing silently on the screen. A wildly muscled balding young man was in a sling in what looked like a very nicely equipped dungeon, with a whole battalion of admirers ready to make use of what he had on offer between his spread legs.

The view was not that much different when he returned his gaze to Walter, who had doffed the boxers and lay across his bed, smiling. He had pulled his legs up to his shoulders and said nothing. He didn't need to. His posture—and the hungry set of his eyes—was all the invitation Donald needed, and he wasted no time shedding jeans and T. He was still very hard, and he came to Walter, positioning himself between his spread legs, grabbing each of them and throwing them roughly atop his shoulders. He let a big gob of spit fall from his mouth to the head of his dick and rubbed himself, although he needed no prepping. The visual had him already leaking precome. "Condom?"

"On the nightstand," Walter whispered, his voice hoarse from need and impatience. Donald wondered how long he had been up here watching pornos, working himself into this state. On the nightstand were three or four Trojans, and he grabbed one, ripped it open with his teeth, and unrolled it slowly over his cock, never taking his gaze away from Walter's intense stare. He snatched up a bottle of Wet and lubed his cock up with it, then carelessly dribbled a line of it over Walter's open and waiting crack. Donald paused to massage the lube on Walter's slightly hairy crack and the taut ring of brown muscle nestled there, slipping first one finger and then another inside Walter's heat and tightness.

He positioned the head of his dick and slid inside. All thoughts of work tomorrow, of Mark, of lives destroyed and lives on the mend were banished by the tight heaven of the muscles of Walter's ass surrounding him, gripping him in the most delicious embrace. The heat was intense, like a warm glove surrounding him. It felt so good Donald wondered for a second if the condom had broken. But he didn't take the time to check. He drove himself powerfully into Walter, who cried out and grabbed onto his asscheeks, drawing him in deeper.

The whole enterprise took no more than five minutes, and when it was finished, the men lay side by side, gasping and sweaty, both staring up at the ceiling. Neither spoke for several moments. A scent of musk and sweat rose up around them.

Walter rolled toward Donald, so that he was nestled up against him, his head resting on his shoulder. Walter's breathing was slowly coming back to normal. Walter played with the hair on Donald's chest, and Donald had to admit, if only to himself, that he was finally relaxed. It felt good to be lying here next to another man, the warmth of his body pressed against him. He slid his arm around Walter.

"You know, I've wanted to meet you ever since I first saw you from your window when I was moving in. God, that was a horrible day, trying to lug all my stuff up by myself."

"I'm sorry I couldn't help you then." Donald debated whether he should tell Walter what had happened to him, why he was not only emotionally unprepared to lend a hand to a neighbor in need, but that he was simply too sore from his injuries to contemplate such strenuous physical exertion. He thought it was too soon to be sharing that information, yet at the same time recognized the need to unburden himself. So much had backed up inside, making his emotions like a dam, sloshing over its confines. The quiet and the dim lighting allowed him to speak. He stared up at the ceiling and, almost without realizing he was doing it, traced circles on Walter's shaved pate.

"I should tell you why I couldn't help." Donald took a breath, giving himself one more opportunity to ask himself if he really wanted to share his story. He plunged on. "Not long before you moved in, my boyfriend and I were fag bashed just outside the Brig...well, a block or so over, by St. Boniface Cemetery." Donald closed his eyes. His voice seemed disembodied as he recounted what he could remember of the night: the horror and the fear, the suddenness of it, and how such a momentous event, life-changing, could take mere minutes to complete. He blew out a big sigh and said, "Mark—that's my boyfriend—was killed that night."

Walter's hand stopped moving on Donald's chest, and he got up on one elbow to stare down at Donald with sympathetic eyes. "I'm so sorry, man. I don't know what to say. Did they catch the assholes?"

"Not yet. It was late, dark, and no one was around. Unfortunately, I haven't been able to remember much detail about that night. My doctors say that's normal, a combination of shock, the blow to my head, and my mind just wanting to protect itself."

Walter lay back and said nothing for a while. Donald debated whether he should tell him about seeing Mark since his death. He decided it really was too soon for that. The guy would think he was crazy. And maybe he was. More than once, Donald had entertained the idea that it was not Mark appearing to him but just his own desperate mind conjuring him up. Even as he thought it, he knew, deep down, that his encounters with Mark post-death were no hallucination. There was still an energy hanging around, and he knew Mark couldn't leave him. Not yet.

"I should probably be getting back downstairs." He moved a little, so their contact was broken.

And Walter snuggled back up to him. "No, don't go. This was nice. Hang around for a bit. Maybe we can sleep for a couple hours. And then I'll fix you a nice breakfast. You like buttermilk pancakes? I make great ones."

Donald smiled. Mark also made great pancakes. Walter's words were both a comfort and a painful reminder. He did nothing, just lay back and closed his eyes. After a while, he could hear the deep, even rhythm of Walter's breathing that let him know Walter had drifted off. It wasn't long before he fell asleep himself.

It seemed like only moments had passed when bright sunlight was shining into the room. Donald sat up. "Jesus! What time is it?"

Walter sat up beside him and picked up a little alarm clock from the nightstand and glanced down at it. "It's almost eight."

"I need to get ready for work. Today's supposed to be my first day back, since…"

"It's okay. You should have plenty of time. Wanna use the shower? I'll put some coffee on."

"No, no I can't be bothered with breakfast right now. It's sweet of you to offer. But I have to get downstairs and get myself ready." Donald swung his legs over the side of the bed and rubbed his eyes. He looked back at Walter, splayed out on the white cotton sheets. He really was a very handsome man. "Thanks for last night. I needed that, in more ways than one."

Walter grinned lazily. "Anytime. I'm just upstairs."

"Don't be so easy!" Donald punched Walter's chest.

Walter batted his eyes at Donald and whimpered, "I just can't help myself." Then, more seriously, "I hope I do get to see you again."

Donald didn't want to make any promises he couldn't keep. So he said simply, "We'll see."

He got up and dressed quickly, reminded of younger days and many mornings like this one, dressing to leave a one-night stand's apartment. Once upon a time, he had thought rashly that those days were behind him. The bright light of the day banished the warmth and contentment he had felt just before drifting off in Walter's arms.

He paused at the doorway and tried to think of something to say. He couldn't, so he just whispered, "Later," and hurried out the door.

Outside Walter's apartment, Donald was dismayed to run into Walter's nephew, who was just coming up the stairs. The boy was dressed in cargo pants that were too big for him, an oversized T-shirt, and a blue parka. He remembered him from the night they had come to borrow some spice from his kitchen. What was the kid doing here so early?

The pair regarded each other for only a moment, and then the boy whipped out a key ring, unlocked Walter's door, and went inside.

Donald stood in the hallway, wondering what the boy had thought. "It doesn't matter." He took the fire-well stairs down to his own apartment.

When he opened the door, he found Mark waiting for him. He was sitting in a chair by the window, wearing jeans and his purple Northwestern hoodie sweatshirt. His feet were bare, and the sunlight lit up his blond curls like a halo. He stared out at the day, and Donald wondered if he could really see it: the brilliant-blue sky, the cirrus clouds, like streaks of chalk, up high.

His heart was filled with love, not fear. He wanted to run to Mark, to collapse at his feet and beg forgiveness for not being in their home, for being off with another man. But he stayed frozen, door open, staring, his keys still in his hand.

Mark turned his head toward him and smiled. "Are you going to come in or what? You want to pay to heat the hallway too? Close the fucking door and get in here."

Donald kicked the door closed and stood, staring. Was this real? He almost felt like doing one of those movie double takes, blinking his eyes rapidly. But he knew this was genuine. He knew that no matter how many times he opened and closed his eyes Mark would still be there—at least for now.

Wasn't there a way to make him stay for good?

Donald moved cautiously toward Mark, as though he were approaching a wild animal. He was afraid that, if he got too close, Mark would vanish. He took several steps like that, with sureness and slowness, and then couldn't stand it. His feet quickened, and he did just what he imagined: knelt at Mark's feet and tried to gather him up in his arms, his face wet with tears.

The reaction to touching Mark was immediate. Instead of a rapid influx of joy and warmth, Donald immediately felt a flash of pain behind his eyes, and then an almost overpowering nausea coursed through him, making him fear he would vomit. White-hot twinges of pain assaulted his ribs and the back of his head, where he had been kicked and battered. He held on to Mark, who felt as solid to him as Walter had just a short time ago, clinging, hoping the nausea would pass and he could enjoy this moment with his lost lover. But the nausea and the pain only grew in intensity, causing him to gasp in agony. He shut his eyes, breathing through his mouth and moving his head closer to Mark's stomach. His heart was hammering so hard it felt like the organ would burst, sending an explosion of blood raining down on his innards. He would not let go—he could not let go—it didn't matter that it pained him. This was Mark. He could feel him, touch him once more. The value of that was worth riding out whatever pain and misery this mere touch brought on.

But then the images started flashing in his mind, as if he were watching them walk down the side street off Clark that night they had been bashed. He could feel the chill in the air and hear, in the distance, the bass throbbing of a souped-up car engine. And then the scene shifted and he was watching Mark's terrified face. Someone had grabbed him from behind and was making kissing noises in his ear. The face was in shadow, completely obscured. But the next face he saw, the one stepping up behind the pair, was clear. A young guy sporting a bandana, wearing a leather jacket and brandishing a baseball bat. He could see the guy was probably in his twenties. He couldn't hear the foul words he was mouthing but could see the gap in his front teeth and the heavy unibrow above his eyes. He looked intent, grim, and full of purpose as he raised the aluminum baseball bat...

Finally, Donald let go and fell back to the hardwood floor as if he had been electrocuted. He couldn't bear to see any more. He was gasping, and in those few instants, his body had become drenched with sweat.

Mark was still there, but his image was wavering, becoming insubstantial. Parts of him were fading away, revealing the fabric of the chair on which he was sitting.

"No," Donald croaked. "Please don't go."

But there was a shift in the air, almost like wind rushing through the room, and Mark vanished, as if he had never really been there at all.

Donald crawled to the window, flung it open, and took in great lungfuls of cold air. The bracing air helped his body return to normal. His heart rate slowed, and the queasiness abated. He turned around and slid down, legs splayed out before him, facing away from the window.

And he realized something. He started speaking aloud, hoping that Mark, wherever he had gone, could hear him. "I've seen you now, you son of a bitch. I know what you look like. And if it takes me the rest of my life, I will find you and I will see that you pay."

Donald rolled over onto his side on the floor and drew his legs up to his chest, wracked with sobs.

Chapter Twelve

Walter was surprised when he heard the key being fitted into his front door. He scrambled into a pair of sweats lying on the floor by the bed and pulled a T-shirt over his head.

"Uncle Walter? You there? Sorry to be coming by so early, but I left a book here I need for school. Don't get up. I'll just be in and out."

Good God. Justin. What if he had come in earlier and found him in bed with Donald? What a pretty scene that would have been! He knew the boy, in spite of having known Walter was gay since he was a child, was still squeamish about the whole thing. Seeing him in bed with another guy would probably really fry his brain. Walter grinned and hurried to shut off the TV, still playing a porno, and to get out to the living room before Justin walked in on him. There were still condoms, wrappers, and lube on the nightstand.

Walter entered the living room, where he found Justin sorting through the newspapers, magazines, and other detritus that tended to accumulate on his breakfast bar. "Didn't expect to see you here." Walter smiled at his nephew, but Justin wasn't returning the smile. He was barely, in fact, looking at him.

Justin pulled out a geography textbook from the mess on the bar and said, more to himself than to Walter, "Here it is." Still not looking at him, he started toward the door, the book tucked under his arm.

What was going on? "Hey, wait a minute. You just gonna rush in and out like that? You want some breakfast? If you don't have time for me to make you something, I've got Cheerios and Frosted Mini Wheats." Walter opened a cabinet and started pulling out cereal.

"I already ate. I gotta go. I'm gonna be late for school." Justin paused at the door, his back turned and staring straight ahead.

Walter came close to his nephew, blocking his exit out the door. "Hold on, what's wrong?"

Justin turned his head to eye him. There was something burning and new in his gaze, and Walter did not like what he was seeing. It almost seemed the boy was furious with him.

"Nothin'," Justin snapped. "Now would you get out of the way? I told you. I'm gonna be late for school."

"What?"

"Can I go?"

"No. Not until you tell me what's wrong."

Justin paused for a moment, looking lost in thought, like he was choosing his next words. Finally, he spat, "Have a date?"

"What do you mean?" In spite of himself, Walter felt heat rise to his face. Donald's leaving and Justin's arrival had coincided so closely that there was no doubt the boy had seen Donald leaving his apartment. He was sure his nephew was savvy enough to know why a man was leaving his home so early in the morning. But still, what business was it of Justin's?

"I saw. I saw him leaving."

Walter sighed. "So what? Your uncle's no saint, Justin. And what you saw is really none of your business."

"I don't want it to be, but when it's thrown in my face..."

"Nothing was thrown in your face."

"I gotta go." He brushed by Walter, shouldering him out of the way. He stopped once he had the door open. "What's his name?"

"Why?"

"I just want to know who my uncle is sweet on." Justin's tone was mocking, dripping sarcasm.

"Donald. You remember him, right below us? In 3B?"

"Yeah, I remember. You got chummy fast." Justin's face was all sneer.

"Look, Justin, just come in and sit down and we can talk about this." Walter put a hand to his forehead; it was way too early in the morning for drama.

"I don't want to talk about it. And I don't know how many times I have to say this before you get this through your thick skull, but I...am...going...to...be...late." And with that, his nephew rushed out the door without looking back.

Walter watched him go, thinking that the two of them would have that talk, if not now, then very soon.

*

Jesus. Justin couldn't believe what he had just witnessed. It made his stomach ache. Was his uncle just like his mom? Some fuckin' slut? He knew Uncle Walter was gay but most definitely did not like having the evidence staring him in the face, such as it was. He knew it was stupid to think Uncle Walter didn't fuck, but it was pretty easy when Justin rarely saw him with another guy or even heard of one in his uncle's life. He shuddered to think what the two of them had been doing as he took the bus over there. He hurried down the stairs, almost tripping over the hem of his cargo pants. He felt a curious mixture of emotions all at once, rage foremost among them, but also betrayal and a very childish need to cry.

When he got to the lobby, he paused by the rows of metal mailboxes. He scanned the names on the boxes until he came to 3B: D. Griffiths. Donald Griffiths in 3B. He stared at the name for a moment, memorizing.

Maybe Ronny would like to have this information. Maybe it would come in very handy for his friend. And what allegiance did he have to that fag who lived below his uncle, anyway? Justin stormed out of the building, already fishing his cell phone from his pocket. He punched in Ronny's number, not really sure his friend would even answer, what with it being so early in the morning.

But Ronny picked up. His voice was deep and muffled; Justin had obviously awakened him. Too bad.

Without any preliminaries, Justin said, "We need to talk." He had already decided, in the instant he pulled his cell from his pocket, that he would blow off school that day. With his overcrowded classrooms, he would scarcely be missed. And even if the school called Patty, he was pretty sure his mom would cover for him, although she would expect an explanation later. That was, if she didn't have a date for the evening and was preoccupied with other, more pressing, matters. For once, Justin wished for even more men in his mother's life.

"'Bout what, dude? I was sound asleep here."

"I have some information I think you might be interested in having. Can I come over?"

"In a bit."

"No. Now. When I get there, you'll be glad you said yes."

There was a pause, and Justin could hear Ronny shifting around, the flick of a lighter and Ronny's inhale. "Shit, man. Can't you just tell me now?"

"No."

"Well…"

"I can be there in ten, fifteen minutes." Justin clicked the phone shut, tired already of trying to persuade Ronny to see his point of view. He began walking briskly toward the Thorndale L stop, the one closest to his uncle's. Once he got on a northbound train, he would be at Ronny's stop at Morse in fewer than five minutes. He felt like crying, and he wasn't sure if it was from the shock of seeing his uncle fresh from the embrace of another man or if he was already having second thoughts regarding what he was about to do. His head was a jumble; he wasn't sure what to think. He only knew he was sickened by what he had seen and wanted someone to pay.

There was a small rational voice inside him, chattering. *You know what you're about to do, dude. You're going to write a death sentence for Mr. Donald Griffiths. You know what Ronny will want to do with the information.* But he cast aside the thoughts as quickly as they arose, his stride impatient and purposeful. As he neared the L stop, he could hear the rumble of an approaching train. He lifted his feet and began an all-out run to the station. Once there, he flew inside, his transit card in hand. He rushed through the turnstile and up the stairs just as the northbound train was pulling into the station, making gonging noises he thought echoed the pounding of his heart.

He hopped onto the train and was too jazzed to sit, even though there were plenty of open spaces. He held onto a pole as the train lurched into motion. *Why are you so impatient, man*? He knew the answer to his own question. If he didn't go through with this quickly, he might not go through with it at all. And if he didn't go through with it, he didn't know what would happen. He wasn't sure which was worse: the idea of his uncle and that fag hooking up again (it was just so fucking convenient and so fucking *gross*) or the guy from downstairs seeing him again and finally putting two and two together and recognizing Justin from the night of the attack.

It was a couple stops to Morse. Justin continued his manic trajectory, running/walking to his friend's studio on Morse, above a Chinese take-out joint. Breathless, he leaned on the buzzer, staring up at Ronny's window. He saw one of the miniblind slats go up and then heard the metallic bark of another buzzer, the one that would admit him.

He dashed up the stairs two at a time and arrived at Ronny's door breathing hard, sweating in spite of the cold, and still wondering just what the hell he was doing. Ronny swung open the door. He was wearing a pair of ripped jeans and no shirt, holding a can of beer in one hand. He opened the door wider and stepped back to admit Justin.

When they were seated in the mess of Ronny's little studio, Ronny on the bed and Justin on a leaking beanbag at the foot of it, Justin tried to slow his heart rate and breathing.

"What the fuck is up with you, man? What's the emergency?"

Justin closed his eyes, telling himself it was not too late to turn back. He knew that once he uttered the words, he would be setting in motion a chain of events that could have—would have—deadly consequences. He waited a couple more seconds and decided he had no choice. This, he decided, had to be the best course of action.

"I know something," he spat out.

Ronny took a swig of his beer and grinned at him. "Do tell. There must be a good reason for getting me out of bed at the crack of dawn."

Justin was tempted to correct him in his interpretation of dawn, then decided against it. "I know the guy's name. I know where he lives."

Ronny cocked his head, listening. "I don't know what the fuck you're talking about. What guy?"

Justin blew out a big sigh. "The other guy...the one who lived." He stopped there, letting the words hang in the air. He knew he had just crossed a threshold; there was no turning back now.

Ronny's eyes widened, and he set the bottle of beer on the floor. "You shittin' me? You mean the other guy from that night? The other *witness*?"

Just the fact that Ronny had put such emphasis on the word "witness" gave Justin a chill and made his stomach start to churn. He knew immediately where delivering this information would take Ronny and knew what he would want to do. "Yeah," he mumbled. And now he wished he could take it all back. He felt like he had stood on a precipice and had just jumped into the abyss.

"Who is it? How did you find out?" Ronny was leaning forward, hands on his knees. Any vestige of sleepiness was gone.

Justin didn't want to implicate his uncle, so he would leave out the part about running into Donald Griffiths coming out of his uncle's apartment. But the only other way he could put forth his discovery with any credibility would be to tie the two together, because otherwise how would he know? He supposed he could just say he saw him in the lobby or something, but he thought Ronny would see through that. Besides, Ronny already knew about Uncle Walter's preferences and would make the connection anyway. In Ronny's mind, all fags were like cockroaches. And like cockroaches, needed to be exterminated. He even had a black T-shirt that had what looked like the insecticide Raid's logo on it, except Raid had been replaced with AIDS, and there was the new tagline: "Kills fags dead." Ronny thought the shirt was a scream when he'd found it in a Goodwill store.

Justin swallowed, feeling reckless. "Remember that night you dropped me off at my uncle's and he was with that other guy?"

"Yeah? That was *him*?"

Nervously, Justin nodded.

"Why the fuck didn't you say something sooner, man?"

Justin thought. "I just didn't put two and two together. I was too worried, I guess, about you knowing my uncle was gay."

"Are you sure?"

Here's an out, Justin thought but continued anyway. "Yeah. It's him. I found out which apartment was his from my uncle. He only knew because he had seen him getting mail one day." *Lame*. Justin had to get through this. He forced his breathing to slow. He rushed the next words out. "His name is Donald Griffiths. He lives in the building my uncle just moved into. In apartment 3B."

Ronny slowly shook his head. "Good work, my little man. You would make a fine detective."

Justin wasn't exactly glowing at the compliment. "What should we do?"

"Well, I think we need to work out a plan to pay Faggot Griffiths a little visit and make sure he doesn't go telling tales, especially if he sees you and recognizes you."

Hoping against hope, Justin said, "You mean throw a good scare into him." He pondered, chewing on a hangnail. "Or maybe make a clear threat that tells the guy, in no uncertain terms, that if he talks, it will be the last time." *Hey, it could work.*

Ronny leveled a dead gaze upon Justin. He spoke so slowly and tonelessly, a shiver ran up Justin's spine. "No. I mean we need to make sure he doesn't talk. To anyone. Ever again."

It felt like the temperature in the room had dropped by a few degrees. "You sure we have to be that drastic?"

"Don't be stupid. You said it yourself, Justin. We murdered a guy. We need to make sure the eyewitness doesn't go pointing fingers. Threats and scares ain't gonna keep this guy away from the police." Ronny sat back. "Once we take care of him, we're free and clear. Nothin' more to worry about."

Justin felt sick, but he nodded, wondering if his eyes were open wider than usual. "We can't get caught."

"Oh no, we won't. That's why we have to come up with a perfect plan to *execute* this just so."

Justin shivered and again, nodded. It was all over now. His life would never be the same. He hung his head and stared at the floor. It was one thing to do a little taunting and torture of a couple of fags while high and drunk one night, quite another to plot out a murder. Man, that shit was *premeditated*.

"Just let me think. That's what I'm good at." Ronny lay back, putting his hands behind his head.

Justin turned away from his friend. So it would happen. But there was one thing Justin wanted to be sure of: his uncle could not get mixed up in this. Fag or not, Justin didn't want Uncle Walter hurt.

Chapter Thirteen

"I've remembered one of the guys who attacked us." Donald said these words to Grace on the morning when he was supposed to return to work. He had taken a quick shower and changed into jeans and a button-down shirt. Before telephoning his sister, he had called his supervisor and told her he needed just one more day. She tried to sound understanding, but Donald knew he was pressing his luck. They would not wait forever for him to come back, no matter how much trauma he had suffered. *Tomorrow, tomorrow*, he told himself, *tomorrow is just one more day; they can wait*. What had been revealed to him was just too important to put off.

Grace was talking. "What do you mean? What brought this on? After all this time, I mean?"

His sister sounded leery. He couldn't blame her. It had, after all, been six weeks since the attack. Memories usually didn't get better or sharper with the passage of time. Often the inverse was true. But Donald knew he'd had help remembering and debated if he should tell his sister the real journey to his recalling one of his attacker's faces in such detail. But then she really would be suspicious and would have even more reason to think he simply needed psychiatric help, rather than police intervention. It was plausible, Donald thought, that the trauma and the blow to his head had merely delayed his clear memory, wasn't it?

"I just remembered, that's all. Last night. I woke up, and it was clear in my head: the guy who actually hit Mark with the bat. An aluminum baseball bat. I saw it. Clear as a picture...in memory." Donald then told a lie. "The doctor said I might one day remember, that sometimes these things took time to work out in our brains and that, sometimes, it can take months or even years before these trauma-repressed memories resurface." *God*, Donald thought, *I am impressed with the conviction and detail of my own falsehoods. But I need Grace to believe me.*

"I guess that could happen," Grace said. Her voice was still tinged with uncertainty, and Donald had the suspicion that his sister was just sitting at the other end of their telephone connection wishing this whole ugly mess would go away, that she could get her brother back and the two of them could once again laugh together over a good meal or a shared memory, a pleasant one, from their years of growing up together. She didn't have to say anything. Donald knew. She just wanted to put this all behind her and wanted her brother to do the same. It made sense, and Donald could understand. We all strive for equilibrium. But maybe, just maybe, Mark was bringing him that equilibrium by showing him, in clear detail, the face of his killer. It was the first step, after all, toward apprehending him. And maybe once that happened, Donald could truly begin to move on. He would always hurt; there would always be a void, but maybe catching the monster that stole Mark away could begin the closure he needed.

"It happened, Grace. Listen, I called in to work. I was supposed to come back today, but they were cool about it. I was wondering if you could do the same and take me down to the police station. I want to look at those mug shots again. And if that doesn't work, maybe see if they can hook me up with one of those sketch artists."

Grace was silent, and Donald rushed in, "I really need your support, sis. Can you do this for me? I don't want to wait too long, in case my memory should start to fade." The odd thing was, his memory was doing anything but fading. Unlike a dream that evaporates over the course of the day, this memory was only crystallizing, sharper and sharper as more time passed. Odd.

"Of course, honey. Give me, oh, half an hour to an hour to call in to work and get myself ready, and then I'll be right over."

"Thanks, Grace." Donald replaced the phone in its cradle and looked out the window. *Today, things will change.* For the first time in six weeks, he felt something positive right down to his core: optimism.

*

The sound of the front door buzzer startled Donald. All the time he had been waiting for her, he had been doing nothing but sitting and thinking. Grace was his sister, he eventually concluded, and deserved to know the truth. She might think he was crazy. She had never taken much stock in things like psychics, ghosts, or things that went bump in the night. But then, neither had he, which was a point in his favor, he thought. Whether she believed him or humored him, the end result was the same: she should know from where his recollection came. They did not have to tell the cops. They did not, in fact, have to tell anyone else. But he had never been good at keeping secrets from his sister—and never really wanted to—and was not about to start now.

He got up from his perch on the couch and pressed the intercom button near his front door to admit her. He remained close to the door, listening for Grace's footfalls as she climbed the stairs. When he heard her approaching, he swung the door open.

She smiled when she saw him, and it warmed Donald. Grace had been a constant in his life, stabilizing, and just to see her smiling face calmed him, letting him know he could tell her anything. She looked good, fresh and clean in jeans and a pink button-down oxford blouse.

"All ready?" she asked. She still clutched her car keys in her hand.

"Not yet." Donald stepped back to admit her. She came into the apartment, regarding him quizzically, waiting by the couch.

"Sit down. There's something I want to tell you before we head out."

"Okay." Grace took a seat on the edge of the couch, leaning forward.

Donald seated himself beside her. He didn't say anything for several moments and couldn't imagine what his sister was thinking. Whatever it was, he was certain it had nothing to do with what he was about to say.

Finally, he turned to her. "Remember what I said on the phone? How I said I just woke up and the memory was there?"

"Yeah. I thought about it, and it made sense. You could very well have repressed the memory. You also took a blow to the head."

"Well, I wasn't quite truthful."

"Okay..."

Donald sucked in a deep breath. "Try to listen with an open mind, okay?"

Grace said nothing, simply sat and stared. He knew she was waiting for him to continue.

No time like the present. "Well, I had help getting that memory back."

"What do you mean?"

"Just let me tell you. You can call the loony bin after I finish."

Grace didn't laugh.

"I don't know how to say this other than just spitting it out. Mark has been coming to me."

Grace's face clouded over. He wasn't sure if it was with concern or pity, but he was pretty sure her expression had little to do with sympathy. She simply nodded, and he noticed she crossed her arms across her chest.

"Mark has appeared to me several times. I know how nuts that must sound. I know you're probably thinking it's a weird kind of wishful thinking or that blow to my own head is inducing hallucinations. I thought the same thing after the first couple times I saw him. But I don't think that now." Donald gazed out the window in front of him. The sky was gray, heavy with clouds. It looked like the kind of sky that promised snow before the sun set. He turned back to her. "I don't know how to explain. I don't know much about these things. Until now, I kind of scoffed at people who talked about this stuff with any trace of seriousness. But I've heard it said that people's energy could hang around after they're gone, and maybe that's what's happening. Maybe Mark can't really rest until the creeps who did this to us are exposed for the cowards and animals they really are. It makes sense to me, you know?"

Grace's eyes were shiny with tears. *Don't start crying now. I need you to be here with me. I just need to get through this.* Donald continued, "Anyway, whatever you think of this, I have come to believe that this isn't a hallucination, is not wishful thinking, but that Mark, or some essence of him, has really come to me." He swallowed. "See, something weird happens when I touch him."

Grace cocked her head. "You can touch him?"

"Only for a minute. But when I do, I don't feel good about it. In fact, I feel sick and in pain...pain very similar to the pain I endured that night. And I get flashes...things I didn't remember start coming clear to me." He caught and held his sister's gaze. "That's how I remembered. I touched Mark and saw one of the guys...saw him very clearly." He sat back on the couch, feeling a sense of near giddiness. He almost wanted to laugh. He knew how preposterous what he had just said must sound to his levelheaded sister. He scratched at his neck, rubbed his leg. Finally, "Will you please say something?"

Grace still didn't say anything. Instead, she leaned forward and wrapped her arms around him, pulling him close and tight to her small frame. She stroked his hair. Finally, she released him and sat back. "I don't think you're crazy. Well, maybe a little, but no more than me and no more than anyone else in our family. I don't know what I believe, but you being certifiable isn't it. Maybe what you said *is* possible. Maybe what you said—about Mark and unfinished business—is true. There's some logic to it, a basis that makes it all kind of believable." She took in a quivering breath. "You might not know this about me, but I think there's a lot that goes on in this world that we don't know about or can't really understand, and maybe this is one of those things."

His sister's words hung in the air. Her belief seemed almost magical, a gift.

"Thank you, sis."

She didn't say anything for another long moment, then leaned her face close to his. "But has something else occurred to you?"

"What do you mean?"

"Maybe Mark isn't hanging around to just let you know who did this to you guys, so it can be avenged or something like that, but maybe he's coming to you because he wants to protect you. I'm not trying to scare you or anything, but those guys are still out there, and maybe he's appearing to you to help you avoid what happened to him."

The thought paradoxically chilled and warmed Donald. On the one hand, what Grace had said made sense...and maybe those guys were still out there, gunning for him, making sure he didn't do what he and his sister were about to do this very morning. On the other hand, and what brought a sudden rush of tears to his eyes and heat to his heart, was the fact that maybe Mark was unable to let go because he loved Donald so much he couldn't bear to see him hurt, even after he, Mark, was dead.

Donald nodded.

Grace picked up her purse from where she had set it on the floor and placed it in her lap. "I think we should go now." She stood.

And Donald stood to follow her out the door.

*

"We'll never find him." Donald and Grace were standing outside one of the interview rooms at the police station. All around them, people were milling about...and no one seemed to give a damn that Donald had struck out once more with the mug shots. It seemed he had looked through hundreds of faces, one blurring into the next, and not one of them jumped out at him with any sense of familiarity. He had even tried to fit his perception to some of the photographs, but it was like trying to force a piece of jigsaw into a puzzle where it didn't belong. He had failed. And it made him miserable.

"Now don't say that. Just like I said—and the officer too—this guy may not even have a criminal record, so he wouldn't have a mug shot."

Donald rubbed his temples. "I have a headache. I'm just afraid this is never gonna happen. I'm never gonna get any kind of closure. Mark will continue to haunt me, which is both a curse and a blessing, and meanwhile, this guy is running around scot-free to bash and kill other guys. Who's gonna be next?"

Grace put her arms around her brother. "Listen, they said we could come back and see a sketch artist. If you really do remember so well, maybe working with one of them will create our own mug shot...one that can be put out there so that if someone sees this guy and recognizes him, he can be caught."

Donald stared at the people in the corridor, all rushing by, as if he and Grace weren't leaning against a cinder block wall, looking both distressed and despairing. He felt invisible. Would his life never get back to normal? Or would he continue to sink into this black hole created one night almost two months ago now when his whole world exploded because some guys decided it would be fun to beat the shit out of a gay couple?

Grace pushed him a little. "Come on, let's go. I'll call the station later and see what I can set up for a sketch artist. Right now, I'm buying you lunch. We're both playing hooky today, so we might as well try and have a little fun. There's a new Vietnamese place up on Argyle I hear is really good."

Donald acquiesced. It was the least he could do for his sister.

They started down the corridor toward the brightly lit exit sign. Just as they had almost reached the stairwell door, a voice called them back.

"Mr. Griffiths? Mr. Griffiths, can you hang on a second?"

The detective assigned to Mark's murder investigation caught up to them. His name was Milton Byrne, and he was a veteran, overweight, with a bald pate and a cheap suit that fit him badly. Right now, he was panting with the exertion it took to run ten to twenty steps down an interior corridor. Sweat was even popping out on his forehead. The odor of stale cigarettes clung to him.

Donald spoke. "What can we do for you, Detective? I suppose the officer told you we struck out again on the mug shots?"

"Yeah, yeah. Sorry you didn't have any luck. That's why I stopped you. I know Officer McKee told you we could set up a time with a sketch artist, and I was hoping I'd catch you before you left the building. See, one of our freelance artists is here, Wendy Brennan, and she's very, very good. Your timing is perfect. She just finished up with another vic and would be willing to talk to you if you've got the time right now."

Grace smiled at him. Donald's headache vanished, and he felt the beginnings of an upswing in his mood. He wasn't sure he'd call it elation, but it felt a lot like relief. Maybe now they could begin to get somewhere. "We've got the time." He glanced over at Grace just to make sure. He didn't even need to say anything. Already, she was nodding.

"Just come along with me, and I'll get you set up with Wendy."

They followed Byrne down the hallway to a different room than the one they were in before. This room was a little smaller, brightly lit, and spartan, the walls painted white, green industrial tile on the floor, and no windows. There was a laminate table and blue plastic scoop chairs. When Donald saw Wendy Brennan sitting at the table, he thought at first he had come across a little girl. She was petite, almost elfin, couldn't have been more than five feet tall. She had short light-brown hair that was highlighted with blonde. Even her jewelry and makeup did little to give her the appearance of an adult. It was more like she was a kid playing dress up. When she looked up at him, though, he felt a connection, even though they had yet to speak a word to one another. Her blue eyes seemed to reach out to him and draw him in. And when she smiled, the deal was sealed. He would have an easy time communicating with this woman, even if the topic of their conversation was so unpleasant.

The detective made quick introductions and left them alone. Wendy stood. "Have a seat, you two. I promise you I'll make this as easy as possible on you, but not so easy that you won't come out of here with something. I'm just not satisfied if we don't come up with a good resemblance. I'm kind of obsessive-compulsive that way."

Donald and Grace sat down, and Wendy tore a page off her sketchpad, exposing a pristine white sheet. She had several pencils laid out before her. She trained her gaze on Donald.

"Donald, I know this might seem stupid to say, in light of what you've been through—and I don't even need to know what that was—but I want you to try to relax.

Take a few deep, cleansing breaths and just let your mind go blank. Take your time. There's no pressure, no rush. We have all the time in the world. We're just going to sit here for a few minutes and not say anything. When you're ready, I want you to begin speaking about what you remember about this person."

Donald looked around the room, trying to take a few deep breaths, but his nerves and eagerness to begin the process made his attempts futile. He knew what he needed to say—the image remained clear and strong in his mind—so he began talking.

"He was tall, kind of lanky. My mother would have called him raw-boned." Donald continued to try to relax, to summon up the image that he still did not believe was in his own memory but the image Mark had provided for him. "He was young. I would say early to midtwenties." Donald began to feel afraid, as if this verbal summing up of his attacker would conjure him up and he would open his eyes to see him standing in the interview room, grinning, an aluminum baseball bat held casually at his side. He opened his eyes to assure himself that he was safe. Grace sat perched on her chair, leaning forward. Wendy eyed him, her pencil in hand, sketchpad open, but not yet drawing anything. "Does it matter how he was dressed?"

Wendy cocked her head and smiled. "It all matters. See, anything you see in your mind's eye is going to help you remember better. If you see a hat, you might see his face more clearly. If you see a jacket, it might help you better remember how he was built. The devil is really in the details." Wendy grinned. "I'm sorry. I guess that cliché is more apropos for this than in most situations. Go on, Donald. You're doing good."

"Okay. Funny thing was he was dressed like he could have been at the Brig...that was the leather bar where we were the night this happened." He looked at Wendy. "You know about leather bars?"

"Oh yeah, I hang out in them all the time." She laughed. "Not really, but I'm familiar with the concept and the general attire."

"Well, anyway, as I said, he was tall and lanky and was wearing a bandana, black I think, but it was night and hard to say for sure. He was also wearing a leather biker jacket that was kind of loose on him. Baggy jeans and boots. The baggy jeans would not have gone over well at the Brig."

"Okay. Let's see if you can kind of zoom in on his face. Can you do that?" Wendy's pencil scratched against the paper and Donald wondered what she was doing. She drew a few lines, stopped, and then drew a few more. She rotated the pad so Donald could see. "Check it out, Donald. Think. How close is this to the general shape of his face?"

Donald looked down at the oval she had drawn. It was kind of long, almost exaggerated, not heart-shaped, not square. But exactly like the face of his attacker. Donald gasped and wondered if somehow Mark was guiding the sketch artist too. He glanced back up at Wendy. "That's pretty spot-on."

"Good. See now how things like body type play into facial structure?"

"Uh-huh."

"So tell me more. Can you see his face?"

Nervously, Donald closed his eyes once more, and there was the man, the one who had killed Mark. He was looking up at him, and even though in his mind and in reality it was a dark night, there was still a shimmering moon to cast enough light to see detail. "Couple things stand out. He had a gap in his front teeth, big enough to notice. His nose was crooked, just a little off, like it had been broken."

"You said it was crooked. Did it go one way or the other, left or right?"

"Right. I'm sure."

"And how about the shape of the nose?"

Donald pondered. "In spite of being a bit crooked, it was very straight. I guess you might call it a Roman nose, kind of big but very straight, almost pointed."

"Very good, Donald. Now, how about the lips around that mouth? What were they like?"

Donald saw the guy grinning. It chilled him, even though the room was a bit on the stuffy side. "Thin. They were thin lips, barely there. The kind—and this fits—you would call cruel." Donald scratched his head and continued. "His face was heavily stubbled but not yet a beard. His chin, like his nose, was almost pointed, very sharp."

"Good. Good." Wendy was busy sketching. Donald could hear the scratching of pencil against paper. The sound was almost comforting, and he wasn't sure why. Maybe it was because he was certain that, this time, things would come out right. "What about his eyes, Donald?"

"Heavy-lidded, almost hooded. I wouldn't be able to say a color; it was too dark and he wasn't close enough."

"Doesn't matter. Anything else about his eyes? Long lashes? Eyebrows? Any wrinkles or scars? Just relax, breathe, and let it come."

Donald really didn't have to try very hard. The guy was right there before him, clear as a photograph or, God forbid, standing right in front of him. "He, uh, had what people call a unibrow. His eyebrows were bushy. That, combined with the heavy eyelids, made his eyes almost hard to see, like they were hidden. I don't remember anything in particular about the lashes. He didn't have any scars or wrinkles. He was too young, for the wrinkles at least."

"Close set or far apart? What was the shape of the eyes?"

"Kind of close set, I'd say, and the shape of his eyes was Caucasian, you know? They were just plain ovals." Donald sighed and opened his eyes for a moment. It was surprising how draining this all was. He could feel a headache restarting behind his eyes, and his temples begin to throb.

"Can you see his forehead, Donald? Was it big, low? What?"

Donald shook his head. "That's hard to say because of the bandana. It was pulled over his forehead, so I can't remember that. I can't tell anything about his hair either."

"That's okay, Donald. You're doing great."

Donald went on, adding a few more details, like his attacker's sharp and almost protruding cheekbones, the dimple in his chin (a detail that came to him just then), and the fact that he could see a portion of a tattoo emerging from the collar of his leather jacket, on his neck. Wendy pressed him for details on this, but all he could tell her was that it was like a flame, pointed upward.

And then Donald was quiet. He glanced over at his sister, who smiled and nodded at him, silently, he thought, indicating her encouragement and approval. In spite of Grace's obvious pleasure and how successful Donald just knew this session would turn out to be, he was exhausted. He wanted to go home, but more, he wanted to see the picture.

Wendy continued to draw, the sketchpad out of Donald's view. Grace's chair was positioned so that she could see, and her gaze returned to it, intense. Wendy sketched for several minutes more, her head bent low over the paper, deep in concentration.

At last Wendy swiveled the pad toward Donald.

His heart skipped a beat, and a chill washed over him, so intense he shivered. He believed that somehow it was not only his description that helped her nail the guy's face so perfectly, but also Mark's guiding force and presence in the room. Even though he couldn't see Mark, Donald could feel him there with them, even now.

"That's him," Donald whispered. "What you've done—it's incredible."

"All in a day's work. You sure I got everything right?"

Donald glanced down quickly again, then away. Looking at the face, rendered so exactly, made him queasy. "You got everything right."

"Okay, then. We'll get copies made and see that these are distributed, especially around the neighborhoods in question. You did a great job, Donald."

"Do you think this will help?"

"Time will tell. But this is a pretty distinctive-looking dude, and if someone who knows him sees this, I think they'll know who it is, especially since you say it's such a good likeness."

Donald didn't know if this was good news or bad. He wanted the guy caught—desperately and for many reasons—but it seemed like it was opening a door and inviting him back into his life.

And, for Donald, that was a very terrifying prospect.

He turned to Grace. "I'm really tired. Can we go home?"

"Sure, sweetie." Grace stood up, gathering her purse and jacket. "Thanks so much, Ms. Brennan."

"As I said, all in a day's work. I just hope what we did here today will have a positive outcome. Do you know the way out? I'd say stop by and talk to Detective Byrne, give him a little update, but I can see that Donald here needs a cup of tea and a warm bed, preferably with flannel sheets and *Golden Girls* on the tube." She winked at him and smiled kindly.

"Thanks. Come on, Grace. Let's go."

Chapter Fourteen

Ronny caressed the knife. It was a thing of beauty. It made his heart race. It made him want to sing and dance. Holding the knife in his hand, the heft of it, its smooth deadliness, made him hard. He couldn't help it. It was truly sick, but in a good way. He had ordered the knife off the web about a week ago. It was a spring-assisted batwing switchblade with a rosewood handle. With shipping, it had set him back almost sixty bucks, but the investment was worth it.

It was much better than driving around with an aluminum baseball bat in the trunk. The knife was so much more easily concealed and so much more lethal.

He loved his new knife. He hoped to use it tonight.

It was Saturday night, and Ronny was planning a night out alone. He thought it would work better that way, with far fewer complications. Justin would only get in the way. The kid had demonstrated himself to be a bit of a pussy anyway.

Like many north side Chicago fags, Ronny was preparing to go out for a night at a gay bar, the Brig, to be precise, where all the leather fairies hung out and did the most disgusting things to each other. (He had heard about the back room and could barely believe such things could go on in public. Talk about twisted!) But Ronny's mission differed in one important aspect from all the gay boys'. Unlike them, his interest in meeting up with a certain Mr.

Right had little to do with wanting to get laid (that particular idea always made him feel just a little queasy...and just to be contrary, his body would revolt by giving him an erection) but everything to do with seeing that a certain Mr. Right didn't talk anymore. Ever. To anyone.

He hoped that Mr. Right, aka Donald Griffiths, might also choose to frequent one of his favorite haunts tonight. From Ronny's observation of him over the recent past, it seemed like a fairly safe bet. Catching the man out in public would make it a lot easier than messing with all that breaking and entering crap and its attendant 911 risks. Going to Griffiths's home was definitely Plan B.

Plan A was simple. Go to the Brig. Watch, observe. See Donald Griffiths. Watch Donald Griffiths, never losing sight of him, even if it meant following him into the bathroom. Then, when Mr. Griffiths had had enough booze and come in his belly, follow the man at a discreet distance, hoping that he parked on one of the many dark residential side streets to either the east or west of the Brig. Ronny would have to act fast. There could be no hesitation. Unstrap the knife from where he had it concealed with a strap along his right calf and have it at the ready in his hand as he tracked his prey through the shadows. When the perfect time came—perfect defined as a moment when no one was around and before Griffiths was able to get inside his vehicle—walk quickly up behind the fag and plunge the knife into his back. It would be messy, he knew, not as quick and sure as a gun, but it could be effective. All Ronny had to do was be a man. Come up behind Griffiths, cover his shrieking mouth with one hand, slice across his throat, and continue to jab at him anywhere it was tender...and keep jabbing until the little queen stopped breathing. Let him drop to the frozen ground. Grope in Griffith's pocket, remove his wallet. Take his watch and any rings he might be wearing. The point was to make it look like a robbery, a common urban disaster. A crime that was anonymous and never solved. Wear gloves. Leave no prints. Make sure to smooth over any footprints. No smokes anywhere near the scene of the crime. No traces.

If all went well, he would walk away clean. He pictured himself whistling a little tune as he walked down Magnolia or maybe Argyle with extra money in his pocket, the satisfaction of a job well done, and a future of not having to worry about a knock on his door and someone calling out "Open up! Chicago police!"

Ronny had laid out his clothes for the night across his bed. Clothes and how he looked were especially important, because it was just today that he had seen his own likeness looking out at him from the window of the Quik Mart on Morse, on one of those "wanted" posters. The resemblance was so terrifying that Ronny had had to stop dead in his tracks and grip the brick wall of the store for support, gasping. As curious passersby looked at him in concern, Ronny stared down at the ground, not wanting to be recognized. His heart thudded, and his breath came in little hiccups. It took him a while to pull himself together. He had immediately forgotten the Marlboros for which he had originally headed out and hurried home, running, casting glances over his shoulder. He felt exposed, as if the world was watching out for him now, never mind that most people paid no attention to those signs. He took a long overdue shower, then pulled out the Edge gel, his trusty Gillette Mach II, and shaved his face and entire skull completely bare. Rinsed and dried, he admired himself in the mirror.

"Mr. Fuckin' Clean," he had whispered, smiling at himself and reaching up to caress the smooth pate. "No one will recognize you now."

At least he hoped not. He wondered all afternoon where else the posters had been put up and who had seen them...most importantly, who had seen them that would recognize him. Were they already calling the cops? "Yeah, I know that guy. He lives in my building." Or, "I see him at the L stop at Morse all the time." Or worst, "That guy used to be a buddy of mine. His name is..."

But on his second trip out for smokes later that afternoon, he carefully gauged the reaction of other people on the street, and none seemed to recognize him.

And now he felt safe, picking out his clothes for a special night on the town. *Oh yeah*. Everything was black: jeans, long-sleeved T-shirt, socks, combat boots, and biker jacket. He even had a pair of black briefs laid out across the bed: 2(X)IST. He heard the fags wore that brand a lot. *So what*? In this outfit, he would fit right in at the Brig. Better, the black attire would make him blend into the night shadows, rendering him virtually invisible.

"He won't even see me comin'." Ronny giggled and took a drag off his cigarette. He would lay off the weed for tonight (at least until much later, when he hoped to have a little celebration). For now, he needed to be aware, sharp, like a soldier or undercover operative.

He dressed slowly, taking time to ensure his metal-studded belt hung just so at his hips, that the outline of his dick was visible beneath the faded denim of his jeans, that the T-shirt fit his lanky form like a second skin, pushing up the sleeves to expose the muscle and sinew of his tattooed arms, even if no one would see them should he decide to keep his jacket on. He wished he could somehow hide his face, make it look different. What if someone in the bar recognized him? Ronny had a vision of a guy turning away from him, cell phone to his ear, casting surreptitious glances over his shoulder as he phoned in his suspicions to the cops. But what was he gonna do anyway, wear a veil over his face? He knew there were some bars where that might go over, but not the Brig. He would just have to hope the shaved head and clean-shaven face would be enough to throw anyone off who might have seen the flyer with his likeness on it. He thought about a baseball cap but then decided the shaved head would make him look even more different, since he was pictured in the flyer with a bandana.

He took one final look at himself in the mirror and was pleased at the manly and handsome young man who looked back at him. He was tough. All male. The fags would be drooling. He caught himself and chided: *that's not what you're goin' there for, man. You have a job to do. A little surveillance that will hopefully pay off big in both cash and peace of mind.*

But still, he couldn't help but admire how lean and mean he looked in the all-black leather and denim. It was a wonder he didn't have a girlfriend.

Ronny set off into the night.

*

Ronny lit a Marlboro and proceeded through the truck flatbed that led to the front door of the Brig as if he did this all the time. He kept his expression neutral, bordering on surly, and only hesitated briefly when the doorman asked to see his ID. The doorman glanced down at the Illinois driver's license, back up at Ronny, then frowned. Ronny's heart skipped a beat, thinking maybe the guy recognized him. After all, the picture on his license was much closer to the likeness on the flyer.

The doorman, a grizzled guy with bleached blond spiky hair and—Ronny had to admit—some pretty awesome tattoos above his leather jeans, continued to frown.

"What?" Ronny finally spat out, a little trickle of sweat running down his back. Would he look too stupid if he just turned and ran?

"Where you been, bud?"

"What do you mean?"

"I mean the butt in your hand. Don't you know you can't smoke in here? Or in any bar in Chicago? Not that I care, but I don't make the rules. You need to put that out before I can let you in."

Ronny sighed with relief, stepped back, took a final drag, and flung the cigarette outside. "Better?"

"Come on in."

And Ronny was inside the Brig for the first time. It was around eleven thirty, and it looked like it was just getting busy. In the short conversation he had had with the doorman, a line had formed behind him. The place was filled with all sorts of guys, and Ronny thought he might not have guessed many of them were gay, except for all the leather most were wearing. Truthfully, it didn't look that different in here than in some of the biker bars in Daytona he had gone to the previous winter.

Ronny walked up to the bar, again thinking how he was acting like he was an old hand at this, and ordered a Budweiser. Beer in hand, he found a spot along the wall on which he could lean and observe.

The guys here were all different shapes and sizes, some pumped up, guys who obviously spent many hours at the gym finessing their bulging pecs and biceps, their six-pack abs. Almost to a man, none of them wore a shirt. If they had anything on at all above the waist, it was either a leather vest or, in some cases, a harness. Sick. There were also a lot of fat guys with beards, which surprised Ronny. Even some of these guys with their big hairy bellies had their shirts open and their sagging tits on display. Didn't they have any sense of decency? He shook his head and took another swig of beer. There were, of course, a lot of the little fairies he so despised, mincing around in their biker gear, which didn't make them look any less effeminate. They made him sickest of all. Ronny could feel a rage building up within him as he watched a lithe blond guy, wearing some sort of latex vest, dog collar, and leather jeans, give him the eye. When he winked, Ronny looked away in disgust.

But of all the assembled men, he saw none who even looked close to Donald Griffiths, whom he remembered well enough that he was certain he'd recognize him if he saw him. There were a couple who came close, but Ronny had a sharp mind and good memory and knew he would know for sure if Mr. Griffiths stood before him. He hoped the night wouldn't be a total waste of time. Jesus Christ, he had better things to do than hang out in fag bars.

In the next couple hours, Ronny drank only one more beer. He wanted to keep his mind sharp. In spite of his clear, unclouded mind and his exceptional eyesight, he never saw Griffiths enter the bar. And he was watching as each man came in, the place getting closer, hotter, and louder with each one. Ronny held steadfastly to his spot along the wall, sometimes getting jostled because it afforded one of the best views of the entrance. No one would come into the Brig tonight without his scrutiny.

However, Ronny did notice that several of the men disappeared into a darker room at the back of the bar. He figured this was where all the perverted action went on and shook his head when he thought about it. Maybe Griffiths had been in there since before Ronny arrived, sucking as many dicks as he could?

Ronny thought he should check. If Griffiths was in there and he didn't look for him, the night would have been a total waste. But could he do it? Could he actually go back there and watch sick fag sex without throwing up or wanting to bash someone's skull in?

He wasn't sure. He stayed standing in his spot for the longest time, debating, trying to reason with himself that to check the back room was his duty. Another part of him said that even Griffiths wouldn't spend more than two hours back there, which was how long Ronny had stood there, nursing two beers.

Even fags had to come up for air, right?

There was a darker force in Ronny's mind that he didn't want to acknowledge, but it was there, almost taunting him. He would never say this aloud, would never even admit it to his closest friend, but he couldn't deny that he was curious about what took place in that back room. He tried to reassure himself that his curiosity was of the clinical sort, just wanting to see how some other life-form lived, and not of any sexual nature. Fuck, no. He shoved this last thought deep down into the recesses of his brain as, at last, he put one foot in front of the other and headed toward the back room.

It wasn't what he expected. The room was tiny, hardly bigger than a closet, and jam-packed. *The temperature must be at least ten degrees hotter in here*, Ronny thought. Already he could feel the sweat gathering in his pits and wished he could take off his jacket. It took him a while for his eyes to adjust to the almost pitch darkness of the room, but they eventually did, and he waded in farther, feeling nauseous as he was forced to rub against the churning bodies. There were the sounds of sucking. There were little cries and whispers, all tainted with the heat of fucking. There was the slap of skin against skin. Ronny's face felt hot; his ears burned as if they were on fire. He could see men in various positions. Many of them were like him, just loitering and observing, but some had already gotten busy and were on their knees. One couple was in a corner, the guy in front bent over and gripping his knees while his buddy plowed him mercilessly from behind. Ronny stared, and for several moments didn't even realize his own mouth was hanging open.

He quickly shut it.

Several guys were taking hits from small bottles while they watched or while they were being blown. Ronny had heard of poppers but had never seen them in such obvious and flagrant use. He wondered what the drug did for these guys. Was it anything like weed? Or meth?

He sidestepped, pushed, and wiggled his way to a wall, where he could find a good vantage point to try and examine faces. The initial shock of the room and its raw sex had made Ronny momentarily forget his original mission to find Donald Griffiths. But now as he settled against the wall, letting his shoulder blades rest against the smooth concrete, he could at least try to make an orderly round of the shifting, packed-in bodies in this small space to ensure that Griffiths was not present.

He had just been trying to methodically move from face to shadowed face, his heart pounding and an uncomfortable, undeniable tightness in his jeans (it's just nerves, he told himself), when he felt something touch his thigh. It was just a whisper across denim, but it was enough to make him gasp and stiffen in surprise.

He looked down to see a little guy on his knees looking up at him and grinning. He was Hispanic, about Ronny's age, with a moustache and thick close-cropped black hair. He took a hit from the bottle of poppers he had clenched in his hand and then reached up to offer them to Ronny.

What the hell? Ronny wasn't sure what he should do. He didn't want to, pardon the pun, blow his cover and react the way he wanted to, which was to reach down and pull the disgusting queer up by his armpits and punch his face in. Ronny's own face was already out there on the streets in shop windows, restaurants, and bars, and such a reaction here could plant suspicions in minds that were already occupied with more pressing matters.

And again—and this made him furious and sick to his stomach all at once—he couldn't deny the erection in his pants and the blatant curiosity about what it would be like to take a hit off the poppers. Almost dizzy, he accepted the proffered bottle and brought it to his nose, took a big hit in each nostril.

It took only a second or two for the rush to hit him. He was filled with a wave of heat that caused an electric tingle throughout his body and, oddly, made him feel very sexual. His head lolled back, and he swore his heart had moved up nearer to his ears to thud rapidly. His dick grew even harder.

And the guy on his knees was reaching for his zipper. Part of him wanted to knee him away, catching him on the chin and hurting him. The other part didn't want him to stop. The other part told him to just be cool and to not give himself away. He knew it was all rationalization. But he let the guy pull down his zipper and briefs, and before he knew it, the guy had lowered his head to his jutting-out cock and was sucking.

The sensations were incredible, especially when combined with the poppers, a hot swirling and intense pressure that felt almost better than any sex Ronny had had before. He wanted to push the guy away but couldn't stop him. He thought briefly of closing his eyes and just trying to imagine Glenda, this chick he used to fuck over the summer, but everything was happening too fast.

He felt the tingling starting in his balls and spreading out like a wave through his body. In only seconds, he was shooting his load into the guy's mouth, bucking and jerking. He knew people were watching and couldn't help himself.

The guy leaned back, wiped his mouth, and whispered up to him, "That was quick."

And this time, Ronny did knee him, hard, in the face, sending him over sideways to crash onto the sticky floor. As he yanked up his pants, he hoped he'd bloodied the guy's nose. Like a bull, Ronny charged through the crowd, shoving anyone that blocked his path to the pale rectangle of light that was the door. There were a few angry murmurs, and once, Ronny even felt a fist land on his back.

But he had to get out.

Now.

Once outside, the cold air was a blessing. Ronny rushed, heedless, around the corner, where he vomited into the grass, on and on into the dry heaves, not knowing whether the tears rolling down his cheeks were from the puking or the shame or both.

Finally, his stomach quieted enough for him to stand upright and wipe at his mouth with the back of his hand. His breath was coming in ragged bursts, and he was trembling all over.

He noticed someone standing near him. It was an older man, wearing jeans and a leather biker jacket, probably on his way to the Brig. Even in the dark, his eyes were bright with concern.

"Too much to drink? You okay?"

"Fuck you!" Ronny shrieked, pushing the guy hard enough that he almost lost his balance. He would have fallen on his ass if he hadn't hit a row of parked cars. He stared at Ronny in surprise and, Ronny thought, fear. The fear made him feel better. The guy pushed away from the car he had slammed into and ran.

"Fuckin' queer!" Ronny called after him. "Get back here! I'll kick your ass."

The guy disappeared around the corner.

Ronny, with shaking hands, lit up a smoke and groped in his pocket. He took a deep drag to calm himself, then withdrew the sheet of paper from his pocket. He brought it close to his face, where he could see Donald Griffiths's address.

"Time for Plan B," Ronny whispered to himself and headed off into the night. He could feel the knife strapped securely to his calf. That sensation and meeting up with Griffiths was all he allowed himself to concentrate on.

Chapter Fifteen

At first he thought Mark had come to visit him again. Donald opened his eyes to darkness, listening. He knew he had heard something, that a noise had brought him up from slumber to his present alert state, but he didn't know what the noise was. He was on edge, on guard, but had nothing concrete to go on except the defenses his subconscious had obviously erected. There was a difference in the atmosphere of the room.

He wasn't alone.

The room was dark. Donald had closed both blinds and curtains to make it pitch black. Now he wished for some light. His gaze darted about, wondering if the fuzzy gray shape in the corner was not, after all, a chair, but a man crouching, waiting for just the right moment to pounce. Maybe that even darker rectangle leading into his closet held something sinister. Gradually, Donald's heart quickened its pace.

"Mark?" he whispered hoarsely into the shadows. Already, his hopes and excitement at seeing his lover were beginning to ebb. When Mark appeared to him, there was something different and ethereal, a charged atmosphere that was present even before Mark appeared.

There was a charged atmosphere now, too, but this was different. There was none of the electricity in the air that accompanied Mark's presence, yet Donald could feel something was amiss. Something was different in the condo from when he had gone to bed that night.

He sat up a bit straighter in bed, listening. And then he heard it, the familiar creak of a floorboard in the living room, followed by another. There was the clear sound of footsteps.

Donald drew his legs up to his chest. He wiped a trembling hand across his face. This was no appearance from Mark. This was no nightmare remnant. This was real life. Someone had gotten into his apartment while he slept. The simple sound of the footsteps and the ominous pauses between them was terrifying. To be alone like this, in the dead of night, and realize an intruder had violated your space was a realization that set Donald's heart to pounding. What should he do? Should he hide, pretend to be asleep? He had heard somewhere that pretending to be asleep was often not a bad idea if you were being robbed. The thieves wanted to run into you even less than you wanted to run into them. But how could one just lie there, feigning slumber, while someone crept around you in the darkness? How could someone stand the potential for harm? The risk?

There was a crash, and something shattered on the floor just outside his bedroom.

Donald covered his mouth with his hand, stifling the cry that wanted to emerge. *What should I do? Hide*? He reached over and flipped on the lamp on the bedside table, squinting at even this soft glow. He called out, "Who's there? I'm calling the cops right now. And I should warn you: I've got protection in here." Donald was surprised at the strength and confidence he managed to convey, when already his face was slick with sweat and he felt his pulse rate surge. Never mind that the only protection he had was a box of Trojans in the nightstand drawer and the telephone—the damn telephone—was on the dresser across the room.

All was silent in the apartment. Whoever was out there wasn't leaving, nor were they moving any closer to his bedroom door, at least not at the moment. Maybe he had frightened whoever it was. Maybe it was just a burglar who had the mistaken idea the apartment was empty, its owner out for the evening. Maybe, when the thief found out the truth, he would beat a hasty retreat.

Except he wasn't. The silence was creepy, portentous. What was happening just outside his door? Who was out there?

And then, with genuine horror, Donald remembered his time with the sketch artist and how she had promised they would canvass the north side neighborhoods with them. He could see Wendy Brennan's earnest face in his mind's eye as she reassured him: "We'll get signs up all over Andersonville, Rogers Park, and Edgewater. If anyone who knows this guy sees one, we'll get some results." What if this was Mark's killer? What if he had seen the signs and was coming now to ensure that Donald didn't talk to any more sketch artists?

But how would he know where to find him? The press had been kind and had not mentioned Donald's name in any of their articles, so his identity was not public knowledge. But still, there would be ways of finding out who he was. It was not even beyond the realm of possibility that their attackers already knew who they were and where they lived before they attacked them.

Anything was possible.

There was another creak of a floorboard and then what sounded like a stumble and someone clutching at a wall for balance.

Enough. I have to do something. I can't just stay here in bed, paralyzed. Donald groped on the floor for his boxers and slid them on. *What do I do now? Where should I hide? Under the bed? In the closet? Whoever is out there already knows I'm in here because I called out. What good would hiding in such obvious places do me? I would be a sitting duck. What then? Jump out the window?* Briefly, Donald eyed the window opposite his bed, wondering how much damage a three-story drop would do. Could he even survive?

The solution was obvious, but Donald's panic made it difficult to do what needed to be done. In spite of the fear making his heart race, he sidled across the room, trying to be as quiet as possible, heading toward the dresser, where the cordless rested on its base. It seemed to take a long time to cross the wide plain that his bedroom had suddenly become, and he stopped once in his tracks and gasped when he heard another click of shoe heel on hardwood. He reminded himself to breathe and got himself to his dresser.

And his mind was blank. What was the number to call, 411? No, that was information. He finally wrapped his terrified mind around the digits 911 and had just pressed the nine when the doorknob of his bedroom turned.

Donald stared at it, mouth dry, trembling, phone clutched in his hand like a weapon. What if his intruder had cut the phone line? He poised his shaking finger on the one, and the door swung open.

Donald screamed and dropped the phone. It clattered to the floor. Donald gasped for air, groping for the phone, eyes wide and staring.

It was him! The guy who had killed Mark! Even with the shaved head, Donald recognized his lanky form and eyes, his expression of relentlessness. Donald backed against the wall, feeling so vulnerable in his boxers, holding up his hands. His mind refused to form coherent thought. The best he could do was whisper, "No."

The guy drew closer, and finally Donald screamed once more when he noticed the switchblade held aloft in his hand. *And this is where I die.* The thought echoed as Donald raised his hands in futile self-defense.

Chapter Sixteen

Why wasn't Ronny answering? Justin punched the speed-dial key he had programmed in for Ronny's cell, and an expression of annoyance darkened his features when once again he got his friend's voice mail. How many calls had he made on this early Sunday morning? Six? Seven? And he had texted Ronny just as many times.

And each time, there was no response. Ronny *always* had his cell with him, no matter what, no matter where. The fact that it was ringing and not going directly into voice mail told Justin that the phone was not turned off for charging or whatever.

So why wasn't he answering? It wasn't like him. Justin had a bad feeling and told himself to stop being stupid. There were no grounds for his fears. Not really. Well, maybe one or two.

Justin had left his apartment early that morning when he had run into another one of his mother's playmates, this time a skinny black dude with cornrows, coming out of their one bathroom. He was naked and didn't even seem embarrassed. In fact, the guy acted like Justin wasn't even there and went into his mom's room. He slammed the door behind him. In a minute or two, he heard both of them laughing softly.

He didn't want to hear any more.

So he threw on some jeans, a sweatshirt, a parka, and a woolen beanie and headed outside. It was a maliciously cold morning, with bright sun belying the wicked wind whipping off Lake Michigan, picking up its scent and chill, lowering the temperature into the teens. Before he was even outside for five minutes, Justin was kicking himself for forgetting his gloves. But he would not—could not—go back in there. He just didn't have the stomach for it.

So he checked his pockets and found a few rumpled singles and knew it was enough for coffee and maybe a bagel at the coffee shop on the corner of Jarvis and Greenview. More to get out of the cold than anything, he ducked gratefully into the little establishment, happy that it was open this early and happier still that it was empty.

He didn't want to see Uncle Walter. Every time he thought of him, he remembered seeing that fag sneaking out of his apartment and his mind would start playing a porno DVD of the things they were doing to each other before Justin's arrival. It made him feel hot and flushed and sick all at once, like he was coming down with the flu or something. He knew Uncle Walter would want to talk about it, and he knew he wasn't up for that. Not yet, not when he could very well say something he might regret later, something that would really hurt Uncle Walter, something that could never be taken back.

No, he knew it was best to keep away from his uncle for a while.

So he had tried Ronny. He was pretty sure he'd wake him up, but too bad. He could go back to sleep while Justin hung out in his studio. Justin could watch TV or even read one of Ronny's comic books while he slept, and then maybe they could get up and go do something. Long enough for his mother to fix her Mr. Right-for-the-Night bacon and eggs and get rid of him, anyway.

But Ronny was not answering. He always answered. Even when he had been asleep and made no secret about how pissed off he was at being awakened. Even if he was out and about.

Justin stared down at his cell, wondering if he should try again, and then knew just how futile that would be. He was tired of banging his head against the wall. He sipped his coffee slowly, wanting to stay in here where it was warm as long as he could. He wished he had his own place. It sucked being homeless, especially when you technically had a home.

Where could Ronny be? Why wasn't he picking up?

And then he saw it. Even backward and through the glass, he clearly saw the little flyer taped to the window of the coffee shop. The flyer with the image of his buddy Ronny's face bigger than life below one huge word: WANTED. Justin's hand trembled, and his cup clattered when he tried to set it back in its saucer. Some of the sweet, milky liquid sloshed over the side.

He stood and ducked outside to examine the paper taped to the glass more carefully. The poster said something about "the man" being wanted for a "hate crime." Anyone with information should call the Chicago police department. It was too fucking cold, and he hurried back inside, remembering in detail the last time he *had* talked to Ronny.

Last night. They had argued. Justin had wanted to come over, spend the night, and Ronny had been vague, saying he had things to do.

"I'll do 'em with you."

"Nah, man, I need to be alone."

"Why? What kind of things?"

"Never you mind, little man. Just the kind of things a guy needs to do by himself. Do you need me to fuckin' spell it out?"

They had gone back and forth, Justin coming close to pleading, not wanting to be stuck out in the cold while his mom "entertained." But Ronny wouldn't budge. Whatever he wanted to do, he wanted to do on his own. He had made that fact crystal clear. Justin had spent the previous night at a Cineplex in Evanston, buying a ticket for one movie and sneaking into two more, until the place closed and he could come home and hope that at least his mother's bedroom would be quiet.

At the time, Justin thought maybe Ronny had a date or something. After all, he was a man, midtwenties. Surely he must need some female companionship from time to time. He talked about it enough, pointing out the tits on that one, or the ass on this other one, or the legs on the one crossing the street. Ronny seemed to have a whole cache of past sexual escapades with which to dazzle Justin.

It just seemed like, since he had known him, Ronny never actually went out with any girls. Maybe last night was different.

Or maybe not, Justin thought with a chill that had nothing to do with the air sweeping in when a blond guy with a laptop under his arm entered the coffee shop. He was thinking further back, to other conversations he and Ronny had had, about the attack back in October...

And how Ronny needed to silence their only witness.

And Justin—with a feeling that made his stomach churn—recalled how he had rushed over to Ronny's with the information about the guy's name and address when he had freaked out after seeing him leave his own uncle's apartment.

Ronny didn't actually do something to the guy? Or at least tried to? Last night? He wouldn't do that without him, would he?

Justin's mouth was dry, and his face was damp. It all fit together: their conversations, Ronny's intent on getting the guy, his unusual evasiveness last night.

Oh my God. Did he actually go there? If he did, what happened? Did he hurt the guy? Had there been a struggle and the guy hurt Ronny? Maybe killed him? Is that why he's not answering? Because he can't? Or maybe Ronny succeeded in "silencing" the guy and was now on the lam, getting as far from Chicago as he could.

Justin let out a little cry that caused the blond guy two tables over to look up, startled, from his laptop.

Justin covered his face with his hands. Ever since that awful night in the fall, he knew there was no way for things to go but bad. Sure, there were a million things Ronny could be doing, including fucking some girl, but Justin had a heart-stopping certainty that something awful had happened. He stood suddenly, realizing he didn't know what to do next or where to go. He looked around the coffee shop, dazed, as if he didn't know where he was.

Thoughts bounced around in his head. How would this implicate him? If Ronny wasn't dead, just caught, would he throw him under the bus? Justin had seen on TV how they were always offering deals if the bad guys would just turn on each other. Would Ronny do that to him?

He knew his friend well enough to know that the answer was yes, in a heartbeat, if it would save his pathetic ass. Justin was kidding himself if he thought Ronny would make any sacrifices for him.

Justin wanted to cry. As much as he wanted to stay away from Uncle Walter, he knew there was nowhere else to turn. Uncle Walter would help him. He had to. He loved Justin.

But he would need to tell his uncle the whole story. And could his loving uncle still love him after he knew the truth?

It was a chance he'd have to take. Justin picked up his cell phone once more.

Chapter Seventeen

Walter groped in his pocket for his keys while Hank clawed at the door. The German shepherd mix was just as eager to get inside as he had been to get outside a half hour ago. Walter laughed at the dog. "I told you it was cold out. You wouldn't listen." The dog stared up at him with mournful brown eyes, as if he understood, then resumed clawing at the door.

"Gimme a chance to get the frickin' keys out, boy," Walter said affectionately. He heard the phone begin to chirp behind his locked door. "Oh shit," he whispered and threw his gloves on the hallway floor, fished his keys from his jeans pocket, and hurriedly unlocked the door. Without bothering to unleash Hank, he dashed over to the little breakfast bar and snagged the cordless off its base just before it went to voice mail.

"Hello?"

For a moment, there was silence. Walter immediately thought it was telemarketers, then glanced down at the Caller ID display. It was Justin's cell. "Justin? You there?"

"Hi, Uncle."

Walter closed his eyes, grateful the boy had phoned. Things had been so strained when he had last seen him. He was afraid the blatant evidence of his homosexuality might cause a longer-lasting rift. It was one thing to talk about it, quite another to have it staring you in the face. "Listen, buddy, about the other morning?"

Justin cut him off. "We don't need to talk about that right now, okay?" Justin fell silent once more.

Walter cocked his head. Justin's speech, even in the few words he had spoken, sounded tense, anxious. What was up? Something with his sister, Patty? Honest to God, the woman did not deserve a son like Justin. She didn't deserve a child at all. "What's goin' on?"

"I need to talk to you, Uncle Walter."

"Okay..."

Justin let a few more moments pass without saying anything.

"Is everything okay? Your mom?"

"Yeah, yeah. It's nothin' like that." Another pause. "Can I come over?"

"Sure you can, bud. You know you're always welcome here. I'll put the kettle on."

"Thanks, Uncle Walter. I'll be there as soon as I can."

And the boy hung up before Walter had a chance to say anything else. He had been about to tell him to hop in a cab and he would pay the fare. He supposed he could call him back and tell him that, but he had a feeling the boy would consider it yet another instance of babying him, as if Justin were incapable of getting himself to his uncle's house on his own.

So Walter turned and filled a kettle with water and pulled two mugs from the cupboard. He dropped a Typhoo teabag in each one. He pulled out a loaf of sourdough from the bread drawer and a jar of strawberry jam from the fridge. He thought about cooking but knew Justin would roll his eyes.

Or would he? There was something definitely bothering the boy this morning. And it didn't seem like it was their run-in on Monday morning.

He hoped Justin hadn't been trying to get in touch with him since last night. Walter had gone out to Big Chicks, a bar close to his place, and had ended up going home with a very cute and very drunk boy half his age, a Loyola grad student. It was a disappointing evening. When they got back to the young man's apartment, the guy sat next to him on the couch, and, instead of reaching for Walter, reached for his laptop. He brought up Manhunt and said, "Let's see who's online, okay?" When he brought out a little glass pipe and a clear envelope filled with what was most likely crystal meth, Walter had decided he'd had enough. He wished his new friend good luck and headed toward the door. He cast one look back before he closed the door behind him and was saddened to see the guy already busy online, as if Walter had never been there.

Walter sat at the breakfast bar, eyeing Hank enviously. The dog, who had commandeered a corner of the couch, curled into a tight little ball, and fallen into a deep sleep, replete with loud snores. It seemed like everyone was getting lots of sleep lately! Walter would probably be doing the same thing right now, beneath his own flannel sheets and down comforter, but Justin's phone call had worried him and acted like a hit of speed on his nerves.

After about twenty minutes, the boy's arrival was announced by the barking of the intercom box near Walter's front door. Walter switched on the gas under the teakettle and went to buzz his nephew in.

When Walter opened the door, Justin was already outside. He must have raced up the stairs yet didn't seem out of breath. Walter gave him his broadest smile and couldn't stop himself from saying, "It's so good to see you. I was afraid you were mad at me."

Justin brushed by him and refused to meet his gaze. He waved Walter's fear away with his hand. "Nothin' like that, Uncle. Forget it."

Justin slumped down on the couch, head back, legs splayed before him. Hank lifted his head to regard him, then replaced his snout between his paws and went right back to sleep. Justin unzipped his parka and stared out the living room window, as if there was something fascinating about the bright-blue sky and the crystalline snowflakes just beginning to dance in the air.

"I'm making tea. And I can toast up some sourdough. I got some really good jam. Strawberry...your favorite." Walter smiled at the back of his nephew's head. It wasn't just his constant need to feed and nurture those he loved that kept him blathering, but also a weird sense within him that wanted to avoid whatever was coming. He didn't have a handle on what it was, but whatever Justin was going to say, he knew it would not be good news. "It'll only take me a couple minutes. I can—"

Justin cut him off. "Will you stop it? I'm not hungry."

Walter switched off the gas under the teakettle. "What is it, Justin? What's the matter?" He wished the boy would look at him, but he continued to gaze forward, almost as if mesmerized.

Justin sighed and then spoke slowly, as if he needed to be understood by someone not too quick on the uptake. "Will you please just come over here and sit down? Quit fluttering around like some fuckin' housewife."

This most definitely wasn't going to be good. Whatever it was, this was not going to be a positive thing. Walter felt the acid rise in his stomach, and his heart began to beat a little faster. What could be wrong now? There was only one way to find out. He walked to the living area and sat in the easy chair across from the couch.

Still, even though Walter was facing him, Justin would not give him the benefit of returning eye contact. He continued to stare out the window. Walter turned to see what so fascinated the boy and saw only other buildings and naked trees reaching their limbs to the placid blue sky, like many others in Chicago winter. He turned back to his nephew and saw that the boy's eyes were glistening with tears.

"I have something to tell you." Justin took in a deep breath.

"I'm listening."

"You're not gonna like me after I tell you."

"Why not just spill it and let me be the judge of that? You might be surprised."

Justin let loose a world-weary sigh worthy of someone twice his age. "I think the only one who's going to be surprised is you." Finally, Justin leveled his gaze on him. Walter could see a war of emotions going on beneath the boy's acne-pitted skin: terror, sadness, and extreme anxiety among them.

Walter leaned forward. "Sometimes, honey—" Walter bit his lip, knowing how Justin hated the endearment. "Sometimes, Justin, the best way to say a thing is just to say it."

Justin nodded. "Okay. You remember last fall?" Justin rubbed the thighs of his jeans rapidly. His gaze wandered everywhere around the room. The only place he didn't look was into his uncle's eyes. Justin's breathing became more rapid and shallow. "I—I don't know if I can do this." At last, he aimed his stare at Walter. Although the rest of Justin was agitated, his eyes were dead, soulless.

Walter began to be very afraid, feeling a chill in spite of the comfy seventy-two at which he had set his thermostat. Part of him wanted to just get up, cross to the couch, and take the boy in his arms, telling him that he needn't say anything more. Walter didn't need to know. But the other part *did* need to know. If there was something wrong—and it was obvious there was—Walter had to find out what it was so he could fix it. "As I said, Justin, just tell me. There's nothing you can say that will make me feel any different about you."

Justin rolled his eyes and gave him a mirthless grin. "I'm not so sure about that." The boy sighed. "Last fall, there was a fag bashing over near that bar you hang out at sometimes. The Brig?"

Walter closed his eyes. He didn't want Justin to go on. His stomach churned. Walter knew what was coming and didn't want to hear it. Once the words were spoken, how could he turn back? Indeed, could what he had said about anything Justin would say not changing his feelings about him still hold true? He nodded for his nephew to continue, nausea beginning to rise up within him.

"There was this attack, I guess, and one of the guys didn't, um, make it out alive. Did you hear anything about it?"

Walter tasted vomit at the back of his throat. Again, he nodded.

Justin stared down at the floor, and his next words came out in a rushed whisper. "It was me, uncle, me and a couple other guys. I didn't actually hurt anybody, but I was there. I was part of it." Justin went quiet.

Walter, for once, didn't know what to say. The two of them sat in silence for what seemed like an hour but was really only about five minutes. When Justin finally lifted his head to regard Walter, his face was wet with tears.

"I never wanted anyone to get hurt. I sure as fuck didn't want anyone to die." He swallowed and hiccupped out a little sob. "I wish I could take it back! I wish it had never happened!"

Walter knew it was his turn to offer some words of encouragement and support but could say nothing. The words lodged in his throat, mysterious. Walter didn't know if they would be expressions of concern or pronouncements of rage. He sat and simply stared at his nephew. He closed his mouth when he realized it was hanging open. Hank let out a whimper and a snore.

"Do you hate me now?" Justin stared at him.

Walter looked down at his hands. A lump in his throat made it hard to swallow. He felt a couple of tears drip from his eyes. How could he answer the boy's question? He didn't know the answer himself. He slowly shook his head. "Justin, Justin." He looked up at his nephew. "I don't know what to feel. I don't know what to say. It's a horrible thing. I would never imagine you being involved in something like this." Walter went quiet again, then asked, "You ever think about the fact that the same thing could happen to me? You could be going to my funeral some day because some losers decide it would be fun to beat up a fag?"

Justin didn't answer. He bit his lower lip and made a close inspection of a piece of lint on his parka.

"I don't know what to tell you, buddy. I don't know what you want me to do with this. Do I still love you?" Walter paused to consider, to make sure of his feelings. "Yeah. You're my family, like a son to me. I could never not love you. But right now, I also am not sure who *you* are. And I guess that's what I need to think about. I need to consider if the person I love is really the one sitting here right now telling me he did something beyond belief. Something so terrible that it's making me wonder if I made up my own idea of you."

"Oh, Uncle Walter, I'm still me. I swear it. I was fucked up that night. I used bad judgment. I was going along to try to be cool..."

"Do you think that would be any comfort to the guy you helped kill's mom? Or his lover? Or anyone that his life meant a lot to?"

Justin had no answer.

Again, the pair fell to silence. Walter heard footsteps in the hallway, doors opening and closing, someone yelling outside, the blare of a car horn. A bank of clouds passed in front of the sun, almost as if sympathetic to the drama unfolding in Walter's living room.

"So, why bring me this now, Justin? Because, man, I don't have a clue. And if you wanna know if I wish you hadn't told me this, the answer is yes."

"I needed to tell you because there's something more."

A tremble, like a spasm, passed through Walter. Could he take any more news? He didn't know. He bit his lip. "What? What more?"

Justin took in a deep breath, held it, and let it out with a great whoosh. "That guy that lives downstairs from you, Donald Griffiths?"

A jolt went through Walter, actually feeling like someone had pressed a live wire to his skin. And it all clicked together. He flashed back to lying in bed with Donald and Donald telling him about the fag bashing that had taken his partner away from him...in October...near St. Boniface cemetery, which was also near...the Brig. "Oh my God," Walter whispered. He wasn't sure if he should run for the toilet. He felt very close to throwing up. "Not...not Donald?" Walter whispered.

"I'm sorry...yeah, him. And his boyfriend." Justin's voice had become toneless, almost as if he were in a trance, as if someone had hypnotized him and he was recounting all of this from a distance.

"So you told me this because Donald lives downstairs? Because I know him?"

"I told you because he might be in danger. My buddy, Ronny, wants to, um, wants to make sure he doesn't talk." Justin became as still as stone, then looked at his uncle, spitting out the next words as if some exterior force compelled him. "I told Ronny who Donald Griffiths was. I told him where he lived."

Before Walter could begin to process the enormous danger and horror of those two simple declarative sentences, his hearing perked up. He could hear sirens in the distance, growing closer. There were a lot of them.

He shut his eyes and waited, finally lowering his head down close to his knees and covering his face with his hands. He could barely breathe. In minutes, the sound of the sirens was near deafening, and when Walter removed his hands from his eyes, he saw swirling blue and red lights reflected on his white walls. Walter stood to look out the window, where several police cars and an ambulance had pulled up. Uniformed men and women were rushing into their building. Accompanying the sirens was the squawking of walkie-talkies and police radios. People were already gathering on the curb to watch the drama unfold. Walter wondered how they'd gathered so quickly.

"God, please no," Walter whispered and turned to look at Justin.

But his nephew was gone. The door to his apartment hung open. Distantly, Walter heard the slam of the fire door and footsteps.

Walter crumpled to the floor.

Chapter Eighteen

Donald turned away from the window. He had moved close to the glass moments ago, alerted by the slam of the front door downstairs. He watched dully as his neighbor and, lately, sex partner, Walter, emerged from the building to walk his dog. He envied the guy's jaunty, carefree walk and the way the dog tugged at the leash, wanting to go faster. Walter called to the dog, laughing, to slow down and then ran to catch up with his canine companion.

Another world.

Like a zombie, Donald walked back to his bedroom. He stood in the archway that led into the room and surveyed a scene of chaos. A lamp, a black one with a mica shade Mark had found at the Brown Elephant thrift store, lay shattered on the hardwood, its ceramic shards reflecting back dull illumination from the window's diffuse light, creeping in from beneath closed blinds. The nightstand was overturned, and its drawer had spilled its contents of hand towels, lube, and condoms.

Happier days.

The mirror above the dresser had a large diagonal crack running through it, throwing back an image Donald almost didn't recognize. His eyes were wild, almost bulging. Until he saw evidence of his chest rising and falling, he hadn't even realized how hard he was breathing. A slash sliced open his cheek on the left side, and dark blood, beginning to clot, still ran down his face and onto his neck and chest. One of his eyes looked puffy and made a prediction of a black-and-blue shade that would mar his features before even an hour had passed.

And finally, Donald allowed himself to glance down at the floor, where the body of a young man lay, blood pooling beneath him, a sticky scarlet pond. The guy's eyes stared dully up at the ceiling, not seeing, already beginning to film over. His face too bore the scars of battle, slashed and broken. His pallor was a sickly white, and Donald knew if he turned him over, the parts of him closest to the floor would be crimson, where the remaining blood inside him had pooled after he had... after he had...

Died.

He didn't die. I killed him, Donald thought, staring at the body. *I killed him, and now I don't know what to do.* Donald was paralyzed there, near the entrance to his bedroom. He was sure he couldn't move, not right then anyway, and he was even less certain he could speak, or scream, or pray, or whatever utterances murderers made after they vanquished their prey.

But you killed him to save yourself. You didn't even kill him to avenge Mark, which would have been okay, understandable at least. Maybe not in a court of law, but in your own heart. Eventually. But the fact that this young man, hardly more than a boy, lay dead at his feet, his life snuffed out by Donald's own hand, made him tremble. The fact of the killing, however justifiable, placed a heavy and almost surreal burden on him. He was in a place he had never imagined being. That was happening a lot lately.

Donald flattened himself against the wall, staring, remembering the young man coming at him with the knife. The memory was like a clip from a movie. Donald could see some of the action but felt removed from it, as if the emotions that should be there were inaccessible to him.

There had been a struggle, falling over furniture, raw punching, adrenaline, and self-preservation taking over. The skirmish was over in a matter, Donald supposed, of two or three minutes, but in his mind it seemed to go on for much longer, hours perhaps. Already, minutes after it all ended violently and then silently, Donald was finding it hard to remember details. The memories were like a movie out of which someone had edited crucial moments...so all that remained were jump cuts.

Somehow, he had won. Somehow, he had managed to pull the knife away from the intruder. Or had it simply dropped to the floor in their struggle and Donald, acting on instinct, had been the first to grab it? And somehow, he had plunged it into his intruder's throat, after missing and slicing open the guy's face, his chest. Donald could not for the life of him remember how most of this had happened.

And had there really been no words? Just grunts and groans, sharp exhalations of air as the men struggled with one another?

Maybe it would all come back. Maybe not. Donald had enough presence of mind to know that the memory lapses and the trembling were warning signs, the early onset of shock. He needed to get to the phone, needed to call someone official. He needed help.

The young man was beyond help. But he too would need tending to.

Donald's gaze moved back up to the mirror. He had stared for entire minutes in its distorted silver surface. He didn't know when Mark had appeared, but now, in the glass, Donald saw Mark standing behind him, wearing a black T-shirt and jeans. For the first time, Mark's image did not seem as solid as it had in life. He was wavering at the edges, as if he were crafted from light, a paranormal hologram. His eyes looked tired, his expression sad. Donald felt that if he turned to him, Mark would vanish, like a puff of smoke caught in the wind, so he continued to stare at his dead lover's reflection in the mirror.

Just seeing Mark restored some warmth to Donald's limbs, gave him a small measure of comfort. Their eyes met in the mirror, and Mark smiled. Donald smiled back.

"What do I do now, honey?"

"You know what to do." Mark's voice was weak, barely above a whisper, sounding not as if it came from directly behind Donald but as though it were traveling down a long corridor. "You cross the room. You pick up the phone. You call 911." Mark's smile vanished, he crossed his arms, and Donald knew he was waiting for Donald to follow his instructions.

So he did. When the 911 operator came on the line, Donald was surprisingly calm, his voice clear and confident, albeit toneless and hollow. He answered her questions, gave his address, told her there'd been an accidental stabbing, in self-defense. He assured her that he was all right. He told her there was no more danger. But then: "They should hurry. I think I've gone into shock. I think I need help." She told him they would be there in a matter of minutes and to keep warm and to "hang on."

He hung up the phone. Mark crossed the room and took him in his arms. For just a moment, there was comfort, and then, like a nightmare flashback, the whole scene of their attack in October replayed in Donald's mind. He felt sick. He saw it all this time, the Hispanic youth and the other one, someone barely out of childhood, a kid with an acne-marred face and eyes that conveyed confusion and regret.

And he knew him. His upstairs neighbor had introduced them once upon a time. His name was Justin. "Oh, God," Donald whispered, clinging to Mark's form, which was feeling less and less substantial with each passing moment.

"Don't leave me," Donald whimpered. It was starting to feel like hugging fog.

"I have to. It's time for me to go. I love you, sweetheart. Live, okay? That's all I want from you. *Live.*"

And Donald began to weep. When he went to lay his head upon Mark's chest, there was nothing there. His arms made a great empty circle in front of his chest. Donald dropped his arms to his sides and slid to his knees, sobbing, as he heard the wailing of sirens in the distance.

Chapter Nineteen

Walter rushed out the door, almost tripping as he hurried down the stairs, grabbing at the cinder block wall to keep himself from falling. Justin could not have gotten that far ahead of him. He dashed through the lobby and out the door. He didn't know what he planned to do when he caught up to his nephew and certainly did not have a clue as to what he would say, but he needed to talk to him, needed to save Justin from whatever peril awaited him outside Walter's care.

The police, onlookers, and now media (a Channel 7 news van was rolling up) didn't give Walter a second look as he hurried by them, pushing through the growing crowd. When he emerged from the building, he knew Justin could have gone north, south, east, or west, getting lost quickly in Chicago's grid-like maze of streets, but a flash of blue, the color of Justin's parka, caught his eye, so Walter headed north.

Walter put out of his mind that the person wearing the parka was also taller than Justin and walking much too slowly for what he would have imagined for the boy, and chased after the figure. Nearly out of breath, he caught up to the blue-parka-clad man and threw a hand on his shoulder to stop him. Walter was filled with the hope of the desperate. He prayed the details that were wrong were just mistakes in his traumatized mind. But a man, much older than Justin—at least thirty-five—turned to glare at Walter at his unwanted touch. He shrugged Walter's hand angrily off his shoulder. "What the fuck?"

Walter waited a moment to catch his breath. "I'm sorry, man. I thought you were somebody else. My nephew has a coat just like yours."

The man shook his head, eyeing Walter up and down as if he had just escaped from an institution. "Whatever." And he continued on up the street, casting suspicious looks back.

Walter closed his eyes and stamped his foot on the cold sidewalk. "Damn," he whispered. Too much time had passed. Justin could be anywhere. Still panting, Walter looked south, where the cop cars, ambulances, and news vans were still gathered, making something of a macabre street fair of his otherwise ordinary street. He watched as two EMTs wheeled a stretcher out. Atop its chrome and padded surface was a black rubber body bag, zipped closed. A white sheet had once been placed atop the body, but the wind had snatched at it until it dangled in folds over the side of the gurney.

Walter whimpered. This wasn't happening. This was a nightmare. Was Donald Griffiths in that bag? Was Walter's own nephew partially responsible for the man's death? Donald was a man he really liked and had hoped to get to know better. Could he really be inside that body bag? Would Walter never see him or touch him again?

And where was Justin?

Walter felt sick to his stomach. In spite of the cold, his face was coated with a slick sheen of sweat. He didn't know if he had the energy to chase after his nephew, did not know if he had the strength to entertain the flashes of possibility that were racing through his mind regarding Justin: running away, suicide, another hate crime. He leaned against a cold brick wall and continued to stare at the circus in front of his building.

And he got a reprieve. Donald was alive. Walter lifted his eyes heavenward and whispered, "Thank you. Oh, thank you." A pair of female paramedics was leading Donald out of the building. It was unmistakably him, and he was unmistakably alive...and able to walk. Even from his perspective of a block and a half away, he could see the man looked shell shocked, his pace slow and stiff, like an old man's. Walter could imagine a glazed expression on his face as his eyes stared straight ahead reliving whatever horror he had just gone through.

And just what the hell *had* happened?

Walter shook his head. He had a good idea and wondered if it was Justin's friend in the body bag. Had it been he who had broken in and confronted Donald, to ensure, as Justin had said, that he didn't "talk"? Or was it something else, a random urban crime, a burglary gone wrong? Or a crime of passion, something Walter wouldn't even know about because, beyond the sex, he didn't really know Donald Griffiths well.

And then it occurred to Walter that maybe he could have done something to prevent all of this. If only he hadn't been tomcatting around last night! If he had been home, in his own bedroom directly above Donald's, maybe he would have heard something, sounds of a struggle, a groan or a scream traveling up to him through the heat duct.

Would he have done anything? Would he have gone down to intervene or at least picked up the phone? Or would he, like so many documented urban witnesses, have turned a deaf ear to the struggle? Would he have chalked it up to Donald's TV? After all, would he really think someone was being *killed* in the apartment below him? Things like that just didn't happen to Walter. He supposed everyone thought things like that didn't happen to *them*.

Until they did.

He continued to watch as Donald crawled into an ambulance and stared as the vehicle passed right by him, siren off.

He had to find his nephew, had to find him before one of the platoon of police did. Maybe there were clues now that linked Justin to whatever crime had occurred. Perhaps Donald himself knew something about Walter's nephew and was now recounting his story, complete with description and Justin's relationship to Walter, to the paramedics tending to him.

Walter turned the corner and began walking east, toward the lakefront. Perhaps the boy had gone there, to be by himself on the beach or the green spaces that lined the water. He didn't know. He couldn't imagine the boy's state of mind, couldn't begin to put himself in his place. But the lakefront was as good a place to start as any.

As he walked, he pulled his cell from his jacket and punched in his sister, Patty's, number. He prayed the ringing would not morph into her cigarette-scarred voice and message. Halfway through the fourth ring, she picked up.

"'Lo?" Patty sounded sleepy, almost angry.

Walter didn't care. "Patty? It's Walter."

"What do you want?" She laughed. "Do you realize how early it is, little brother? And besides, I got company." Her laugh was throaty, deep, and sounded dirty. Walter wondered how he had wound up with her for a sister.

"Never mind that. Is Justin there, by any chance?" Walter wasn't sure if the boy had had time to get home yet, but it was worth checking, and he still needed to warn Patty, hopefully without tipping his hand. He did not want his sister any more involved than she had to be. Walter knew he was the best person to take care of this. He was the only real parent the boy had ever had.

"Fuck if I know. I've been busy."

Walter rolled his eyes and tried to control the rage he felt welling up inside him. He took a deep breath and told himself she didn't know. She had no idea of the gruesome horror that had just transpired in his building...and her own son's involvement in it. "Well, could you do me a huge favor and just check?"

"Oh sure, no prob." Patty's voice dripped sarcasm before she set the phone down. In a few seconds, she was back. "He's not in his room...and the bathroom's empty, so I'm gonna go with, 'No, he isn't here.' What's up? You had plans or somethin' and he didn't show?"

Walter took the easy path. "Yeah. That's right. If he does show up, will you do me a favor and make sure he doesn't leave again? I need to talk to him. It's important."

"Okay." Patty snorted, as if trying to clear her nostrils. She was a real class act, his sister. "What's this all about?"

Walter mumbled, "Nothin'. But I may drop by in a bit. Tell Justin if you see him to call me right away. Tell him I'm not mad at him."

"Okay. But what the fuck is goin' on?"

"Don't worry, sis. Just get back to your guest."

The advice was obviously good enough for Patty. She hung up.

*

Justin was not at the lakefront. He had not returned home to Patty's. His cell phone went directly to voice mail. Thoughts of betrayal and outrage were crowded out of Walter's mind by concern for his nephew's well-being. *Just let him be all right. We can deal with the other stuff later.* As Walter trudged up his street, all traces of the carnival of urban crime that had taken place just hours ago was gone, as if it had never happened.

Would he never find the boy again? In spite of what he had done, the prospect was an agonizing one for Walter. He really loved the boy. Other than Hank, he was all Walter had. The thought of a world without Justin was a grim one.

He opened the door and took the steps slowly, as if his boot heels were filled with lead. He paused at his door and laid his head wearily on the frame. Had it only been hours ago that he had cheerfully walked Hank, looking forward to such a simple pleasure as getting back inside and going to bed? Walter wondered if life would ever be the same. It seemed to take minutes for him to fish his keys out of his pocket and to unlock the door.

When he opened the door, Justin was on the couch, waiting. The scene almost didn't seem real, like something that would vanish if only Walter would blink a couple of times. The TV was on, flickering images before the boy. Walter stared at the screen and saw that Justin was watching news, which was surprising, considering the boy favored the Cartoon Network and wrestling. But he was even more surprised to find him here, in his living room. He remembered, of course, that Justin had his own key, but he never expected him to come back, at least not so soon.

The boy turned and looked at him. He did not smile but simply stared at Walter. Then he turned back to the TV and said, "Ronny's dead. Your friend downstairs killed him."

Walter took a deep breath, then closed the door behind him and set his keys on the secretary desk. He and Justin had a lot to talk about, and he hoped the boy realized that too. For now, though, they had immediate issues with which to deal. These issues would have to be handled with the greatest of care, and Walter was glad Justin had gone to him and not to Patty.

He went and sat next to the boy on the couch. Even though a part of him was telling him not to and that by doing this he was betraying himself, he wrapped his arms around the boy. They sat in silence for a long time, the muffled voices of a news anchor in front of them. After a while, Justin began to sob. Walter pulled him closer, thinking Justin was both the enemy and the only family he really loved. It was a tough space to be in. But love triumphed, and he stroked the boy's back while he cried, rubbing his hand in circles over and over, whispering, "Sh-h." He pressed his lips to the boy's stubbly pate.

The crying went on for a while. Walter supposed it was the first time in a long time the boy had actually let go (maybe even since he had taken part in the attack last October). He knew Justin had been traumatized by all the violence, the secrets, knowing his own uncle was a target for just the kind of mayhem he helped perpetrate, and the loss of his friend, however evil and wicked this Ronny character really was.

As his nephew sobbed, Walter wondered what he should do next. He first thought, like that of a trapped animal, was of fleeing. He could pack bags for himself and

Justin, take whatever meager funds he could find in his apartment, and head down to the Greyhound station. They could get away from all this, be the father and son Walter had always dreamed of them being. He could even imagine the pair of them in some small town somewhere no one would ever look—West Virginia, maybe—leading quiet lives. Walter could clean houses or something to make money, something where he was paid in cash, under the table. Weren't there people one could turn to for fake birth certificates, fake IDs and the like? He and Justin could become whole new people, start over. Walter knew, at heart, the boy was not a bad person, just impressionable and caught up with the wrong people. He would make sure the boy finished high school and then, maybe, college, or at least a good trade school. Walter would work hard to support him, to give him the good start he had missed here in Chicago. He could make it all work out.

Justin was sniffling as he sat back on the couch, freeing himself from Walter's grip. Walter looked over, and the boy, underneath his despair, looked stunned. It was no wonder he had yet to say a word. Walter squeezed his shoulder and sat back, giving Justin his space.

The fantasy of running away was the wrong one. Walter knew it. He probably knew it all along, but in his current state, he thought it was okay to allow this little fantasy before plunging forward into grim reality. Besides, he didn't have the know-how or the resources to do the things he dreamed about. They would only get caught on the lam, getting Walter into deep shit, Justin into deeper.

No, the only way to make things right was to face the music. Even if the music was a dirge or a cacophony of crashing cymbals, it had to be faced.

Walter cleared his throat and angled his body toward his nephew's. "Justin, listen."

Justin eyed him. His lower lip quivered, and Walter remembered the boy as a toddler. He saw in his mind's eye a towheaded boy running on the beach, pointing upward at a kite his uncle was flying. Could he do this? Could he say the words and see them through?

Walter swallowed to try to relieve the ball of pressure that had built quickly in his throat. "Justin...we need to take care of this."

Justin continued to simply stare. Walter wondered if the boy had been so traumatized by what had occurred that he had lost his power of speech.

Walter glanced down at the floor to compose himself, then back at his nephew. "I'm going to get up now and grab the phone. Then I'm going to call the police." Walter sighed, staring out the window at a perfectly normal winter's day that was anything but. "You are going to turn yourself in. It's the only way you can begin to make things right." He put his hands on Justin's shoulders, to pull him closer, and spoke to him in a voice barely above a whisper. "I don't want to see you in this kind of trouble. But honey, there's no alternative."

Justin bit his lower lip. His eyes welled with tears. He was really just a little boy, after all. "I'm scared."

"I know you are. And I promise I will stand by you through everything. And maybe things won't be so bad. Things might go better if you turn yourself in. And I don't know, maybe you'll be treated as a juvenile and not an adult." Walter doubted this, but he wanted to offer what little comfort possible to his nephew.

Justin simply nodded.

Walter got up to get the phone.

Chapter Twenty

Although only a few days had passed since Donald had killed—in self-defense—Ronald Hanks, the time seemed much longer. In fact, it was like it had really never happened at all. Again, Donald's memory was fuzzy, and their fighting and the chaos that ensued once Ronny came into his room wielding the knife came in fragments, like pieces of a dream barely remembered as the hours of wakefulness passed.

It all had an air of unreality about it: the attack in October, Mark's funeral, Mark's appearances to him, his two-month fog, the attempt on his life, and finally, the news that Justin Wakefield, his upstairs neighbor's nephew, had turned himself in. The good thing was that Donald was back to work. They had told him not to come back so soon, to take time. But work was like a balm for Donald, offering oblivion, distraction, an escape. He had cleaned his apartment from top to bottom. Although he was battle scarred and ravaged by all he had been through, he felt he was joining the ranks of the living once more. *Why, in no time*, he thought, *I'll be right as rain. Yeah*, he answered himself, *if "no time" is measured in decades.*

Donald sat on his couch in flannel pajama bottoms and a T-shirt. Outside, it was snowing, and the forecasters predicted accumulations of more than eight inches. The steady flakes coming down, big and fluffy, were pretty and kind of a distraction for Donald, who didn't want to think about much. He didn't want to consider of what his "new life" would consist. Didn't want to ponder "next moves" or words like "goals" or even "happiness."

All he could do right now was survive. He had gone to work that day, put in his eight hours, and supposed his boss would have said he was productive and that his performance was satisfactory, yet Donald could remember little of what he did. Hadn't there been some kind of meeting in the afternoon? Had he bought coffee from Starbucks in the concourse of his building that morning? Had he looked like just another corporate drone in downtown Chicago?

Thinking he would relax and fix himself dinner later (something that would appall his sister, Grace, something like a Lean Cuisine or a sandwich and chips), Donald had loaded up the VCR with one of his favorite movies, *Rosemary's Baby*. He thought Rosemary's otherworldly troubles and her suspenseful trajectory would spare him from thinking for a couple of hours. He also thought the drink on the arm of the couch, J&B on the rocks, would ease the work of having to think like a normal human being.

But neither the drink nor the movie was successful. The alcohol simply made him feel sluggish and lethargic. He lost the thread of the movie shortly after Rosemary and Guy moved into their fateful and improbable Manhattan apartment.

He couldn't help but think about Mark. He was glad he had come to him and wished he would come to him again but knew, as the hours and days passed, that the last time he had seen him really was the last time. Mark had come to help him resolve things, to protect him...and when that job was done, he had gone somewhere else. It was a place, Donald hoped, where Mark would be free from care, and the horror that had ended his life would completely fade away, to be replaced by quiet joy and contentment. He liked to think of Mark in such a place. He deserved it. Yet Donald also imagined Mark still watched him from time to time and felt like he could feel him near.

Donald still hugged the pillow next to him on the bed before drifting off to sleep and again the next morning. Yes, he even kissed it at times and called it Mark. And he still searched for the scent of his dead lover's hair on the linen. It had faded away, but that didn't deter Donald from trying to find one small sense memory of Mark. Someday, he supposed, he would put away that pillow and replace it with a new one, one upon which Mark had not lain his golden-curled head.

But he didn't know when he would be ready for that. He didn't know if he'd ever be ready.

The first thing he had to do, he thought, to make any progress forward, was to let go of the unfairness of what had happened to him and Mark in October. He didn't quite know how to go about setting free the rage and the injustice of it. Donald had thought that knowing who did this to him and his partner and seeing them "punished" would bring closure, but it hadn't. It was just more of the same story: a young life taken, another destroyed. And still, Mark hadn't come back.

Even the arrest of Luis Martinez, based on testimony from Justin Wakefield, had not brought any kind of relief. Donald just wanted to forget them all and had promised himself he would do only the minimum in order to see the remaining pair got what was coming to them, which was to cooperate with the district attorney's office and testify in court when the time came. He would read no news accounts, would submit to no interviews from newspapers, gay or otherwise, would really never speak of this again.

Was that healthy? Donald wasn't sure. He was sure, though, it was the best thing for him now.

A knock on the door interrupted his thoughts. "Who the hell?" Donald craned his head back to look at the door, as if he could see through it and find out who had come to call. He paused the movie, even though he had long ago lost interest, and got up to answer the door.

Walter Wakefield was standing outside. He looked bigger somehow than when Donald had last seen him, but he supposed it was just due to the fact that seeing him here, at the threshold of Donald's own home, was a bit surreal after all that had happened. The man looked good, though, smiling brightly, his body thick and his pale eyes alert and probing. He cocked his head.

"Hey, Donald. It's really coming down out there. Cold too. Weatherman says wind chills are, like, thirty below."

Walter shifted his weight from one foot to the other, grinning for all he was worth. "Anyway, I made a big pot of beef stew, way too much for just one guy, and thought you might like some."

Donald looked down to notice for the first time Walter was carrying a casserole dish swathed in a dishtowel. Donald grinned and thought: "Connie Casserole." The reference to *Boys in the Band* caught him unawares, and he laughed. The mirth sounded strange, as if it had come from someone else.

"That's awfully nice of you, Walter." Donald took the casserole from him and stooped to set it on the floor behind him. He stood back up and met Walter's gaze. He hoped the guy didn't expect him to ask him in. "I was probably just going to eat a sandwich, if I ate anything, so this'll come in really handy. Especially on a night like this."

"That's what I thought," Walter said. The two men lingered at the doorway for several moments, neither saying anything. Walter crossed his arms and rubbed himself, as if he was chilly, then let them drop. Finally, Walter broke the silence. "Well, I just wanted to drop this off. You enjoy it, now."

"Thanks a lot, buddy." Donald closed the door on Walter's smiling face. He shook his head as he picked up the casserole dish and walked into the kitchen with it. He was surprised that the scent of beef, vegetables, and herbs wafting up to his nose was making him hungry.

And then he stopped. He didn't see Mark, but he heard him, only in his mind this time, but it was clear enough. What he heard was Mark's final word to him.

"*Live.*"

And Donald hurried back to the door and threw it open. Walter was just about to open the door to the stairwell between their apartments, and he looked back. Donald was touched by the hope he saw on the other man's face.

"Hey! I just looked and there's way too much here for me. You wanna come back and eat with me?"

Walter's face broke into a wide grin as he hurried back. Donald stepped aside to let him in and then closed the door.

Afterword

Getting *Bashed*: Where Book Ideas Come From

It doesn't matter what you write, whether it's crime, suspense fiction, literary fiction, or some other genre where you make stuff up, the most frequently asked question writers get from readers is: "Where do you get your ideas?"

Usually, I give them some smartass answer, like "Off eBay. Some guy there sells plot ideas, six for a hundred bucks, minimum bid." Or "The dollar store. It's all I can afford." But the truth is there's usually a different inspiration for every story or book I write, so the question is one that's truly difficult to answer without sitting down and taking it on a case-by-case basis. Ideas come from all over. It seems the more of them I get, the more of them I have. Inspiration comes from dreams, snatches of conversation overheard on public transportation, a news item on the Net or in the paper, and asking myself the one question writers ask themselves more than any other: "What if..."

And sometimes, ideas come from real life. Such is the case with my novel, *Bashed*. For a lot of gay men and women, hate crimes are a fact of life. Many gay people have either themselves experienced the terror, violation, and persecution of being attacked simply for who they are (whether the attack took the form of words, fists, or something more lethal) or, at the very least, they know someone who has. I've been lucky. I have no permanent physical scars. But I did come very close to experiencing a hate crime up close and personal (and I suppose one could argue that what I did experience was actually a hate crime), and that was the inspiration of my novel, *Bashed*. The title, of course, refers to being fag bashed.

My close call came one October night several years ago, back when I still lived in Chicago. I was once into what's affectionately called the "leather scene" and owned chaps, biker jacket, boots, and other accouterments that passed the dress code in either a gay leather establishment or a biker bar. That particular night, I had been hanging out at the Eagle, one of Chicago's foremost leather establishments. I had stayed late, arriving after midnight and leaving near closing, at close to four o'clock in the morning. I had made a new friend, and we were making our way to my car, which was parked on a side street that ran parallel to St. Boniface Cemetery. It was a very dark and quiet side street, made all the more so by the late-night hour. My companion and I weren't thinking about things like fag bashers or hate crimes.

But we suddenly were when we noticed an idling old car parked just opposite from my own. The car was a souped-up muscle vehicle of some sort, and inside it, we could see several dark figures, all turning their heads, alert, as we approached. Both of us tensed and quickened our pace. Even in the middle of a metropolis like Chicago, it was easy to feel vulnerable and alone. And we felt even more vulnerable when the still of the quiet night was broken by the sound of car doors opening. Suddenly, my friend and I stopped, feeling exposed in our leather gear, as four young men emerged from the car. To a man, they all sported shaved heads and were dressed in uniforms of baggy jeans and hoodies.

And one of them was carrying an aluminum baseball bat.

They didn't call us "fags" or "queers." They didn't say anything. Their silence was perhaps more disturbing than if they had hurled epithets our way. To reach my car, we would have to walk right by them...and it didn't appear as though they were planning to let us pass.

It was like being confronted by a grizzly in the woods or a lion in the jungle. What do you do? Run the other way, knowing that four strong men are on your heels? Try to get to your car and hope the baseball bat was for a late-night game of sandlot?

We froze. The four, as a unit, moved closer. One of the guys, the one with the bat, grinned, swinging the bat slightly.

This was a moment of terror. My heart pounded. A trickle of sweat ran down my back.

In books, they call what happened next predictable or *deus ex machina*, but at just that moment, one of Chicago's finest rolled down the quiet street, very slowly, toward us. The men got in their car quickly. And so did we.

Thankfully, I do not know what the outcome of that night would have been had not the police come along on such a fortunate patrol.

But the incident did stick with me for many years, until I got around to dramatizing it as the opening to *Bashed*. But in my fictional world, no police car came to the rescue, and the pair of guys emerging from the leather bar end up bashed very badly...with an aluminum baseball bat. It's chilling to think that one of your characters could have been you, a you who might not have survived to tell a tale again.

About the Author

Real Men. True Love.

Rick R. Reed is an award-winning and bestselling author of more than fifty works of published fiction. He is a Lambda Literary Award finalist. *Entertainment Weekly* has described his work as "heartrending and sensitive." *Lambda Literary* has called him: "A writer that doesn't disappoint..." Find him at www.rickrreedreality.blogspot.com. Rick lives in Palm Springs, CA, with his husband, Bruce, and their fierce Chihuahua/Shiba Inu mix, Kodi.

Email: rickrreedbooks@gmail.com

Facebook: www.facebook.com/rickrreedbooks

Twitter: @rickrreed

Website: www.rickrreedreality.blogspot.com

Other NineStar books by this author

Unraveling
Sky Full of Mysteries
The Perils of Intimacy

IM

Chaser

Raining Men

Blue Umbrella Sky

Third Eye

Legally Wed

Hungry for Love

Big Love

A Face without a Heart

Bigger Love

Torn

The Secrets We Keep

The Man from Milwaukee

Coming Soon from Rick R. Reed

The Couple Next Door

CHAPTER ONE

How many disappointing dates will I endure before I just give up?

I mean, here I am, a perfectly attractive, fit, self-sufficient thirty-year-old, and I'm *still* waiting to meet the man of my dreams. Mr. Right. Hell, tonight I'd even settle for that character who seems to come along on dates for most of us, the all-too-common Mr. Right Now. But even he isn't on the seat beside me. In fact, I strongly doubt he's anywhere in the vicinity of the Capitol Hill neighborhood of Seattle where I live.

Believe me, I've looked.

Mr. First Date pulls his Ford Fusion up to the curb in front of my apartment building on Aloha Avenue. We sit in awkward silence for several long moments, listening as the engine ticks down as it cools. I can feel him looking at me. As he's done most of the evening, he waits for me to speak. I turn my head and, in the dark, give him a weak smile. The date, dinner at a little sushi place on Broadway, had not gone well, full of uncomfortable silences, awkward pauses, and desperate looks around for avenues of escape—on both our parts.

Do I need to say we just didn't click?

I didn't think so.

So what he says now surprises me.

"Do you want me to come up?"

Really? We've just spent an hour and a half of agony together, trying to find a snippet of common ground that doesn't exist, and he's wondering if I want him to come up, which we all know is code for "Shall we make the beast with two backs?"

Seriously? The most irksome thing is, I'm considering it. I mean, he's cute in spite of our lack of social connection. He's a games developer for a software company here in town and looks it, with a sort of hipster/geek vibe going on. He has red hair, which I love. He has a beard, which I love. He wears retro glasses, which make him look paradoxically goofy and sexy—which I love.

Would it be *so* terrible to sleep with him? I mean, it's been at least two weeks since I've enjoyed the charms of anyone other than Mr. Thumb and his four sons, so at least in terms of a release, maybe I should just say "Sure" and open the car door. If things go like some of my dates in the past, he'd follow me upstairs to my apartment and be back in his car in, like, fifteen minutes.

No, I tell myself. And then I tell him, shaking my head, looking sad, and saying the words countless heartbreakers have used over the years to stop ardent passion in its errant tracks.

"I'm sorry, Neil. But I have to get up early." Lamely, I pat his hand. "Maybe another time."

I don't need to be psychic to know that we both know another time ain't gonna happen.

Neil seems relieved as he restarts his car. He shrugs. "It's okay. Club Z's just a couple minutes away, right? Down Broadway and a right on Pike—easy."

He grins at me, and I wonder if he expects me to laugh. Club Z is one of Seattle's filthiest bathhouses, and yes, it's only a few minutes away. He doesn't seem to need directions.

It's my turn to be relieved that I didn't actually succumb to the temptation of inviting this jerk upstairs. Wordlessly, I get out of the car and slam the door behind me.

Neil roars off into the damp and still night.

I pause and sigh, staring up at the building in which I've lived for the past five years. It's an okay place, an old redbrick three story with none of the modern amenities—no stainless steel, granite countertops, or gas fireplaces. My apartment is homey. It even has the original tile, sink, and claw-foot tub in its single bathroom. The living room is large, with three big windows that look out on Aloha and let in lots of light—on the days when we have sun in Seattle (that means usually summer days). The floors are scuffed original hardwood. The kitchen actually has a pantry and built-in china hutch. I've painted the place a cheery, soft yellow.

Upstairs, the TV, with its DVRed episodes of at-odds *Sons of Anarchy* and *Downton Abbey*, awaits. Upstairs, there's the gelato I love from Whole Foods in the freezer—hazelnut dark chocolate.

Such is my life. Comfortable and a little lonely.

Sometimes I wonder, like Peggy Lee, if that's all there is.

I head toward the glass-paned front door. I grope in my jeans for my keys. The mail had not yet arrived before I left for my date, and I wonder if there will be any surprises in the vestibule mailbox. You know, like an actual letter from someone, standing out from the usual assortment of bills and solicitations by the cursive spelling out of my name—Jeremy Booth.

My problem is I always have hope, even when there's little reason.

I open the front door, and that's when everything changes. My life turns upside down. I go from bored discontent to panic in a split second.

The first thing I hear is someone shouting "No!" in an anguished voice. I look up from the lobby to see two figures on the staircase above, on the second-floor landing. One is a guy who looks menacing and so butch he could pose for a Tom of Finland poster. An aura of danger radiates from him. Aside from his imposing and muscular frame, he's even wearing the right clothes—tight, rolled jeans and a black leather biker jacket with a chain snaking out from beneath one of the epaulets. His high- and tight-buzzed hair gives him a military—and mean—air. He has his hands on the shoulders of a guy who looks a bit younger and much slighter, making me want to call up the stairs, "Why don't you pick on someone your own size?" The smaller guy, blond and clad only in a pair of pajama bottoms, struggles with his attacker, looking terrified. Their movements, clumsy and rough, would be comical if they weren't so scary. The smaller guy is panting and batting ineffectually at the bigger one.

"Please! No! Don't!" the smaller guy manages to get out, his voice close to hysteria.

I have never seen either of these men before. In fact, the whole scene has the quality of the surreal, a dream. The danger and conflict pulsing down the stairs makes my own heart rate and respiration accelerate, causing feelings of panic to rise within me.

And then the worst happens. The big butch guy shoves the smaller one hard, and all at once he's tumbling heavily down the stairs toward me.

The fall is graceless, and it looks like it hurts. It's over so fast that I'm left gasping.

I look up to see the leather-jacket guy sneer down at his mate, lying crumpled and crying at my feet, and then turn sharply on his heel to go back into a second-floor apartment that had been vacant yesterday. He slams the door. The sound of the deadbolt sliding into place is like the report of a shotgun. Both slam and lock resound like thunderclaps, echoing in the tile lobby, punctuation to the drama and trauma of this short scene.

I switch into Good Samaritan mode and drop to my knees at the sniveling, crumpled mess of a man lying practically at my feet.

"Are you okay?" I ask and reach out to lightly touch his shoulder.

He jerks away and, wincing, pulls himself up into an awkward sitting position. He stares at me with clear blue eyes for a moment, almost as though he's trying to place me. He finally looks away.

"My ankle is throbbing. It hurts like hell. Maybe I twisted it."

I don't know what to say, other than to ask, "Would you like to try and stand? Test it out?"

He nods.

I lean over to grip him under the arms—it's damp there, and I can smell the ripe aroma of body odor, probably inspired by fear or panic—and pull. He comes up with me and then stumbles, wincing and crying out.

"Damn. I might have sprained it when I fell." His eyes are so appealing, in both senses of the word, as he stares at me, as though seeking direction for what to do next. He leans on me, taking his weight off the injured ankle.

I keep my arm around him, and together we limp over to a bench set beneath the bank of common mailboxes. We sit.

"What do you want to do?" I ask.

"I don't know. I think Cole may have locked me out for the night."

I look up the stairs at the closed door and imagine the frame vibrating from its recent slam. I notice then that my new acquaintance is shivering. It's a typical Seattle winter night—chilly and damp—and the vestibule has poor heat. Good thing, I think, that I've worn a hoodie over my T-shirt. I unzip it and take it off and then hold it out to him. "You could wear this."

"Are you sure?" Without waiting for an answer, he takes it from me and puts it on. He zips it up to his throat and pulls the hood up over his thick blond hair.

"I'm sure." I grin. "I'm Jeremy. Jeremy Booth. I live here in the building." I stare down at the lobby's worn linoleum floor, not sure what else to say or do.

"Shane McCallister. I just moved in today." He casts a nervous glance up the stairs. "Well, *John* and I just moved in this afternoon. From Chicago." He tries to give me a smile, but it comes out sad.

I nod. "I thought you said his name was Cole."

Shane laughs and his cheeks redden. "Did I? I meant John. Sorry."

We stare at one another for a second—a second in which I feel as though I've fallen down the rabbit hole.

They must have done their moving while I was out working this afternoon. I rub my chin and then say, because my mama taught me right, "Well, Shane, I can't just leave you here like this. Do you want to come up to my place?" I think for a moment, get a better idea. "Or maybe I could take you over to First Hill, where all the hospitals are, get you to an emergency room so you can have that ankle looked at. It could be something worse than a sprain. You should do that, you know. I have a car. It's parked in the back."

Suddenly, chauffeuring this downtrodden stranger to one of the hospitals in the next neighborhood over seems more appealing to me, more exciting, than the date I just came home from.

"Oh, I couldn't ask you to do that."

I wave his protest away. "Yes, you could. You're new in town, right? Do you have someone else you could call?" I pull my iPhone out of my jeans pocket and hold it out to him.

He looks at it strangely and just shakes his head. "We haven't really made any friends here yet."

"Well then, it's settled. Let me run you over to Virginia Mason or Swedish." I peer into those icy blue, yet magnetic, eyes. "Okay?"

"We don't have health insurance," Shane blurts out.

"Let's not worry about that right now." I stand and comb my fingers through my dark hair. "If your ankle's broken or even sprained, you need to get it taken care of. That's not something that heals on its own."

He simply stares at me.

I sigh. "Look, I'm gonna run up to my place, get you some shoes—I have some shearling-lined moccasins that will probably fit—and they won't hurt...much. I'll grab you a shirt too. Are you gonna be all right here?" I glance nervously back up the stairs, but there's no John, or anyone else, glowering down at us. The apartment building is still this Thursday night, caught in no-man's-land between people getting home from work and departing for an evening of revelry farther south on Broadway at the gay bars.

"I'll be okay," Shane says softly.

He seems to shrink into himself, and my heart goes out to him. Poor guy! I have never understood why anyone would allow himself or herself to stay in an abusive relationship. At least that's what I assume this pair have going on. I can ponder—or maybe even ask the guys themselves, although I already think I'll be avoiding John—more about their situation later. Right now, duty calls.

I start up the stairs, and Shane calls out, "Jeremy?"

I turn, halfway up the stairs, realizing suddenly that these two are my new next-door neighbors. "Yeah?"

"Thanks. Not everyone would do this."

"Sure they would," I say, not at all sure that I speak the truth. I pause for a minute, still uncertain about what I'm getting myself into. That John character looked pretty menacing. What if he comes after us? Comes after me? What if he thinks my Good Samaritan act is an attempt to go after his lame boyfriend? I shake my head and continue trudging up the stairs. Sometimes life offers us very limited alternatives. I can't just leave the guy on his own, friendless and hurt. And even taking him into my place is out of the question—he could be seriously injured. There are a million questions on my lips, and for right now I think the best course of action is to leave them unasked. "I'll be right back."

And then I hightail it up the stairs. In quick succession I unlock my door and dash into my apartment to hurriedly gather up the things I promised, fearing that at any moment John might return. He looked like the type who might do even more harm to Shane, and I don't want any part of that. He appears to be a man who talks with his fists as much as his mouth, and my sympathy for poor Shane has manifested itself quickly and completely.

In record time, I return with a plain black T-shirt and the aforementioned moccasins. I help Shane stand and get everything on. "My car's out back in the lot. It ain't much, but it'll get us there." I slide my arm around Shane and guide him down the central corridor that leads to the back door and the parking lot.

Somehow I have the feeling my life is about to change.

*

We get back a little after eleven. The ER was busy and the wait was long. No insurance? Get thee to the back of the line! Fortunately for Shane, his ankle was just mildly sprained, and he's added only an Ace bandage to his ensemble. They offered him crutches, but he told me he already had a pair at home, which chilled me.

During the ride to Swedish Medical Center and even in the ER waiting room, Shane was quiet, distant, and reserved, staring off into space. When I would try to engage him in conversation, even about the mundane, stuff like asking if he wanted a soda from the vending machine, he would answer only in monosyllables and then look away, as if it was painful to talk.

And what do I know? Maybe it was. After all, I had just witnessed the guy being flung down a flight of stairs by a man I assume is his lover, partner, boyfriend, husband? It's understandable that he would have been shaken up and wanting to withdraw. Who wouldn't?

But now, as we enter the lobby once more in the dead of the night, Shane becomes more talkative, perhaps because he has no other choice. He looks up the stairs and then back at me. In a voice barely above a whisper, he says, "I don't know if I'm welcome up there tonight."

I want to shake him. I want to ask what's the matter with him. *Not welcome?* It's his home, and this asshole just beat him and flung him down a flight of stairs without an ounce of concern. I want to ask why he's even with this guy, why he would allow himself to be treated so horribly. Instead I stick my neck out, knowing I might be putting myself smack dab in the middle of a domestic relations problem that does not have to be my own and say, "Listen. You can stay at my place tonight. You don't want to go back there anyway, do you?"

"Oh, Jeremy, that's really nice of you. But I can't impose on you any more than I've already done. Maybe you could just call me a cab and send me to the nearest hotel or motel."

He looks into my eyes searchingly, and what he says next also chills me.

"I've done it before."

Again, there's a lot I want to say to this young man, about standing up for himself, about not allowing himself to be abused more than once. Having grown up in a house where my father abused my mother physically, I know the soul-sapping destruction this kind of abuse can wreak firsthand. I also know, sadly, how the abused can often feel trapped, even going so far as to make excuses for their abuser. How many times had my mother urged me to be more understanding about my father when he hit her, or shoved her into the car, or said something so cruel it was as cutting and painful as a physical blow?

But again, I only met Shane a few hours ago. We've exchanged little more than a few banal words. I don't really even know him. Maybe the opportunity will come up sometime to talk more to him. Or maybe this night will be an anomaly and we'll become simply ships that pass in the night—or at least the common bank of mailboxes in the lobby. "Don't be silly. There's no reason for you to stay in a motel." I grin at him and try to lighten the situation. "Your virtue will be perfectly safe with me. I won't expect you to share my bed."

Shane laughs at that, and the laughter and the smile make me feel a little better. I like the way his smile lights up his face, erasing all the darkness that was there just moments before.

"Are you sure?"

"I wouldn't have offered if I wasn't."

"And I will be fine on the couch," Shane offers.

"You'll do no such thing. You're the injured party. You take my bed, and I'll sleep on the couch."

Sleeping arrangements settled, we start tentatively up the stairs, Shane clinging to me as he makes his way, trying his best to avoid putting any weight on the sprained ankle. We go quiet as we head upstairs, and I think it's because we're both afraid John will open the door. I strongly suspect Shane would not like that. And I know I wouldn't.

"Which apartment is yours?" Shane asks, and I notice he's whispering, which lends credence to my suspicion that the last thing he wants is to see John again tonight.

"I'm right next door to you guys."

Shane's hand on my arm tightens. "That's nice. I already have a friend in the building."

I smile and nod. "You sure do, Shane. But I wish we didn't have to meet under circumstances like these, memorable as they are."

"You and me both," Shane says. He continues, voicing words that fill me with dread. "But you probably got the wrong idea about John. He's not so bad, really. He just has a temper, and sometimes I get in his way."

As I grope in my jeans pocket for the keys to my front door, I look at Shane and fail to keep the expression of slack-jawed amazement off my face. I slowly shake my head. I can't help myself from voicing the truth. "Don't. There's no excuse for pushing someone down a flight of stairs. There's no excuse, really, for laying your hands on another person to do them harm."

I don't wait for a response. I unlock the front door and help Shane inside. "Why don't you just sit here on the couch?" I lead him over to the beat-up couch I picked up at Goodwill and that I like to kid myself is "midcentury modern" when it's really just tacky and an embarrassment.

After he's settled on the couch with his ankle up on the coffee table, I ask, "Do you want anything? You're probably worn out and just want to get to sleep, huh?" Although Shane might be tired, the events that transpired tonight have left me feeling strangely restless and energized. "I could make us some tea."

"That would be nice. I'd like that."

I start toward the kitchen and call over my shoulder, "I have some English breakfast, which has, of course, caffeine and some Sleepytime, which, of course, does not. Which would you like?"

"Give me the English breakfast, please."

I head into the kitchen and hear Shane mutter, "I probably won't sleep much tonight anyway."

I just want to wrap my arms around him and tell him things will be okay, which even I know, this early in the game, is most likely a lie. "Coming right up!"

I busy myself in the kitchen, filling the teakettle, setting it on the stove to boil, pulling down mugs from the cupboard (Fiestaware, made across the river from where I grew up so many years ago), and grabbing a couple of tea bags from the canister on my Formica-topped counter. I lean against that same counter as I wait for the steam to rise from the spout of the kettle, hoping to arrest the kettle before it begins to scream. I also want these few minutes alone to think about the evening, to think about my new neighbors.

Curiously, or maybe not, my date earlier this evening barely registers as a significant event. Hell, my workday cleaning apartments and condos here in the neighborhood seems more memorable. But what really sticks out, of course, is the recent events I've borne witness to. I've been so busy all night taking care of Shane and worrying about him that I haven't really had time to catch my breath, to stop and consider what's happened, how this night has been a game-changer.

The big question I have to ask myself is if I'm sure I know what I'm doing. My sister, Deanie, back in Ohio, would tell me I was being a fool, although she would first praise me for my compassion. Deanie's a professor at the local community college back in Fawcettville, teaching an introductory-level psychology course. She also does counseling at the student clinic. She makes about the same money I do cleaning, but she's really my mother's pride and joy because she's got her PhD, and more important, she never left our little hometown to pursue bigger dreams like me. Look where my pursuit got me! I look around my run-down kitchen, watching a cockroach skitter into the sink drain.

But I see Deanie in my mind's eye, her dark hair and luminous brown eyes. She's not only smart but also beautiful. I imagine I've just relayed tonight's events to her.

"Jeremy, are you crazy? You should keep out of this! You don't know what that John character might do, not only to this Shane person, but to you." She makes a *tsk* sound and fashions her lips into a frown. "He's already proved he's a violent man. How do you think he's going to like you taking in his 'friend' for the night?"

In my imagination, this is the point where Deanie gives me a hug and strokes my hair for a moment, then pushes me away to issue her stern yet sensible advice.

"You don't owe these people anything. It's nice that you want to help, and Shane sounds like he can really use that help, but sweetie, it's not your place. You're sticking your neck out for someone you don't even know. Be his friend. That's okay. But also keep your distance. You leave yourself so open to pain." Deanie bites her lower lip and stares at me with those intense eyes that say more than words ever can. She whispers, "You were always the one to stick up for Mom, and where did it get you?"

To answer her question, I glance down at my left wrist, at the way the bone protrudes ever so slightly because it never healed right after Daddy—

The teakettle shrieks. "Shit," I say and snatch it off the burner. I pour the boiling water into mugs, feeling as though I've just awakened from a bad dream. I wait for five minutes, letting the tea steep, and force myself to think of nothing, not home, not the dreams I have yet to make come true, and not even Shane in the next room, whom I have a sneaking suspicion I'm about to become very involved with, despite common sense and imagined Deanie warnings.

I finally remove the tea bags and toss them into the trash can under the sink. I call out to the living room. "You want milk? Sugar?"

There's no answer. "Shane?"

I put down one of the mugs in my hand and creep to the archway that leads into the living room. Shane's on the couch, injured foot up, head back and mouth open. He's snoring.

"Bless his heart," I whisper. I creep into the living room and stare down at him. There's something of the child about him now, of the innocent, with his golden curls and unlined and carefree face. I think how all the adrenaline his system has probably pumped out recently has left him depleted, and his body simply took over, knocking him out. There's a sweetness to his face. He's kind of angelic, and it actually brings a tear to my eye.

I'm glad I brought him home. The consequences be damned. I move quietly across the room to Shane, trying not to make any floorboards creak. Good luck with that! But any noise I make doesn't seem to bother him; his snores continue unabated. I stop midway through the room and turn back. I duck into my bedroom and go to the closet, where I pull down a soft, old quilt. From the bed, I grab one of the pillows.

I return to the room and set the quilt and pillow down on the couch and turn back to Shane. I move toward him and stand quietly, simply taking in his handsome features, admiring. Is this what motivates me to care for him? Silly question. Yeah, he's attractive, but I know he's brought out my nurturing instinct, something that's lain fallow since the old days back at home, when I would comfort my mom after she and Dad fought, sometimes brushing her hair for her or reading her a few pages from one of the books I was always reading, just to take her mind off things.

Yeah, I was that kid.

I reach out and gently push some of the blond hair off Shane's forehead. He murmurs but doesn't awaken, and I let my hand rest there, feeling the heat transfer. I wonder if he's dreaming, and if he is, I hope it's of good things.

I break the connection so I can kneel at Shane's feet. I pull the slippers from them and set them gently aside. I take both of his feet in my hands and pull them up so I can shift him into a reclining position on the couch.

He says something that sounds like "Don't" and "John," but they are only mumbles, and it's impossible to be sure. The important thing is that he doesn't awaken as I get him situated and put a pillow beneath his head and a quilt spread out over him. I tuck the quilt close to his chin and allow myself one more gentle touch, to his cheek.

I am just about to turn off the light in the living room when the phone rings.

I hurry to quiet it, glancing over my shoulder at Shane, who luckily does nothing more than turn onto his side, his face to the back of the couch.

"Yes?" I whisper, annoyed, hoping my one word doesn't come out as more of a hiss.

"You got Shane over there." It's not a question. It's an accusation. And the gravelly voice making it sends a chill down my spine.

I glance over at Shane, who has somehow managed to stay asleep. I feel a fierce determination not to wake him. He's been through enough tonight. I walk quietly into my bedroom with the phone and close the door.

As I sit on my bed, the deep voice comes through the line again.

"Well? What do you have to say for yourself?"

I whisper, but there's an intensity in my voice that conveys anger as well as if I were shouting. "What do *I* have to say for *myself*? I could ask you the same, although I wouldn't expect an answer that would make any kind of sense."

"You need to send him home."

I want to ask who this is, even though I know. I want to ask how he got my number, even though I know I'm listed and one of the few people on the planet who still has a landline phone.

"I'll leave that up to Shane. For now, he's sleeping."

"You want me to come over there?"

Again, not a question but a threat. It makes me recall my father saying "Don't make me come in there" when Deanie and I would cower in our shared bedroom with the door closed, our hands clasped tightly together, eyes wild.

I feel a twist in my gut, a sudden nausea that makes me want to puke. I swallow down the bile splashing at the back of my throat and force myself to take a few deep breaths. I raise my voice above a whisper and hope it doesn't wake Shane. I keep it level, though, trying my best to keep emotion out of it. "You come over here, you even knock on my door, and I *will* call the police. When they get here, no matter what Shane says, I will tell them what I was an eyewitness to, an act of brutal physical assault that was *not* an accident."

He's quiet, although I can hear him breathing on the other end. The breaths are coming just a hair faster, so I know maybe I've riled him. I don't know if that's a good thing or not. I can feel the sweat gathering in my pits, and

I fear bursting out into giddy laughter that has nothing to do with humor. The guy who avoids conflict at all costs? That's me. And standing up like this for someone I barely know surprises even me. It also makes me feel like I'm about to pass out.

I try to swallow. My mouth is dry. "Did you hear me?"

"I heard."

Before I can think of what to say next, I hear the click of the phone being hung up.

I stand for a long time, the phone in my hand, feeling chilled in spite of the radiators clanking on, the hiss of steam from them. After a few minutes, I tiptoe back out to where the cradle for the phone is and set it back in place.

I turn off the lights in the living room and head toward my bedroom, trying to ignore the fact that I'm trembling.

Just as I get to the door, Shane's voice stops me in my tracks.

"Thank you," he says.

I turn and look toward the dark, huddled mass on my couch.

I don't say anything. I go into the bedroom and close the door behind me. Quickly I strip out of my clothes and, clad only in a pair of boxers, slide under the covers. After a moment I pull the blanket over my head.

Also Available from NineStar Press

Connect with NineStar Press

www.ninestarpress.com

www.facebook.com/ninestarpress

www.facebook.com/groups/NineStarNiche

www.twitter.com/ninestarpress